THE BODYSURFER'S
GUIDE TO LIFE

THE BODYSURFER'S
GUIDE TO LIFE

Mark Wollard

To order additional copies of this book, contact:
Xlibris Corporation
1-888-795-4274
www.Xlibris.com
Orders@Xlibris.com
73057

For my family,
both biological and logical,
with deepest gratitude
for your love, support and lessons
throughout this journey.

The Bodysurfer's Oath:

*Do you solemnly swear to use the secrets of bodysurfing
to enjoy life more? And do you solemnly swear to keep from
hurting yourself or anyone else while riding the energy in the
awesome ocean on the most awesome of waves?*

*Do you solemnly swear to realize that there are an abundance
of awesome waves out there, and to understand that not every
wave's awesomeness is meant just for you? And that there is
enough awesomeness to go around, but when the right wave
offers its awesomeness to you, do you promise to jump in
and enjoy the ride of you life?*

"Due to a reorganization in the company, your job has been eliminated. It's nothing personal." The words still echoed in my head as I drove home from my last day of work.

How could I not take it personally? I had given up dinners with family and friends, weekends at the beach, and even the recitals and soccer games of my nieces because the company needed me to "grow the job for my department." And now it seemed I had grown it so well that they had divided my job into two positions. One I was overqualified for, and the other they felt I was underqualified for. Even the department no longer existed. It was now a subcategory on the flowchart that led to a more favorable bottom line.

huh? How can I be over—or underqualified for positions I had grown and nurtured for eight years?

I was angry and confused. "Now what?" I asked myself. My whole life had been wrapped up in that job. The idea of getting ahead and making something of myself, and that position, was what had dominated my mind during the day. I even dreamed about my job. Hell, I hadn't even updated the little '50s bungalow I'd inherited from my grandmother six years ago. I had managed to make do, because I was so tired when I came home from work that I didn't want to think of another project I had to put any effort into.

I pulled onto the tree-lined street and remembered why I loved my house. This neighborhood reminded me of the fun

I had growing up. A street lined with small one-story, 1950s-style houses and lots of hibiscus, oaks, and palms. Something about it was soothing and familiar, and I liked that. But now I was pulling into my driveway like a stranger. The happy life, I thought my job and home would provide, had been reorganized by my new ex-employer, and I wondered if my life would ever be the same again.

As I emptied the trunk of the boxes containing the personal items I had displayed in my office, I saw a picture of me with my parents, siblings, and nieces on a family vacation and thought to myself, "Was that really five years ago? Where had the time gone? What had I done with my life?"

While I had been working hard to put on the facade of a happy, successful professional, I realized that although I had been successful in the business world, my personal life wasn't that happy or successful. I dreaded telling people. What would they think of me? Would they think I was a slacker, not capable of cutting it in the fast-paced business world?

Fortunately the reorganization came with a severance package that, combined with my savings, would keep me afloat for about a year if necessary. But this really wasn't what I had planned to spend my savings on.

I loaded the boxes into my small dining room that had become more of a storage closet. If I had dinner with anyone, it was at a restaurant because I was always too tired to think of shopping for, preparing, and cooking a meal for company. As I unloaded the last box, a picture of my folks fell out. They were always so proud of me, and I wondered, "What would they think of me as their unemployed, under-qualified/overqualified son?"

Unemployed! I'd never been unemployed my whole adult life. I was unemployed! No new job in sight. Who was I if I didn't have a job? Where did I fit in? Would I be able to get another job? What would the people looking for employees think about me being reorganized out of a job? Exactly what had I become?

And with these questions filling my head, I stumbled forward into what would become a time that would change my life forever.

Over the next few days I made the obligatory phone calls to let my friends and family know what had happened. (Although it seemed that word had traveled faster on its own.) Of all the phone calls I made, the one that I dreaded the most was the one that turned out to be the most important to my next step. It was to my parents. With my mom on one extension and my dad on the other, I laid out the story of the demise of my career.

When I was through, my mother said, "I'm sorry you're having to go through this, but you haven't been happy there for quite a while."

"What do you mean? I loved my job," I replied.

"Well, I could be mistaken, but I really haven't heard you say much positive about your job in a long time."

I was silent for a moment as I realized she was right. I couldn't think of the last time I had something positive to say about my job. The politics were crazy. The worship of the bottom line had overtaken my being able to use my talents to help others, which was why I had gotten into the job to begin with.

"Are you there?" my dad asked.

"Yeah, I'm here. Wow, I think you're right. I really wasn't happy there," I replied.

"Well, to be honest, son," Dad said, "you haven't really seemed happy or yourself for a long time."

"We've both been worried about you," Mom added.

"Are you going to be okay financially?" Dad asked.

I assured them I would be okay for a while.

"So, why not take some time off?" my mom asked.

"I don't think this is the time for a vacation," I replied.

"I'm not suggesting a vacation. I was thinking about just taking some time to figure out what to do next," Mom said.

"Well, it's a pretty tough job market out there," I said. "I need to get out there as fast as possible."

"But what if you get another job like the one you just had?" Mom asked. "Why don't you take some time and figure out what you want in life?"

"But I already have a career," I argued.

"I hope you want more out of life than a career," Dad added. "Son, life is about more than just a career. It's about connecting with others and doing the things that make you smile. Remember, you used to love to paint. When was the last time you picked up a paintbrush?"

"We're not saying retire. Just take a few weeks off to get back in touch with who you are. I know. Go to Daytona Beach. Your uncle has a bungalow there that he hardly ever visits anymore. I'm sure he wouldn't mind you using it," Mom said.

The beach. I used to love to go the beach. I couldn't even remember the last time I had been to the beach. A few days of relaxing in the sun and playing in the ocean could be exactly what I needed to get back on my feet. Plus, I could go into job interviews looking tanned and relaxed.

"That's a great idea, Mom. I'll call Uncle Doug and ask him if I can use the place."

Our conversation drifted to the fun we used to have at the beach, and as we chatted, I was getting really excited about some time away from my home that needed lots of work. And where my life, which also needed lots of work, might take me.

My uncle was happy to let me use the bungalow and asked if I could be there for a few weeks. He was having some work done to update it before he put it on the market to sell and said he would feel better if there was someone to watch over the progress. The lawn maintenance guy had offered to check it over when he was in the neighborhood, but my uncle said he'd feel better if someone was checking on it every day.

I readily agreed and made arrangements to drive to Daytona to stay for three weeks.

And so my adventure began.

DAY 1

There's something exciting about going somewhere new. I think it's partly the anticipation of what can be, combined with our hopes and daydreams. And so it was with a smile on my face that I drove under the overpass that read "Welcome to Daytona Beach."

As I drove toward the beach, I marveled at how Daytona had grown since the last time I had been there. It's funny, it was only an hour and a half away from where I lived, but I hadn't been there in years. Although I loved the beach, there was always something else I had to do, or I thought I'd go after I lost a few pounds, or any number of other excuses. Why had I made excuses for not doing what I love to do? Was I afraid of enjoying life? Or was I a workaholic?

I was pondering these questions when I began my journey across the Halifax River, and at the peak of the bridge I caught my first glimpse of the turquoise waters and white cresting waves of the Atlantic Ocean. I lost my concentration and focused only on the joys that lay ahead as I wound through the small backstreets to my uncle's bungalow.

As I turned onto Hibiscus Lane, it was like going back in time. Not much had changed here since I was a child. The small 1950s cement block homes were still a variety of pastel colors with metal hurricane awnings and front lawns of grass burned by the salt and sun. Up on the left I saw my uncle's place looking a little worse for wear. Its bright yellow paint faded to a dull cream and was peeling. Its lawn more brown than green and its hibiscus plants overgrown and gangly.

It made me sad to see a place of such fond memories had fallen into disrepair. I pulled into the cracked driveway and walked to the front door. The old flamingo screen door made me smile as I remembered my aunt Anita telling me how she thought no Florida home was complete unless it had a screen door with a tropical scene on it. And I smiled thinking of how we had walked to and from the beach on different streets so that we could see the wide variety of screen scenes on the front doors.

The screen door squeaked as I opened the front door, and a hot blast of musty air burst past me into the yard. I took a step back and a gulp of fresh air, held my breath, and headed for the back of the house to open some windows and let the cross breezes cool down and clear out the house.

By my third trip from the car to the house, the rooms were comfortable. I pulled the sheets off the furniture, folded them, put them in the hall closet, and turned my attention to unpacking and getting reacquainted with this bungalow.

Not much had changed since the last time I was there. The bamboo cane furniture still had its "nifty fifties" tropical print upholstery although it was well worn and faded. The kitchen's avocado green appliances had been upgraded to newer white ones a few years back. But the kitchen still had the turquoise-and-white checkered linoleum floor and turquoise countertops.

Each of the two small bedrooms had a double-sized bed and dresser. The master bedroom also had Aunt Anita's vanity with pictures of family at the beach tucked in every possible space around the framed mirror. That had been my uncle's idea so that when she was missing her family, she could sit at her vanity and look at her reflection completely surrounded by these photos to remember how much she was loved.

My aunt had died two years ago from cancer, and it was weird being in her place exactly the way she had left it. With perfume and suntan lotion on the vanity top and her clothes hanging in the closet like she had expected to come back anytime. But I knew she never would.

"Why do things have to change, and people have to die?" I thought to myself and then I heard a knock on the door.

"Hello? Helloooooooooooo?" a tiny elderly woman called out from the other side of the flamingo screen door.

She stepped back as I opened the screen door, and I thought, "Well, not everything has changed."

It was Mrs. Vargas. She had lived next door as long as I could remember and was always in everybody's business. My uncle said he didn't need a burglar alarm as long as Mrs. Vargas was around.

Although she looked older, her skin was still a deep tan with the texture of leather, and her hair was still Marilyn Monroe blonde, and in curlers. I don't ever remember seeing her hair without those big curlers. Even at the beach she wore curlers with a big scarf tied over them, making her head look huge.

"Hi, Mrs. Vargas, I'm Jack, Anita and Doug's nephew. Remember me?"

"Aren't you the one who blew up those Styrofoam cups with firecrackers one New Year's Eve?" she asked.

"Guilty," I laughed. "But you'll be happy to know that I don't play with firecrackers anymore."

Mrs. Vargas didn't seem amused. "Good. I found little bits of Styrofoam in my yard for weeks after that. Your uncle said he didn't see them, but I could. I just came over to remind you that this is a nice, quiet neighborhood, and we don't want a lot of noise or parties going on. We can leave our windows open and our doors unlocked, and we like things just the way they are. Without a lot of outsiders."

I assured her that I would do my best to keep it down, and she turned to go back to her home.

"Oh, by the way, sorry to hear about your aunt," she said.

"Thanks," I replied, but she was already off yelling at a pet owner whose dog had stopped to water her mailbox.

"Change might be a good thing after all." I smiled to myself. "And I hear the beach calling to me."

I quickly changed and walked the two blocks to the beach. As I got closer to the water, I began to feel the gentle breeze coming from the ocean. I sighed and thought, "I need this more than I thought."

After I crossed A1A, I stepped off the sidewalk into the sand and took off my flip-flops and wiggled my toes in the warm sand. I found a good place to set up my towel and beach chair and walked down to the ocean.

As I stepped into the water, a wave came roaring toward the shore carrying what looked like a person with his arms outstretched in front of him. He sailed onto shore about ten feet away from me, yelled "wahoo!" and ran back out into the surf.

I was surprised, but after all, this was Daytona, and I was starting a new chapter of my life, so I decided not to think anymore about it and headed out to play in the surf.

I had made it about halfway out toward the breaking waves when I saw the odd fellow go by me again riding just below the top of the wave. I smiled and kept going and moments later heard "wahoo!" again.

I laughed to myself, shook my head, and continued on past the breaking waves and into calmer water.

I had been floating for just a short time when a small bald head popped up a few feet away from me.

"I'm really enjoying the bodysurfing today," the man said.

"It looks like you're having fun," I replied.

"Oh yes, I am. There's nothing like bodysurfing to remind you of how right the world is," he said. "Do you bodysurf?"

"I did when I was younger. But I've got a bad back," I said, trying to cut the conversation short. I had come to Daytona to relax and start a new chapter of my life, not do all the stuff I did thirty years ago.

"I had a bad back too." The little man continued, "But I find the water helps, and for me bodysurfing is like getting a chiropractic adjustment from Mother Nature."

"I'll take your word for it," I laughed.

"Well, if you change your mind, just let me know. I'm out here most every day," he said. Then he swam off and into a wave that carried him toward the shore.

I had bodysurfed when I was a kid but had never been carried as far as this guy was, and on such small waves. Maybe I should ask him for a tip and the name of a local chiropractor just in case. But then I thought that would be awkward.

"What about starting the next chapter in your life?" I thought to myself. How can you think of starting a new chapter if you're still behaving like the old you—not wanting to ask for help or embarrass yourself? What's the worse that could happen? You hurt yourself and look like a fool. On the other hand, he does look like he's having fun. Yeah, but maybe he's having too much fun. He could be crazy, you know.

My inner dialogue continued like this for quite some time and was getting me nowhere when the bald head popped up again and said, "I have the name of a good chiropractor if that's what you're worried about. Why don't you try it?"

"Maybe tomorrow," I replied.

"Okay," he said. "By the way, my name is Fin."

Then he was off in a flash, and a few moments later I heard another "wahoo!"

I swam back to shore, dried off, sat in the beach chair, and drifted off to sleep. When I awoke, I was staring up into a beach umbrella. I looked around, but there was no sign of anyone. Just a note that read "You were starting to get a little pink."

I waited for a few minutes to see if the owner of the umbrella would appear, but then decided to pack my things and head back to the bungalow to contact the contractor and figure out a game plan for my uncle's renovations. I left the umbrella where it was in the hopes that whoever left it would come back for it.

When I returned to the bungalow, the musty smell was gone, and I surveyed the little place and what I thought needed to be done. Being a self-proclaimed "king of lists" I got out a pen and my notepad and started writing down the things the bungalow needed to spruce it up. It definitely needed to be painted inside and out, and it needed new roofing shingles, and the kitchen could benefit with a bit of an update as well. Structurally it was sound, and the terrazzo floors were in good shape, aside from a few cracks, nothing that a good polish and a throw rug couldn't fix. In all, there were about twenty things—some major, others minor—that needed to be done.

I called the contractor, Vincent Sams, who informed me that the job he was on was taking longer than expected, and he would be available starting next week and not this week. At first, I was annoyed but then decided to make the first week a vacation and not have to worry about the renovation. Then I went off to the supermarket for food, suntan lotion, a good murder mystery to read on the beach, and cleaning supplies.

That evening I popped a frozen dinner into the small microwave on the kitchen counter, opened a beer, and watched TV until I fell asleep on the couch.

# DAY 2

I slept well, but the next morning my back was stiff from sleeping on the couch. I moved slowly toward the kitchen to get the coffee percolating and then headed to the shower.

Looking in the mirror I saw that my face and the front of me had gotten a little pink while the back part of my body was still pale. So today I resolved to lay on my stomach at the beach, in order to even out the coloring and to not get too much sun. I had a few weeks of beach time ahead of me and didn't want to get burned the first few days.

So I sat down and watched television for a while, getting lost in the variety of game shows and reruns daytime programming provides. When I looked up, it was almost 1:30 p.m.

"What am I doing watching TV when I'm at the beach?" I asked annoyed with myself.

Quickly I changed into my swimming suit, applied a liberal amount of the spray on suntan lotion I had purchased at the supermarket, and found that the packaging claim of "easily covers your back with the push of a button" was true, as long as you placed your body at a forty-five-degree angle and sprayed liberally over each shoulder.

Then I grabbed my backpack and beach chair and hurried off to the beach, anxious that I wasn't making the most of my time there.

When I arrived at the beach, I saw that the umbrella that was set over me yesterday had been moved and that someone was lying under it. As I got closer, I saw that it was Fin, the odd little bodysurfer I had met the day before. So I went over to thank him for the use of the umbrella.

He looked up as he saw me coming and waved. I waved back and walked over.

"Thanks for the use of the umbrella," I said.

"No worries," he replied. "You were in a pretty deep, sleep and I didn't want you to get burned on your first day at the beach."

"Well, thanks again," I said as I turned to go find a place to set my chair.

"Why don't you join me?" Fin asked.

"I don't want to intrude," I said, trying to think of a way to be able to sit by myself.

"It's no intrusion at all. In fact, I'd enjoy the company. Besides, you look like you've had a rough time of it lately and could use a friend," he said.

"Well, okay," I replied, wondering just what shape I was in if he could tell by looking at me that I'd had some rough times lately.

I set my towel next to Fin's and lay down on my stomach, determined to get rid of my two-toned appearance.

"Where are you from?" he asked.

"Orlando."

"What brings you to Daytona?"

"I'm here to oversee the work on my uncle's house."

"Are you a contractor?"

"No, I just have some time on my hands right now and thought I could combine a vacation with helping out my uncle," I said.

"Are you one of those guys who retired by the time he's fifty?" he asked.

"I wish," I laughed. "No, the company I worked for retired me early, so I decided to take some time off to figure out what comes next."

"That's a smart thing to do," he answered.

And before I knew it, I had told him the whole story of the demise of my career and how angry it made me feel.

"So you're here to start a new chapter in your life?" he asked.

I was a little surprised that he had used the exact words that I had used when thinking about this to myself, and it must have shown on my face.

"Did I say something wrong?" he asked.

"No, it's just that's exactly what I've been saying to myself ever since I lost my job, but I haven't said it to anyone else because I think it sounds so corny. It's just a coincidence. I guess a lot of people use that phrase."

Fin smiled and said, "Well, I don't ever remember using it before, and I don't believe in coincidences. That was just synchronicity showing you that you are on the right path."

"Synchro—what?" I asked.

Fin smiled and explained, "Synchronicity is the universe's way of giving you signs that you are on the right path. It's kind of like road signs to your future self."

"What?" I asked.

"Synchronicity is the little signs in your life that tell you that you are on the right track. For example, what are the chances that you meet some stranger and he uses the exact terminology that you use to yourself when describing something you're thinking or worrying about?"

"Well, it is kind of a common phrase, isn't it?" I said.

"I guess it could be. But I honestly don't ever recall using it before. I think it's kind of corny too."

"So did it surprise you when you said it?" I asked.

"Nothing I say surprises me anymore," he laughed.

I laughed too. There was something very comforting about Fin and the way he didn't take himself seriously.

"So if you're saying 'starting a new chapter,' is this road sign telling me that I am on the right path, where is my life going?"

"That's a great question. Good for you for asking it," he replied." Of course, a better question would be, how am I living it?"

"So was my losing my job synchronicity too?" I asked.

He thought for a moment and then said, "No, I think that might be more of a wake-up call than synchronicity."

"A wake-up call?"

"Yeah, a wake up call. You told me earlier that you hadn't been happy in your job for some time but that you'd held on to the job for security and the health benefits. That's not living your life to the fullest," he said.

"But it was secure," I objected. "And I knew where the next paycheck was coming from. And do you know the cost of health insurance today?"

"But we weren't put on this earth to be secure, and life is anything but predictable as you well know. I think we are put on this earth to make it a better place, and that means laughing often, taking risks, loving deeply, and helping others. That takes courage, but I believe that the me I'm meant to be is waiting for that courage to kick in. The courage to take a stand and do what I think is right, and not worry about what others think.

"For example, there was a time when I took myself so seriously that I would never even have considered bodysurfing. 'That's for kids,' I told myself because I was worrying about what other people would think of this grown man playing in the water."

"What changed your mind?" I asked.

"I had my own wake-up call and realized that the people whom I had been trying to impress were only interested in me as long as I could impress them. It was more a matter of convenience for them than a bond of friendship with me. I'm not judging them. It was my choice to try to gain their admiration by impressing them. But one day I realized that I had lost myself and the joy of living in the process."

"So what did you do?' I asked.

"Well, for a while I just stewed about it and blamed everyone else for not being a good friend. But then I realized that I had wanted to be friends with them for the happiness I thought I could gain from associating with them. And if that was the case, it was my fault as much if not more than theirs. So I decided to start looking for the happiness that seemed to elude me all of my adult life.

"At first, I couldn't even remember being happy. And just as I was thinking 'there must've been some time when I was happy' I saw a television ad for Daytona Beach, and I remembered how happy I was as a child when my family would vacation at the beach and all the fun my brother and I had bodysurfing."

"So you're saying bodysurfing is the key to happiness?" I joked.

"Well, in a way it is," he laughed.

"You see, that was the last time I remembered really laughing without caring what others thought. So I decided to go to Daytona Beach and bodysurf. Looking back on it, I see that ad as part of the synchronicity of my life. It appeared exactly when I needed it, to help me get to where I wanted to go."

"I guess that makes as much sense as anything else," I agreed.

"Well, it did to me too at the time, but when I got here and ran in the water to bodysurf, it was harder than I remembered, and I was very self-conscious about what people would think of a grown man acting like a child. So I didn't really enjoy it, and that made me angry and feel like a fool for following a folly without a plan."

"But you obviously enjoy it now, and you're really good at it, so what changed?" I asked.

"My attitude. As I was standing in the waves fuming about what an ass I'd been to think this would make my life better. A teenage boy came up and said, 'The bodysurfing is great today. Isn't it?' Then he dove into a wave that took him onto the shoreline. At that moment I hated him. Looking back on it, I can't believe it, but I actually hated that kid for enjoying the water. Well, actually it was for being better at something than I was. I stood in the water and watched the teenager jump in the waves again and again. Not all the waves took him to shore, and I noticed that if he jumped into a wave that didn't take him into shore, he just swam back out and tried again. And then it hit me. I was making finding happiness so serious that I never would find it. So I watched the teenager some more and noticed that while I had been jumping into a wave after it had already started to crash and fought the wave to gain control, he jumped into the wave as it was just cresting and let the energy of the wave carry him up and along. He was letting the wave do the work, and I had been fighting the wave and losing the battle."

"So you tried it, and it took you onto the beach?" I asked.

"Not at first," Fin said. "First, I jumped into a wave, and it took me a little way and dropped me. A couple of waves pummeled me into the sand. But I kept getting up and back out, and my natural curiosity got the best of me as I tried to figure out how to catch the wave. It became a game, and with each failed attempt, I got back up and thought, 'Well, now I know that holding my arms that way won't work, or I jumped into the wave too soon.' It wasn't long until I was exhausted, so I went on the beach and fell into a deep, really sound sleep, and when I woke up, I felt better but was really sunburned. That's why I put my umbrella over you yesterday. I wanted my negative experience to be able to help someone else."

"And my dermatologist thanks you for it," I said laughing. "So then what happened?"

"Well, since I was sunburned, I decided to spend the next day shopping for suntan lotion and understanding more about waves. I went to the public library and found an oceanography book that explained about waves and the energy that creates them. And once I understood the energy of waves and the cycle of water, I realized that I could learn a lot from my time here on the beach. So do you want to try bodysurfing?" he asked.

"Well, if it can be life changing, I don't want to let an opportunity like this pass me by," I quipped.

"It helped change my life," Fin said. "I can't make any promises about yours, but I'll be glad to teach you what I've learned so that you can enjoy it."

"You see," he said, picking up a stick and drawing a circle in the sand, "the waves are just circles of energy in the water. Somewhere off the horizon a wind blows the surface of the water, and that creates a circle of energy moving in the direction of the wind. The energy keeps traveling in a circular form until the circle is broken when it gets into shallower water and hits the sand on the bottom of the ocean floor. Once the circle of energy is broken, the wave breaks, and the energy carries the wave to shore.

"I had been jumping into the wave after the circle of energy had broken and was trying to ride the downward energy, which, no big surprise, kept pushing me down. What I learned is to jump into the energy as it moves up, and its energy will pull you up and keep you on top as you ride to your destination. It's just like life, if you gravitate toward things that pull you down, you shouldn't be surprised to find yourself down a lot of the time. But if you jump into the things that lift your spirit, they will raise you up and carry you to your highest good."

"Whoa! You got all that from a wave?" I asked.

"I certainly did, but that's just the beginning, I'll tell you more later. But for now let's go put my research to the test."

And so we ran into the water and swam out past where the waves were breaking, and I learned to trust Fin's judgment when he told me to jump in a wave. Like anything, it took practice to understand where to jump, but little by little, I got the hang of it. However, the waves didn't carry me as far as they were carrying Fin, and I began to get discouraged.

"If you ride a wave that doesn't carry you far, get back up and out there again. There are more waves coming," Fin said. "And if you don't keep trying, you'll never find the wave that will give you the ride of your life. And by the way, that goes for anything in life."

So I kept trying, and before long I had figured out the best way to hold my arms and head to glide faster and farther through the water. Soon I had ridden several waves all the way onto the beach. It was an amazing afternoon, and it seemed to fly by.

Then we heard a faint roll of thunder in the distance, and we both knew it was time to get out of the water and head home before the thunderstorm got any closer.

"This has been a great day," I said. "Thanks!"

"It's been great for me too, my friend. I'll be out here tomorrow. Maybe I'll see you then."

"Definitely!" I said and headed off toward the bungalow.

The rain arrived soon after I got to the bungalow, and it was nice to sit inside and watch the rain through the jalousie windows and feel the damp, cool air refreshing the house. I couldn't remember the last time I had just sat and enjoyed life without a television or book to occupy my mind. This time of doing nothing was as refreshing to me as the rain was to the salt-covered plants outside.

After dinner I sat down on the couch and was about to turn on the TV when what Fin said about riding waves being similar to life popped into my head. I was gravitating toward things that were pulling me down and then being angry at them for pulling me down. So being the king of lists, I began to make a list of the things that I did that pulled me down and another list of the things I did that lifted my spirits. It was amazing how short the good list was and how long the downward list turned out to be.

"This is crazy!" I thought to myself. You have an enjoyable afternoon with some odd little man and the next thing you know you're taking his advice as if he were your mentor. I started to wad up the two sheets of paper, but something inside me told me to hold on to them. So I folded them and put them in the top drawer of the dresser I was using in the guest room and went to bed. Tired, refreshed, and confused.

DAY 3

The next morning I was up early and ate breakfast at the round cement picnic table in the backyard. I looked around and saw the hibiscus looking perky after yesterday's rain. Even the grass seemed to be greener after just one rain, and I thought to myself, "It's amazing how something that looked so tired the day before can become so vibrant with water." Even I was feeling more alive after my day of bodysurfing.

As I was sitting there, I remembered how much easier it is to pull weeds when the ground is wet. So after breakfast I weeded the flowerbeds around the house. Then went inside, crossed that off my list, showered, sprayed on the suntan lotion, and headed off to the beach only to find the ocean as smooth as a lake. It was close to low tide, and the beach looked huge. There was no one in sight when I got there, so I set up my chair and decided to take a walk down to the pier.

When I got back to my beach chair, Fin was settled in beside it sitting cross-legged with his eyes closed and a big smile across his face. Although I tried to be quiet as I approached, he looked up and waved.

"Did you enjoy your walk?" he asked.

"Yeah, but I'm disappointed that the waves are so lame today," I said.

He laughed and said, "Well, I'll tell you the secret to life that you'll find in these waves, if you answer one question for me."

"I'm not the philosopher. You are," I laughed. "So don't think I'll be giving you the answer to any mysteries of life."

"It's an easy question." He smiled. "What's your name?"

"Oh, sorry. I'm Jack," I said a little embarrassed that I hadn't introduced myself.

"Well, Jack, it's a pleasure sharing this beautiful day at the beach with you," he said. "I apologize for not asking sooner, but I've gotten into the habit of seeing everyone as a friend, and when I see everyone in that way, names don't seem to matter as much anymore."

"How can you see everyone as a friend?" I asked. "Isn't that being a little naive?"

"Well, I'll answer that in a second, but first, since you told me your name, I'll tell you the secret of life that these . . . what did you call them? Oh yes, 'lame' waves tell us. You see, there is no good wave or bad wave. A wave is just a wave. It is our human judgment that wants to define them as good or bad.

"See out there?" he asked, pointing to a father playing with his small child in the almost nonexistent waves as they lapped the shore. "To them this is the perfect type of wave. If the waves were much stronger, the child wouldn't be able to keep her balance in the water, and the father would be afraid for her safety, instead of playing with her.

"Now, for what you want to do, it may seem that the waves are lame, but it is only that the waves are different than what you want them to be. The same is true in life. We label everything as good and bad, when in actuality everything is really neutral, and we label it as it suits our needs."

"Everything is neutral? Do you mean to tell me that if a giant wave came and washed up on shore, destroying people's homes, that it wouldn't be a bad wave?"

"Well, it probably wouldn't be a pleasant experience for the people whose homes were damaged or destroyed. But at the same time if a photographer took a picture of the wave, you could see how beautiful and magnificent it looks as the light bounces off it, showing the power of its energy. In fact, there's a beautiful Japanese woodcut by Hokusai depicting just such a wave as it approaches a fishing village. It's considered a masterpiece. So you see, some would see it as beautiful, and others would see it as horrible, and they would both be right in their own opinion. The truth of the matter is that it is a wave doing what waves do.

"The interesting thing is that if we can do this type of labeling to a wave, imagine what kind of labeling we do to people. For example, yesterday I told you about when I first came to Daytona and saw a teenager bodysurfing and enjoying it, and that I hated him for doing it. Well, I'm sure I thought he was showing off and rubbing my nose in the fact that he could do something better than I could. But looking back on it now, I truly think he was just enjoying the moment. It was my insecurities and ego that were trying to make him look bad in order to make me feel better about myself. So I labeled him a 'show-off' and hated him for being one. But even if he was showing off, he wasn't hurting anyone, and by watching him, I began to understand how to bodysurf. So this person who I was judging as 'show-off' and 'deserving to be hated' actually was a good influence in my life and helped me get to the point where I'm at today."

"You mean a person who sees everyone as a friend," I said skeptically.

"Well, I was going to say 'happy,'" Fin answered. "But yes, seeing everyone as a friend is part of my happiness. You see, once I discovered that just like a wave is a wave, people are just people, I began to realize that it was how I was labeling them that was creating my thoughts about them. This person cut me off in traffic, so they are bad, and a bad driver or this person has a bumper sticker I like, and so they are a good person. The truth is the person who cut me off in traffic could have had a number of reasons for doing so, including not even seeing me in their side mirror. It wasn't a personal attack on me, it was just a person preoccupied and not paying as close attention as he or she should have. The point is, it was just a person doing what people do, which is sometimes driving while they are preoccupied. I know I've done it before."

"Me too," I admitted. "But I don't think I could see everyone as a friend."

"Maybe not right at this moment. But in time I bet you will. You see, what you think becomes your reality, and if you think that everyone is out to get you, when someone cuts you off in traffic, you'll think 'that person deliberately cut me off to slow down my commute,' and fume about it for the rest of your drive. Where as if you think that everyone is a potential friend you might wonder why he or she is so preoccupied and wish the driver a safe journey and continue your commute without thinking anything else about it. Which sounds better to you?"

"Well, when you put it that way. I guess welcoming potential friends into my life isn't so bad," I said. "But these neutral waves sure aren't what I was hoping for today. I want to bodysurf!"

"Me too," Fin said. "But it's important to remember that you are exactly where you are supposed to be."

"Don't tell me you're getting this from the neutral waves that are too small to bodysurf," I said sarcastically.

"Actually, yes," Fin said, ignoring the sarcasm in my voice. "You see, the universe wants you to be happy and has a great plan for you, and right now the plan seems to include sitting here chatting—and perhaps practicing patience—while we enjoy this wonderful day."

"You mean this neutral day," I corrected.

"You're right." He smiled. "But since the day is neutral, and it is only my opinion that makes it good or bad to me. I'm choosing to make it a great day. And how could it not be? I'm at the beach chatting with a new friend about life and happiness."

"In the business world, we call that setting an intention," I added.

"Same in the spiritual world too," Fin agreed.

"Are you some cult guru or missionary or something?" I asked warily.

Fin let out a big laugh and looked at me with such kindness that my wariness eased.

"No. I'm nothing like that. Just a guy on a journey called life," he said still smiling.

"Well, I've had some bad experiences with some religious types," I said, trying to justify my reaction, "and even though they may be neutral people, their actions and words have still hurt me."

"I know a lot of people who have been hurt by organizations labeling and treating God's children as good or bad. But once again those are just labels they use to try and justify their own actions. I believe that whatever child of God I'm with at any moment is one of God's favorites, because I think God loves us all equally. No matter what! God is this great parent who understands the whole neutral thing and chooses to see each of us a wonderful child who can bring the world so much joy, but gives us the chance to choose for ourselves."

"If that's true, I think it might be better if God did the choosing for us," I muttered.

Fin looked over at a little boy throwing mud bombs at green army men sending them scattering around the moat of a sand castle they were positioned to defend.

"God is not like that," he said, pointing to the boy gleefully bombing the toy soldiers. "He's not this tyrant leader who enjoys telling his children what to do or sending his people scattering in terror at his whim. God is a loving parent wincing when his child makes a mistake but allowing him or her to make the mistake and hoping they will learn and grow from it. Understand that God does not create the chaos in our lives. We do. But he sends us signs along the way to help us get back on the right track."

"That's synchronicity. Right?" I said, proud I could actually use the word intelligently in a conversation with this man.

"Very good." Fin smiled. "Now while we've been talking, the waves have gotten larger and are currently just about the size I prefer to bodysurf in. Want to join me?"

And with that we ran off toward the neutral (though what I thought to be perfect) waves.

Although all the waves looked to be about the same, each one was a little different. And I found myself jumping into some waves that just washed over my head and raced on to the beach leaving me behind. So I stood there and watched Fin, who looked like he was lost in thought as he stared out into the oncoming waves.

As I watched him, I noticed that every wave he chose to jump into he was able to ride quite a distance and end it with a "wahoo!"

"What's going on with these waves? Or is it me?" I asked.

"Just because a wave is passing doesn't mean it's the right one for you. If you want to get the best ride from a wave, be patient, feel the energy of the waves, and listen to your gut. When it feels right, jump in and enjoy the ride. By the way, that works in life too."

"Of course it does," I laughed and then worked very hard at being patient.

After a few minutes of working at being patient, I became very impatient. The waves I chose not to ride were the ones Fin rode in. So then I thought I'd just follow Fin and jump into the ones he jumped into. That didn't work at all.

As Fin swam back from yet another successful bodysurfing experience, I said, "Okay, I give. What's the secret to this 'being patient, feel the energy, and listen to your gut thing?'"

"You're concentrating too hard on the lack of the perfect wave, and so that is what you are noticing," Fin said. "Remember life happens between waves too. So stand here perfectly still and just look out at the horizon. Feel the breeze on your face and watch the birds flying by. Just stand here and concentrate on this for right now."

After a few minutes of trying to stand still I became impatient, because while the water forming some waves would wash right over me, other times a current would be tugging at my feet while a building wave would hit my chest and shoulders and knock me over. I noticed Fin was having the same problem and said so.

"Congratulations, Jack! That's what the energy of the wave feels like. For a really good ride, you'll feel a slight tug at your feet by the outgoing current while your body is being carried toward shore by the energy of the wave. When you feel that tug and pull at the same time, and it feels right, then trust your gut and go for it. When the right one comes, jump in, hang on, and enjoy the ride."

And so I did, again, and again and again.

When we were both exhausted and back in our beach chairs, I thanked Fin for being so patient with me, and for my impatience.

"No worries." Fin smiled back. "I've been there before. And had to discover the neutrality of the wave and the outgoing current so that I could see the benefit of both."

"Okay," I said, taking the bait, "what do you mean?"

"Well, when I first came back to Daytona, I was thinking that the world was against me. So when I was having the same trouble you were at figuring out how to choose the right wave, I was even more frustrated than you appeared to be. But being stubborn, I thought, 'I'll be damned if I'm going to give up.' So I stood there looking out to sea, trying to figure it out, when an outgoing current ripped my legs out from under me. At first, I thought, 'Great, now I can't even stand in the water.' Then it hit me that for every action, there is an equal and opposite reaction. So if I felt a tug at my feet that meant that the wave above was going to be more powerful. And too powerful a tug at my feet would diminish the wave's energy. So I put that theory to the test, and it works. What I didn't realize is that in the negative frame of mind I was in at the time, in order for me to feel the energy of the wave, I had to put it into a context where it would bother me. Then I had no problem seeing it. The whole time I was trying to jump into the waves, I was ignoring the very thing that would help make it a good ride. Once I just wanted to stand still and mope, the energy was all I could feel because it was annoying me. That was a good lesson for me. And really helped me understand that sometimes the things that seem to annoy us the most are the very things that can help carry us to our highest good. Or in this case, a really great ride."

"Are you saying I'm in a negative frame of mind?" I asked defensively.

(How could he think I was in a negative frame of mind? I was having fun out there, and I was feeling better than I had in a long time.)

"No, I'm just saying that I know you've been hurt. And I know from experience that when we've been hurt, we're more susceptible to experiencing the things that annoy us, as opposed to the things that enrich us, even if they are the same thing. Our egos say, 'Look, here is more pain for you to enjoy.' We tend to focus on the negative attributes of something instead of the positive things it brings to us. So one day, the waves tossing you around would be fun, no matter the outcome. On another, the same waves will irritate you and make you think the world is against you."

Strangely enough, that made sense to me. "This whole neutral thing is beginning to make sense," I said feeling less defensive. "Of course, it makes sense that our moods would influence our judgment of things. So how do we stay in a positive mood?"

"Ahhhh, Jack, that is the question and a great lesson. But not for today. I've lost track of time and have to be going. I have some things I've promised to do," he said. And in the swift, fluid movement of something that has become second nature, he packed up his beach paraphernalia and was walking down the beach singing to himself in an instant.

I sat on the beach for a while and watched as the waves came in smaller sizes and watched young children with boogie boards laughing as they played in the waves. I smiled because their laughter reminded me of the fun I had experienced riding the waves with Fin, the beachside philosopher. And the idea that everything is neutral popped back into my head. These waves were too small for me to enjoy bodysurfing, but they were the perfect size for these children to enjoy their time in the water. And, in watching them enjoying life, I too was smiling to myself and enjoying the end product of these waves, which I would have labeled as "lame" earlier today.

After about an hour, I did the official suntan poke (pushing the skin of my forearm with my finger to see if my skin is too pink) and decided to head back to the bungalow. After I showered, I made a shopping list and went shopping for some real food. The microwaveable dinners were losing their appeal. I was hungry for fresh fish and some fruit.

When I returned from the store, I turned on the radio only to find that it had poor reception, so I looked toward the old phonograph that sat in the corner. In the wooden storage case were some old records. As I looked through them, I saw the Ella Fitzgerald album I always remembered my aunt playing. Surprisingly enough, it didn't look warped, so I put it on the turntable and smiled as the record crackled, and Ella hit those first few notes of "Over the Rainbow." It occurred to me that Daytona and this bungalow with my aunt and uncle had always been that magical over-the-rainbow place for me. And now, here I was a middle-aged man cooking a real dinner in the bungalow that hadn't changed much since the first time I'd heard Ella sing this song. It's amazing the memories a song can bring to mind. And my thoughts were full of all the laughter my family had shared in this tiny, little building and how my aunt had always encouraged me in drawing and painting.

This was where I first tasted coconut shrimp and ice cream with cherries flambé. (To a young boy, anything flambé is awe-inspiring.) And this is where we would play Scrabble or crazy eights until it was time for bed. Mom and Dad slept in the guest room, and my brother and I slept on inflatable mattresses on the sunporch where it was cooler.

My reminiscing was disturbed by a sharp knock on the door. I could see through the kitchen window that it was Mrs. Vargas.

I sighed, resigned myself to getting yelled at, and went to answer the door, wondering if the music was too loud.

I opened the door, and there stood Mrs. Vargas with her hair in curlers tied up in a lime-green-and-safety-orange scarf and holding a Styrofoam plate in her hands with four cookies on it.

"I'd just finished making some cookies for the homeless shelter, and then I heard that music coming from over here, and it reminded me of your uncle and how he had a sweet tooth. So I thought you might like a couple of cookies to go with whatever it is you're cooking."

I'm not sure what surprised me more. That she was bringing me cookies or that she baked for the homeless instead of kicking them. So I was at a loss for words when she was actually nice to me.

"Well, thank you," I said.

And then my mouth started saying something that my mind couldn't believe.

"Would you like to come in?' I asked.

"Well, I can see you're getting ready for dinner. So if you're just asking me to come into chat, I'd have to say thank you, but no."

(My mind let out a silent sigh of relief a little too soon.)

"But if you're asking me to join you for dinner, since I brought you the cookies and all, I'd have to say thank you, yes," she continued.

My mind raced, but I couldn't think of a graceful way out of asking her to dinner, so I said, "It's a simple meal of just broiled fish and fresh fruit, but you're welcome to join me if you like." (I was congratulating myself on the subtle way of playing on the meagerness of my meal.)

"Well, that's not enough for two people," she said with what I took for disbelief that I would even ask her to participate in such a puny meal.

Then she added, "I was just making myself a salad. I'll go get it, and we can have that too. I'll be back in a second."

And as I stood slack jawed in the doorway, off she ran to her periwinkle blue bungalow to get her salad.

I returned to the kitchen wondering what had just happened and how a perfectly lovely day had taken this turn when I remembered the lesson about everything being neutral and how sometimes the things that annoy you can be the same things that can bring joy into your life.

"Well, the cookies do look good," I said to myself, "so perhaps the evening won't be a total waste."

In a few minutes, Mrs. Vargas was back with a large salad full of crunchy vegetables. "You keep cooking," she called from the yard. "I'm going to let myself in."

Ella was still singing as we sat down to dinner.

"I remember the first time I saw Ella Fitzgerald in concert," Mrs. Vargas said, watching me to see if I was paying attention. "Here was this woman with that enormous voice belting out of her. I never heard anyone that had a voice like that, before or since."

"First time?" I asked. "How many times did you see her?"

"Oh, every time she was in the state. I can't remember how many times, but each time was a real treat. We'd find out where she was performing, and my husband, Hal, and I would make it a minivacation and stay at a nice motel and then get all dressed up to see Ella in concert. One time we were at this supper club, and they had overbooked, so we had to sit at this table they set up on the dance floor. As the band played, people kept bumping into our table and spilling our drinks. If Ella hadn't been scheduled to perform, we'd have got up and walked out. Hal complained about the table, but the maître d' just said, 'If you want to see the show, that's the only table we have for you.'

"So we decided to stay, and boy, am I glad we did." She continued with a sparkle in her eye. "Ella comes out, and she was in fine voice, and she came over to our little table crowded onto the dance floor and asked if we had a favorite song. Hal says 'You Do Something to Me,' and she sung it just for us. It was such a magical moment I wanted to get up and dance, but I thought that would be rude with

Ella performing and all, but it was like she was there just for us at that moment. I'll never forget that," she said in a faraway voice.

I was amazed. Here was nasty, mean Mrs. Vargas having dinner with me and telling me about a night Ella Fitzgerald sang to her, and she was so happy she wanted to dance. Maybe she wasn't nasty, mean old Mrs. Vargas after all. Maybe she was just a person doing what people do.

Was it synchronicity that had me put on Ella loud enough for Mrs. Vargas to hear the music and bring me the cookies to help me learn about neutrality?

"I can't even imagine what it would be like to have Ella sing just for you," I said, truly in awe.

"Well, if you take the most beautiful sunset you ever saw and combine it with the excited feeling you get when you see a shooting star, that was kind of what it felt like," she laughed.

Where was this coming from? Who knew Mrs. Vargas was so poetic?

"What a feeling," I exclaimed sincerely. "And beautifully said."

Then Mrs. Vargas blushed the way people do when they feel they've revealed too much about themselves.

"Well, I guess you didn't think this old broad had any poetry left inside," she said back in her crusty tone.

"I didn't mean that at all," I said. "It's just the way you described that moment I could actually understand how it must have felt."

"It was pretty amazing," she said, "but so was the time I sat and chatted with Eleanor Roosevelt."

"Are you just yanking my chain?" I asked.

"Nope," she laughed. "But I'll save that story for another day. Ask me some other time.

Your uncle tells me you got canned and came over here to find yourself. That true?"

I winced at the harsh sound of the reality, and she laughed again.

"Those ain't your uncle's words, they're mine, but they're true. Right?"

"Well, I prefer to think that I was reorganized . . . ," I began and then laughed and said, "yeah, they canned my ass."

"Well, Jack, I'm gonna finish the rest of my Ella story now. I think you might get something out of it," she said. "After she sang to us and the show was over, I asked the waiter if he'd be so kind as to ask Miss Fitzgerald to join us for a drink, and he looked at me like I had just thrown up on him. 'Madam,' he says, 'this is a whites-only club. We don't serve coloreds.'

"That moment changed my life. Here was this amazing lady with a beautiful voice, and it was okay for her to entertain us, but not for her to sit down and have a glass of wine with us. Just because of the color of her skin. What kind of thinking is that?"

"Stupid," I answered, surprised at where this conversation was going.

"Exactly. But that's the way things were back then. It was the law. Only until that moment I hadn't seen how stupid it really was. Since it was the law, I thought it was all right. Now I know better. The laws are made by people, and sometimes people make mistakes. I sure did by never thinking about how wrong it is to treat people as less than equal just because they are different. Different is just different. Now I think for myself and don't let politicians or anyone else tell me what is right or just.

"The reason I'm bringing this up is, here I was at the height of happiness, and then wham, something bad happened. But that something bad taught me something about being a good person. And the same thing can happen for you. You see, when the civil rights movement took place, Hal and I were right there helping in every way we could. It was the least we could do for Ella. And we made a lot of good friends during that time."

I just sat there amazed at this woman I had judged as old, crabby, and mean and realized that I had only labeled her from my rash judgments, without seeing her as a person.

"Well, don't just sit there a-staring," she said. "Go get them cookies. It's time for dessert."

I cleared the table and brought the cookies, which were delicious. After dinner she said she needed her nicotine fix and beauty rest. As she crossed the yard back to her place, I saw a different person than the one who had invited herself to dinner several hours before. She hadn't changed ⌐   · beginning to.

I did the dishes and went to bed happy and tired. I lay there going over what had happened since I had gotten up that morning. Amazed at how much life can be squeezed into one day.

DAY 4

It was still dark outside when I awoke the next morning. Instead of my usual coffee, I grabbed a bottle of water out of the fridge and decided to walk down to the beach to watch the sunrise.

As I sat there watching the colors of the sky changing from dark to bright, I thought about the past few days and how my life was changing and getting lighter also. Was it really the universe bringing all these changes in my life through synchronicity? It seemed crazy to think so, but how could I explain the past few days? Especially what happened yesterday. Never in a million years would I have thought I'd have dinner with Mrs. Vargas and she'd tell me the same thing as an odd little bodysurfing senior citizen philosopher that I had been hanging out with. Man, talk about starting a new chapter in my life! This one looked nothing like the one I had come from only days ago.

As if on cue, I saw Fin walking along the surf line with a bucket in one hand and a long-handled clawlike mechanism in the other.

"What on earth are you doing?" I asked. "Is that some sort of crab catcher?"

He looked down at the clawlike gizmo, laughed, and said, "How eccentric do you think I am? This is just a garbage grabber."

"You mean, you're picking up garbage? I didn't know you worked for the city," I said a little surprised.

"I don't. Why do you think I work for the city?"

"Because you're picking up garbage," I said, wondering why he would think picking up garbage is less eccentric than going crabbing when you're on the beach.

"I'm just taking my morning walk," he said. "I brought these along in case I come across garbage that might get caught in the tide and pulled out to sea," he said, holding the bucket out so that I could see the contents, which included several beer bottles, a clear plastic bag, and an empty cracker box.

"See that plastic bag?" He continued, "It looks innocent enough to us, just garbage. But as the tide washes that out to sea, it makes it move in a way that's similar to the way jellyfish move. I read that over a million birds and over one hundred thousand marine animals die each year by mistaking plastic bags and debris for food. So I'm just doing my part to help."

"But doesn't Daytona has a sanitation patrol? I've seen them drive up and down the beach in a tractorlike, minigarbage truck," I said.

"They do. But they can't be everywhere at once, so I'm just making sure that one less bird or sea turtle dies from a plastic bag. It's a good feeling and shows a small part of the gratitude I feel for being able to live in such a wonderful place. Believe me, the abundance I get from this little act of gratitude far outweighs carrying around this bucket and garbage grabber."

Maybe it was the lack of caffeine in my system, but I was totally confused. "What does picking up garbage have to do with abundance and gratitude?" I asked.

"Quite a bit," he answered. "I know it may seem strange, but let me explain."

"I'm about to get another life lesson, aren't I?" I laughed, rolling my eyes.

"Only if you want one," he said smiling.

"Of course I do," I said. "These ideas are already making a big difference in my life, and I have some questions for you, but first, tell me what picking up garbage has to do with abundance. And I'm guessing it's not an abundance of garbage."

"Well, unfortunately there is an abundance of garbage, but that's not the abundance I'm talking about. By now you know that I believe that the universe really wants each of us to succeed."

"And that's why synchronicity comes into our life," I added.

"You're a quick study," he laughed. "So for me, life is great because I get to live on the beach and bodysurf and watch the dolphins swim by."

He pointed to where a pod of dolphins was swimming by.

"Oh man, that's cool," I exclaimed, and we watched as they swam by.

"That's what I say every time I see them." Fin smiled "And I see them almost every day. Seeing dolphins always reminds me to come up for air."

"What?" I asked.

"You know, just stop what I'm doing, take a deep breath, and just be in the moment. It's amazing how great it feels to reconnect to the energy of the universe. Dolphins come up for air so gracefully, and they always remind me that I should do the same."

We stood silently on the beach watching the dolphins swim past us and farther northward. It really was a remarkable feeling, very calming, and at that moment I did feel connected to something bigger than myself.

Finally Fin said, "Now where was I?"

"You were about to give me a life lesson about gratitude and garbage," I teased.

"Oh yeah. Well, as you just saw, the beach is an amazing place and brings such an abundance of joy to my life."

I nodded.

"So every morning, as I set my intention for the day, I give thanks for all the abundance that flows—or as you just saw, swims—into my life. You see, it's like the feeling of the tug on your feet of the outgoing current as the wave gets ready to take you for a ride. Abundance is the wave getting ready to give you the ride of your life, and your gratitude is the outgoing current that just makes it even stronger. It's all part of the same cycle of energy—whether it's life's energy or the energy of a wave, it's all the same."

"So what does that have to do with garbage?" I asked.

"Picking up trash so that it doesn't hurt marine life is one of the ways I show my gratitude by giving back to the universe and all its creations."

"So you're telling me that because you pick up garbage, the universe rewards you?" I asked skeptically. (Maybe beach philosophy sounded better later in the day with a couple of jolts of caffeine under my belt.)

"Not exactly. I'm saying that I recognize that I am a part of the universe, and I also know that the universe wants me to succeed and helps me by giving me signs along the way."

"Synchronicity," I chimed in.

"So if you compare the universal energy to that of the waves you experienced over the past few days, you'll see that abundance flows toward you in wave after wave. By sending an outgoing current of gratitude back, you get that little extra energy thrown into the cycle, which helps create a wave that can give you a great ride. But only if you choose to jump in and ride it."

"So gratitude helps strengthen the abundance the universe always has flowing toward you," I said, trying to grasp the concept.

"Right," he said excitedly. "And when you're in a grateful frame of mind, you notice all the blessings flowing into your life. Just like when you were in an angry frame of mind, trying to stand still in the waves, you only noticed the things that irritated you. I know it's a hard concept to follow, but I think you get the gist of it."

"Well, at least I'm trying to," I said. "But where does the garbage come in?"

"I'm so grateful to be a part of the universe and all its wonders that I want to do my part to keep those wonders around. So after I read how many sea creatures die from ingesting plastic every year, I decided that one way I can give back for all that I receive from living on the beach is to collect trash. Who knows? Maybe one of those dolphins we just saw could have been killed by swallowing this plastic bag and having it clog her digestive track. I have to admit that at first I started doing it because I wanted to test my theory and intensify the abundance in my life. But then I realized that knowing I was a part of protecting these creatures just strengthened my feeling of being connected to the universe and the rhythm of life. So I already felt an enormous abundance in my life. I just hadn't noticed it before."

"So by giving, you are receiving," I said.

"Right again," he laughed. "It may sound like a cliché, but it really is true. I think it was Gandhi who said, 'Be the difference you want to see in the world.' I want to see a world with a cleaner environment and healthier marine life, so I do what I can to ensure that happens. Now, why don't you join me on the rest of my walk? It's only about a half a mile."

As we walked along, Fin asked, "So what are these questions you said you have?"

I told him about my dinner with Mrs. Vargas and how she had echoed what he'd told me about good coming from a bad situation.

"Was that synchronicity?" I asked him.

"Well, I'm not the only one who thinks that good things can come out of bad experiences. What do you feel?"

"Well I think that—"

"I didn't ask you what you think," he said. "I asked you what you feel. What our gut tells us is right is often what our minds try to talk us out of for the sake of convenience. So what do you feel? Was it synchronicity?"

"My first reaction is yes, it was synchronicity because it seemed so out of character from the Mrs. Vargas I knew to even come over. It could have been the Ella record that brought her over, but I just feel that the whole thing was meant to happen."

"Why?" he asked.

"Because her story helped me understand how I labeled people, just like I labeled waves. But she seems like such an unhappy person, I'm surprised the universe could use her in the whole synchronicity thing."

"I see what you mean, Jack. But we're all a part of the universe, and everyone has been a part of the synchronicity of other people's lives. Like the waiter who told Mrs. Vargas that they wouldn't serve someone because of the color of their skin. That was an ignorant thing, but it directed Mrs. Vargas on a path of helping others. So synchronicity can use anything to give us a sign that our greater good is waiting for us."

This made sense to me.

"Okay, Fin, here's another question. If giving back helps increase the energy of abundance like you say, then why is Mrs.

Vargas seems so unhappy? She said she was making cookies for the homeless shelter before she came over. Why isn't the abundance of joy flowing to her?"

"It is," he said with a twinkle in his eye. "Remember when you and I were trying to just stand still in the water, before you understood about listening to your gut and feeling for the outgoing current? Remember how hard it was to stand still with all that energy flowing around you?"

"Yeah," I said remembering how frustrated I was as the waves tossed me about.

"Well, maybe the waves are coming at her, but she's trying to stand still, so she just stands there frustrated and feels like she's being tossed in all directions. Just like the ocean, life is fluid and constantly moving and changing, and we need to be constantly changing too. If we try to be rigid in a fluid situation, we're bound to become frustrated by our lack of control. But if we loosen up, feel the rhythm of the energy, and dive into the next wave, who knows where life will take us."

"Well, come to think of it, she hasn't changed much since I was a child," I said.

"Sometimes we find something we like and try to hold on to it to make it last. But it can't last, because nothing is permanent. And when we understand that, and embrace that, change happens. Then we can open up our thinking, and our lives, to all the possibilities available that can bring us closer to our highest good."

By this time we had returned to where I had watched the sunrise, and my stomach was growling.

"From the sound of your stomach, I think you might want to go get some breakfast," Fin laughed.

"Excellent idea," I said. "Would you like to join me?"

"Thanks but I've already had breakfast, and I have some things to do this morning. Make it a great day, Jack!"

And with that Fin headed up the beach singing to himself and picking up garbage.

When I got back home, I checked my cell phone and saw that the contractor had called. I returned the call only to find out that his painter had broken his leg and wouldn't be available for at least six weeks.

I wasn't planning on being in Daytona for six weeks! I needed to get back to reality and start looking for a job. But I knew that my uncle was counting on me to oversee the work on his place. My first reaction was frustration, and then I caught myself and thought, "What is synchronicity trying to tell me? I need to get a new painter? But I don't know anyone in Daytona."

Then it occurred to me that I could paint the place myself. It would save my uncle money, and the bungalow was small enough that it shouldn't take very long.

So I called my uncle with the news and asked him what colors he wanted the place to be painted.

"I trust you, sport," he said. "Your aunt always said you had an artist's soul. Whatever you think best is fine with me. But I don't want you to think you have to do it."

I insisted that I'd be glad to do it as thanks for letting me stay at his beach bungalow.

He told me that I was already doing him a favor by overseeing the project. But I could hear in his voice a kind of relief that he wouldn't have to worry about it.

When I got off the phone, I felt good that I was going to be able to help my uncle and was kind of excited about choosing the colors. I could spend a few hours painting each day and still have plenty of time at the beach.

After breakfast I hopped in my car and headed to the local home-improvement center to get some paint swatches to bring to the bungalow so I could look at them in the varying lights of the day.

When I returned to the bungalow, I got out my trusty pad and pencil and began to make a list of what supplies I would need. I rummaged around the kitchen junk drawer and found a measuring tape and then figured out the square footage of each room's walls. When I was satisfied that I had a plan, I sat down on the sofa, and it suddenly occurred to me I was acting out of gratitude and was happy about spending part of my time at the beach painting walls because it was helping my uncle. Just like Fin had said.

After lunch I packed up my beach gear and headed down to see what lessons the waves had in store for me.

It was a hot day, and the sand burned the bottoms of my feet. I didn't see Fin, so I set up on the beach quickly and sat down resting my feet on my beach towel. For some reason my brain went back to the whole reason I was in Daytona, the elimination of my job. As I sat there thinking of all I had done for the company and how I resented the way I was treated, my mood began to darken.

I was brooding over this and lost in the thought of all the things I wished I had told them, when Fin plopped his chair down beside me.

"Whoa! What's wrong with you?" he asked.

"I'm sitting here thinking about what those jerks at my old job did to me. Who do they think they are? I have a good mind to call them up and tell them off."

"Oh," he said. "I see that your *kleishas* have a hold of you."

"My what?" I said, not really in the mood for a lecture.

"Your kleishas. It's a word Buddhists use to talk about the mind dramas and strong feelings that we all play out in our heads of 'I should've done this or said that to teach them a lesson.'"

"Are you a Buddhist?" I asked.

"I'm a student of life," he answered. "I look for answers everywhere. Now come on, let's sand dance on into the water and cool off. It's too hot out here."

"Sand dance. I'm in no mood for dancing," I said more tersely than I meant to.

"Well, Jack, the way I see it, you have three choices. You can sit here in the heat feeling sorry for yourself and building your mind drama. You can try to look cool as you walk across the hot sand to the water, or you can be creative as you dance across the sand oohing and aahing all the way. When given the choice, I always choose to dance."

And off he went making all sorts of noises and moving his arms like the people seen in Egyptian hieroglyphics.

Watching him made me laugh, and watching others watch him made me laugh even harder.

"Okay," I thought to myself, "it's showtime."

And off I danced, with less flourish, and let out a sigh as my feet entered the cool Atlantic water.

"I'd give that dance about an 8," he laughed.

"Isn't that judging my neutral dance?" I joked.

"Touché," he laughed back. "Now come on, there's nothing like diving beneath the waves to wash off the earthly things that make your feel overwhelmed. Just let them drift off into the sea, and you'll emerge fresh again."

And we both swam off into the waves to bodysurf.

We'd only been out a few minutes when we noticed a fisherman had set up his gear on the beach and was sitting with his fishing pole right in front of us.

"Come on," Fin said. "Let's move up current so that we don't get a hook in us."

"That's not right," I said angry that I had to change my plans because of someone else. "We were here first. He shouldn't be setting up here."

"Well, he is," Fin said patiently. "And if we don't want to be the catch of the day, we just need to move a little up current."

"It isn't right. How inconsiderate of him," I said.

"Come on, Jack. There's an abundance of ocean for us to swim in. We don't have to swim in this exact spot," Fin said as he swam against current.

I followed, but still fuming.

When we were a little way away from the fisherman, we stopped.

I glared back at the man wanting him to see how angry I was. But as I looked back, I saw him standing up and reaching for his cane for support. I instantly felt bad that I had felt so much anger toward him. It was only natural that he would set up as close to the road access as possible. What must it be like to walk on the soft sand with a cane?

Fin saw what had just happened and said, "You weren't really angry at him, you know."

"Yes, I was," I said, feeling guilty.

"You might have been annoyed at being inconvenienced, but you couldn't have been that angry with him. You had been hooked by one of your kleishas, and it was just helping you rebuild the mind drama that life was against you."

"What do you mean I 'got hooked'?" I asked.

"Okay, imagine that fisherman is a kleisha or mind drama. You know he's sitting there, but you go swimming in front of him anyway—like a great big target. He casts his line, and it hooks you, and he starts to pull you in a different direction from where you want to go. You try to swim away, but you're really hooked, and it feels better to swim with the hook instead of swimming away from the hook. So you drift on into shore, and even though it feels better to swim in the direction the hook is pulling, you're letting someone else control where you end up, and that is giving them complete control, which makes you angry. You've given away your power. And you're blaming someone else for it. That's what kleishas do. They get you thinking negatively and make you think you're powerless to make a change.

"So you're saying the anger I felt is really from thinking about how I was treated by my employer. But since I was already angry from buying into my mind drama, it was making me a target, and I wound up taking my anger out on whoever inconvenienced me first."

"Exactly. The good news is, you can always take a breath and change your direction. So instead of buying into the mind drama, you realize it is just a kleisha and pull out the hook so that you can move in the right direction for you. And remember, even if the hook is pulling you in the right direction for you at the moment, it won't do so forever. Sooner or later, you're going to need to pull that hook out and take control of your own journey, and not blame someone else for where you end up."

"But I'm really angry about losing my job," I said.

"Don't get me wrong," Fin said, "you've just lost your job in a way that you think is unfair, and you have to mourn that loss. And part of the way humans mourn is through anger. But to dwell on it and make imaginary scenarios that only intensifies your anger isn't helping you or anyone else."

He reminded me, "Remember, you weren't very happy in your job anyway."

"I know, I really do think it was a wake-up call to move onto better things," I agreed. "But I still don't like the way I was treated."

"And you don't have to like the way you were treated. It's important to forgive though. We have to forgive others to free ourselves. If we don't forgive, and instead hold on to resentments, we are giving them power over us. We can try blaming them, but it's really our choice. So you need to forgive them and move on with your life without trying to hold on to past injustices. Look over there at that sand castle," he said, pointing toward the shore to an elaborate castle that was being eroded by the surf.

"Jack, your losing your job is a lot like that sand castle being washed away by the energy of the surf. No sand castle is permanent, and the same goes for jobs. But once the sand castle is gone, in its place you'll find a wonderful blank canvas full of infinite possibilities. The same applies to your job. You were in a job that you didn't enjoy. Now you have the opportunity to find one that you will enjoy."

"I guess you're right," I said.

"Always lessons and never losses, my friend." Fin smiled. "From your last job, you learned a lot about what you want or don't want in a career path, and how you want to be treated, and how not to treat the people you manage. So it wasn't a loss as much as it was one of your life lessons moving you on to become the masterpiece the universe knows you can become. Life goes by fast, and you don't want to be stuck in a place where you're not happy when you could move on to a place where not only are you living up to your fullest potential, and making the world a better place to live, but you're enjoying life and all its possibilities."

"So how do I keep from getting kleishas?" I asked as we did a less elaborate sand dance back to our chairs.

"If you find out, tell me," Fin laughed. "Kleishas will find you no matter how far along you are on your life journey. So since I can't avoid them completely, I've learned to recognize them and send them on their way."

I looked at him blankly. "Huh?"

"For example, say I'm sitting here in my chair enjoying the view and the next thing I know I'm fuming about something that happened in my past. I can sit here and buy into the whole drama, or I can call it what it is, a kleisha, and decide not to pay any more attention to it by bringing my mind back into the now of life."

"The 'now of life'?" I asked, raising my eyebrows.

"Yeah. In case you haven't noticed, we spend a lot of time dwelling on the past or wishing for happier tomorrows. And all that does is make you miss what's currently happening in your life.

But if I bring my mind back to the now, I realize I'm alive and healthy and am able to enjoy this wonderful moment at the beach. So I let go of the past and stop dreaming about the future. Life takes place in the present. The rest is just memories, or dreams of things yet to come."

"But didn't you tell me you set your intention for the day? Isn't that living for the future?" I asked.

"I set my intentions every day. But then I don't dwell on every little thing and worry if it is making my intention a reality or worry about the past and try to change it. The past is the past. Learn from it. Learn from the kindnesses of those you love and from the strength and wisdom you gained from the hard times. And as you set your intentions for the future, what you learned from past lessons will lead you to who the universe knows you can be. Always lessons, never losses."

"So how do I go about setting an intention?" I asked.

"That's easy," Fin said. "Start out by saying what you intend to happen. For example, this morning I woke up and set my intention by saying, 'Today is going to be a wonderful day full of the joy of life.'"

"Isn't that a little generic?" I asked.

"Well, that's what I want out of today, and every day actually," Fin answered. "Didn't you say you set intentions in business?"

I nodded.

"Was it similar?"

"It was, but it had more measurable goals like number of deadlines met or volume of calls," I said.

"Well, I think having a wonderful day full of the joy of life is a measurable goal. At the end of the day, I can sit back and say it was a really wonderful day and mean it. Of course, you can set your intention for anything really. Even a new job."

This piqued my interest. "How?" I asked.

"By simply putting it out there to the universe. Remember the universe wants you to succeed. So simply state what you want and trust that the universe will help you get it."

"Isn't that a bit naive?" I queried, once again the skeptic.

"I prefer to think of it as trusting that the universe wants me to be happy," Fin said. "Let me ask you this: before you lost your job, did you think about what it would be like to quit and not have to go to work there anymore?"

"All the time!" I said.

"Did you ever think of all the good things about your job?"

"What good things?" I joked.

"So what were you putting out into the universe?"

"That I hated my job and no longer wanted to work there," I said.

"And here you are," Fin said. "You asked for it, and you got it."

"But I did like the steady paycheck and benefits," I said.

"And other jobs offer those too," Fin replied. "So figure out what you want and trust the universe to deliver it, or something even better."

"Or something even better?" I asked.

"Sure, I've found that my imagination can be quite limited, so if I'm setting my intention on a specific thing, I don't want to limit myself to what I think is possible as opposed to the infinite possibilities the universe knows can happen. So I set my intention and then add 'or something even better.' Then I trust that the universe knows what's best for me. Even when I can't imagine it."

"Wow. I never imagined it could work like that. It does work, doesn't it?" I said.

"Yes, it works. But not always how you imagine it works. By letting go of the exact outcome and trusting that the universe will guide you where you need to be, to teach you what you need to learn, in order to reach your highest good, you'll find you live life a whole lot more as you let synchronicity guide you along the way."

"Hey, Fin. Thanks!" I said. "I'm sorry I wasn't very good company today."

"No worries, Jack," Fin said. "Remember, you're where you need to be, so you can grow into the masterpiece you're meant to be."

I didn't really know how to respond to that, so I just said, "Thanks."

Then we both looked out to sea and sat there enjoying the warmth of the sun and smell of the air and the company that was so comfortable that words weren't necessary until it was time to go home.

That night as I was looking at paint swatches and imagining all the possibilities, it occurred to me that this place was my uncle and aunt's dream, and I had always loved it just as it was. So instead of making any drastic color changes, I would try to make it look just like it did when they first painted it and then bring my uncle over to enjoy a little time with him at the beach before he sold it.

I chose the colors I thought were the wall colors, but they looked much richer compared to what I saw were the actual colors on the walls. Had the walls faded? Or had my mind enriched the colors and imbued them with the all the warmth of my memories? I decided it was a little of both and chose colors that were in between the colors I saw on the walls before me and the colors I saw in my memories. In the morning I would go to the home-improvement store with my list and my swatches to buy the paint.

DAY 5

The next morning I awoke to thunder rattling the windows. "This'll be a good day to go shopping for the painting supplies," I thought to myself.

I started the coffee and hopped in the shower thinking of the colors I had chosen. For the inside, tropical splendor (pale green), scent of mango (a golden peach) and dolphin blue (turquoise) and Bermuda sunshine (yellow); for the outside, with island linen (white) for the trim. As I showered, I thought how I would have named the colors differently and then joked to myself that maybe that could be my new job, official paint-color namer.

I was sitting on the sunporch and enjoying my breakfast when I remembered to set my intention. (Part of me was disappointed it had taken me so long to remember, and another part of me was surprised I remembered at all. I was really beginning to relax into my time at the beach, and I had sloughed off my daily routine.) I thought about what Fin had said yesterday about not limiting my intention to my own imagination, so I wanted this one to be a good one. I thought for a few minutes about what I wanted. The list came down to joy, peace from the inner chatter of my kleishas, and to be able to send some sort of kindness back out into the world.

It took my brain a minute or so to organize it, but finally I said softly, "Today will be filled with the joy of life, bringing me inner peace to help me send kindness to all those I meet. All this or something better." (It didn't sound quite like me, but I figured as I got better at setting my intention, either the verbiage would change or I would.)

The rain was already subsiding, and by the time I was ready to go to the store, it had calmed down to a light drizzle.

My trip to the home-improvement store was uneventful, and I returned home with a lot of Bermuda sunshine, the other paint, brushes, and lots of rolls of blue painters tape.

Since it was still raining, I decided to get started on my project. I began in the master bedroom by moving the furniture to the center of the room and taping off the trim. I wasn't the neatest painter in the world, so the prep work took longer than I had expected. By the time I was finished, the sun was out and baking the fresh rain into humid air. Soon, even with the ceiling fan going, it was too hot to stay inside, and I headed off to the beach.

When I arrived, I noticed that the fisherman had already set up for the day in the same place he was yesterday, so I moved farther down the beach toward the pier and set up my beach gear. Fin wasn't there, but the waves looked extremely inviting. The sand was still wet from the rain, so no sand dance was necessary as I headed off toward the ocean.

The water was colder than it had been the day before but still felt good compared to the hot, steamy air. The waves were about four feet and exactly the way I liked them for bodysurfing. Wave after wave took me to shore, and I'd get up smiling and head back out to catch another ride. One ride was so incredible that I actually said "wahoo!" loudly as I got up laughing with the rush of the experience.

Other people started bodysurfing too, and soon there were about fifteen people trying to bodysurf in about a fifty-foot-wide section of the ocean. At first I tried to just mind my own business, but it got increasingly more difficult as I'd catch a wave and another bodysurfer (pulled by the energy of the wave) would smack right into me.

Then I tried moving, but the other bodysurfers moved too. Fin's lesson about being where I need to be was still fresh in my head, so I got out of the water and decided it was life's way of saying it was time to rest.

As I got out of the water, I saw Fin sitting by my beach chair.

"Well done!" he called out.

"Thanks," I laughed back satisfied with life. "The waves were great!"

"And you handled that last lesson quite well," he replied.

"What lesson?" I asked. Had I missed something?

"The lesson of riding your own wave," he said.

"You mean just now?"

"Right. That's one of the most important lessons you can learn in life, and you handled it with aplomb," Fin said smiling.

"I'm glad I handled it well," I said. "But I think I missed the lesson."

"Riding your own wave is one of the most important lessons you can ever learn," Fin repeated.

"You see, so often we get caught up in what other people are doing and latch onto their ride or goal. As you saw out there, if you're trying to ride the same wave as someone else, sooner or later you're bound to run into each other, and neither one of you is going to enjoy the ride as much as if you each rode your own wave. The strongest relationships are where each person involved enjoys his or her own journey and is cheered on by the others in their relationship. When the ride ends, celebrate with each other, but if you try to ride the same wave, someone is always going to get the lesser ride and lose their joy in the process."

"So you're saying grab the wave because it feels right for me and not just because someone else is grabbing it?" I asked.

"Right! Some of the people out there were watching you have fun, and so they figured that if they wanted to have fun too, they should grab the same wave you did since you obviously must know what you are doing."

"I did that at first when you and I went bodysurfing. But I didn't crash into you like they just did to me," I said, congratulating myself silently on my obvious stealth and control.

"Well, I think that was because when you were jumping into the same wave I was riding, it wasn't cresting at the right time where you were, so while the wave was taking me to the beach, it was just washing over your head."

"You've got a point," I said, glad I hadn't said anything out loud about my stealth and control. "Because where you were standing, the wave was just starting to crest, and the energy was going up, and where I was standing it was already crashing, and the energy was going down."

"Right. You see the abundance flowing toward us reaches each of us at the exact, perfect time for our own ride. So jumping onto someone else's wave just because they are enjoying the ride doesn't mean it's the right wave for you. Remember how you felt when I was enjoying the wave and you were pulling yourself back up after being knocked down by the same wave?"

"Yeah, frustrated," I answered.

"Exactly! Now if you look out there," Fin said pointing to the ocean, "you'll see wave after wave flowing toward us. So you see there's plenty for everyone. The important thing is to let each person catch the wave that is right for him or her. And for you to catch the right wave, you have to be in the right place at the right time and willing to jump in and enjoy the ride. Synchronicity will put you in the right place where *your* wave will begin to crest and pull you with it. It's up to you to jump in and enjoy the ride. As you've noticed, the entire wave doesn't crest all at once, and that's the way it is in life too."

"So you're saying that because each of our lives is different, we should celebrate those differences and where they take us. Not try to do the same thing just because someone else is doing it?" I asked, amazed that this was beginning to make sense.

"Right. We humans do it a lot to one another. We want our children to enjoy what we enjoy or our spouse to do what we do with the same gusto. The fact is, everyone has his or her own wave to catch. It's much easier to catch it and enjoy the ride when it's the wave that was meant for you and not someone else's wave you're riding just to try to make that someone happy."

"But don't parents just want to help their children grow by exposing them to things that could make them happy? I asked.

"Quite often, yes," Fin said. "But do you and your parents like all the same things? Same music? Same books? Same sports?"

"No," I laughed.

"And that's the same for everyone on the planet. We're all unique beings, here to make the world a better place. So instead of trying to make everyone just like you, or just like me, I think it's important to expose them to what we enjoy and then see if they enjoy it. If they don't, then help them explore other options and celebrate when they catch their own wave and ride it joyfully."

"So the key to having happy relationships is letting everyone be who they were created to be and rejoicing in their triumphs?"

"And helping them through their hard times. And reminding them of how wonderful they are, but not trying to make them ride the same wave that we're riding."

"Wow! Who knew someone crashing into me could teach so much?" I laughed.

"I know," Fin said. "It's all in how you see it."

"That neutrality thing keeps coming up," I said.

"It always will when you consider that everything is neutral."

"How do you know how to approach something if everything is neutral?" I asked.

"Easy," Fin said. "Look to why you are doing it."

"You mean my motive for doing it?" I said.

"Right. If you're doing it out of love, it's the right thing to do."

"Are you talking about romantic love?" I asked.

"No, I'm talking about the love that inspires you to help a stranger because you see they need help. Not for any reward, but just because you can help make their journey easier. Romantic love often comes with too many strings attached to it. The 'I'll love you if you do this' type of love only makes people lose a part of who they are. That's why letting each person catch his or her own wave and celebrating their individual ride collectively is the best kind of love."

"So are you saying romantic love is bad?" I questioned.

"Not at all, romantic love can be incredible. But if I start trying to control the other person in any type of relationship, I'll lose the respect that I should have for him or her, and then they become more like a possession that I'm using to fuel my ego."

"I had a boss who liked to control people like possessions," I said.

"How did he make you feel?"

"Well, I'm stubborn," I said. "And he was from the 1980s school of management by fear. So the more he belittled me, the harder I worked to show him he was wrong."

"It sounds like a clash of the egos to me," Fin laughed. "And when that happens no one really wins."

"What do you mean? I was just defending my reputation," I said defensively,

"And he got you to work harder by intimidating you. As he was pushing, you were pushing back. No one was trying to help the other or learn, or trying to do their job to serve others. Both parties were trying to force their point of view on the other person, and neither was willing to budge. What was it like going to work each day?"

"Awful," I said. "I dreaded every morning."

"That's how working out of ego makes you feel. It is an uphill battle you'll never win because the ego operates out of fear, fear of not measuring up, fear of being inconvenienced, fear of lack, fear that no one will like who you really are. The list goes on and on."

"But I thought an ego was a good thing," I said.

"Having self-esteem is a good thing. The ego, the way I'm talking about it, is the result of trying to build ourselves up at the expense of others or even ourselves. All those actions come out of the fear that we are not lovable. It's all labeling again. This person said this, so they must not like the way I look or speak or act. It's all kleishas fueling your fear and making you act in ways that'll make you feel bad about yourself. And when we feel bad about ourselves, we try to build ourselves up. Often at the expense of someone else."

"Labeling again? Right?"

"Yes. It turns into a vicious cycle of ego versus ego, and no one wins. But one person can break the cycle by acting out of love."

"You mean when my boss belittled me, I should have said, 'I love you?'" I said sarcastically. "He wouldn't have believed it. No one could love that man."

"Maybe that was the problem," Fin said. "He thought he was unlovable, and instead of giving people the time to reject him, he made them not like him so that it felt like he was in control."

"When you put it like that, it almost makes me feel sorry for him," I said. "almost!"

"You see, Jack. I believe that each of us is created as a loving spirit housed on earth by a fallible body with a mind that tries to justify the body's imperfections. When someone acts the way your boss did, it shows that he's lost touch with who he really is and is buying into the belief that he is only what he can produce or offer or possess to make him seem important. He's forgotten that each of us is a beloved child of God and we should be treating ourselves, and one another, with love and respect. In fact, Jesus said that loving God, loving others, and loving ourselves are the most important things we can do."

"Yeah, and they killed him," I said.

"But he was able to forgive the people as they were killing him. To be able to see the pain of your tormentor and forgive them for what they've done to you is true love in action."

"So when my boss yelled at me, I should have replied, 'I forgive you.'"

"In the frame of mind he was in, it probably wouldn't have helped. But you might want to ask yourself, 'What would cause me to act like he is acting?'"

"I don't even know where to begin. I don't think I've ever been that angry," I said.

"Well, you were pretty angry yesterday," Fin reminded me.

"Yeah, but not like my boss was. And he was always that way."

"Can you imagine feeling angry all the time? That must be awful," Fin said.

"Yeah, I never thought about it like that before."

"So if you ran into him again and he started trying to try to make you feel bad, I'd advise you to think of how hard it must be to be that angry all the time. Maybe even wonder what could have caused him to be that way and then respond out of a feeling of compassion, instead of fear."

"Wow! Have compassion for that man. Now that's a radical concept," I said jokingly.

"It's only radical because we act out of fear so much of the time and then blame the other person for our actions. What I'm suggesting is taking control of our actions and responding with love and compassion, no matter what is hurled at us," Fin replied.

I was quiet for quite a while as I digested all of this. He was right that if someone pushes and I automatically push back, I'm letting that person control me. But if that person pushed and I realized I had a choice of how to react, maybe, just maybe, I might make the right choice and regain control of the situation.

"In theory, it sounds easy," I said. "But I don't think it really will be when I'm in a situation like that."

"It won't be at first," Fin replied. "But like bodysurfing, it gets easier the more you do it."

I nodded still deep in thought.

"I think I've given you enough to think about today," Fin said. "The waves look to be about the right height and the crowd has thinned out, let's bodysurf."

We spent the rest of the afternoon enjoying the waves and the coolness of the saltwater alternating with the warmth of the sun on our skin.

As I was walking back to the bungalow, I realized I hadn't eaten since breakfast. It's amazing how the sun and surf can wear you out and make you hungry.

After showering, I jumped in the car and drove to the supermarket to pick up the fresh catch of the day, which happened to be Atlantic shrimp. I also picked up some lettuce, tomatoes, carrots, celery, and a pint of ice cream. (After all, I was on vacation.)

When I arrived back at the bungalow, I saw Mrs. Vargas in the front yard watering her yellow allamanda vine that trailed up the colonial-style lamppost in front of her home.

"Hi!" I said as I got out of the car.

"Whatcha got there?" she asked, pointing to my bags and adjusting the sky-blue-and-magenta scarf covering the rollers.

"Dinner," I replied. "Want to join me?"

"What is it?" she asked.

"Fresh shrimp and salad. There's plenty for two."

"Never eat shrimp," she said. "They're like the cockroaches of the sea. But enjoy. And be sure to devein them if you don't want to be eating their crap. Besides, it's bowling night."

"I didn't know you bowled," I said, trying to ignore the comment she'd made about my soon-to-be-supper.

"Yep, every Thursday night. It's really hopping on Thursday nights."

"What team do you bowl on?"

"The beach babes," she cackled. "At one time it was fitting. Now I just enjoy the irony."

I wasn't sure how to respond to that without offending her, so I just wished her luck and went in to devein and cook the shrimp.

As I munched on shrimp and salad, I thought about the direction in which my life was going and what I could do to make it a happier one. I was definitely on the lookout for the synchronicity in my life. But trying to figure out how to act out of love, and not ego, was going to be a bit more difficult. Just my conversation with Mrs. Vargas had pushed a button when she was making disgusting remarks about the shrimp. But as I bit into another one, I realized that although she was labeling them in a negative way, I was still enjoying them immensely. So it came to my mind that although the shrimp were neutral, we were each entitled to our opinion. An opinion is just an opinion, being neither right nor wrong, and so shouldn't be taken personally. So I decided I should just try to see her as a person.

Satisfied with my insight, I cleared the table and cleaned the kitchen and put on the same Ella Fitzgerald album I had listened to the other evening.

As Ella serenaded me, I went out to look at the stars in the sky. The streetlights were very bright, and it was hard to see many stars, so I thought I'd take a walk to the beach and see if they looked brighter from there.

When I got onto the beach, I noticed that it was really dark with very little artificial light coming from the hotels. I sat down and listened to the surf and watched the stars. I couldn't remember the last time I had just stargazed. It was amazing! And once again I felt like I was a part of something bigger. Then it occurred to me that I was just a tiny part of something much bigger. Would this huge universe really put out road signs to direct *me* on my way? Was I that important in the vastness of the universe? Or was all this just Fin's beach philosophy?

As I thought about this, I decided to take a walk on the beach and enjoy the coolness of the sand on the bottoms of my feet.

THE BODYSURFER'S GUIDE TO LIFE

Walking along I saw a red light up about a few hundred yards and thought I'd go investigate. As I got closer I saw the shadow of a man shining a red light on what looked like a body on the ground. My first instinct was to not get involved. But my gut was telling me to go see if I could help.

I cautiously approached, and the person with the light looked my way and held up a hand directing me to stop. I stood where I was, and the man walked over to me.

"Is everything all right?" I asked.

"shhhhhhhhhhhh. Hey, Jack," a familiar voice said in a whisper.

Fin. Does that man live at the beach?

"What are you doing?" I whispered back.

"A sea turtle is laying her eggs," he said.

"Can I go see?" I asked.

"Yeah, but you have to be very quiet. She's gone into a trance while she lays her eggs, so if we're quiet and stay out of her field of vision, we won't disturb her."

"What happens if she wakes up?' I asked.

"She won't drop all her eggs into the nest, and fewer baby sea turtles will have a chance of making it. That's why I'm using this red light. It's not supposed to startle them like a regular flashlight would," Fin replied in a hushed tone.

Slowly we crept up to the large turtle and watched as she dropped eggs the size of golf balls into a hole dug into the sand below her shell and right next to the sand dunes. As each egg dropped, I heard her give a sigh that sounded so human I could relate to her discomfort.

"How many eggs will she lay?" I whispered.

"Between fifty and a hundred and twenty-five," Fin said.

I knelt down in the sand and watched as five feet away this huge sea turtle grunted and sighed and laid egg after egg.

Then she just rested there for a couple of minutes. (I think I would too if I had just laid one hundred eggs.) Then she started to fill in the hole with her back flippers.

"Now run!" Fin said.

And we took off running toward the water. I stopped when Fin stopped, and I turned around to see the turtle throwing sand all over the beach with her flippers.

"She's throwing her scent around the beach so raccoons and other animals won't be able to sniff out the exact location of the eggs," Fin said admirably.

After she had thrown sand for several minutes, she turned her body toward the water and grunted as she slowly pulled her body back toward the ocean.

We stood with the waves lapping our ankles for several minutes as we watched the giant turtle pull herself past us and swim away.

"That was amazing!" Fin said.

"It was!" I agreed.

"Every time I see a turtle do that, I am humbled," Fin said.

"Well, isn't she just doing what turtles do?" I asked.

"We just saw a sea creature built for swimming lug her 175-pound body about fifty yards across the land to lay her eggs and then throw sand all over the beach to protect her eggs from predators. And she's done this after a journey of thousands of miles, all without thinking about it. If a reptile can do this, imagine what you are capable of if you listen to your heart and don't let your head tell you all the reasons you can't do something."

Suddenly I too felt humbled. Here we were beneath the stars having just witnessed this amazing feat by a reptile. We just stood there for a while silently lost in what we had just witnessed.

Finally I said, "Do you live at the beach? You're here every time I'm here."

"I could say the same thing to you," he replied. (He had a point.) "What brought you out tonight?"

"I came to look at the stars without the glare of the streetlights," I said.

"Why tonight?" he asked.

"I'm not sure. Just a whim I guess."

"Or was it synchronicity? Maybe you were meant to be inspired by that sea turtle to do something your heart is telling you to do."

"Like what?" I asked.

"Well, is there something your heart is telling you to do that your mind keeps talking you out of? Something that could bring some happiness to yourself or others that you're afraid to do for one reason or another?"

"Not that I can think of," I said.

"Well, don't be surprised if the answer just pops out at you. And don't be afraid to listen to your heart and act on whatever it is."

"I seem to be getting more confusion than answers, though," I replied.

"Remember, know the universe wants you to succeed and be happy," Fin said with a kindness in his voice. "What are you confused about?"

"Well, while I was sitting out here looking at the stars I found it pretty unbelievable that this vast universe cares anything about me," I said.

"Don't you see that the universe is full of amazing things? Look at what we just witnessed. Sea turtles travel thousands of miles in their lives, but they always return to where they hatched to lay their eggs. Don't you think that a universe that helps a reptile find her path is going to help you find yours?" Fin said.

"It's just that the stars in the sky are so vast and make me feel so small," I replied.

"Okay, let's wipe that slate neutral," Fin said. "You're comparing yourself to the vastness of the universe. That's ego thinking. Instead, view the stars with the loving thought that God is like the stars in the night sky. Always there, even when clouds obscure the view or bright lights and earthly things distract us."

"Where do you get these sayings?" I asked, trying to mask how much that last sentence touched the loneliness in me.

"Like I told you earlier, I'm never surprised at what comes out of my mouth," Fin laughed. "I just listen to my heart and act out of love."

"Well, it certainly seems to work for you," I laughed.

"And it'll work for you too," he said.

"I'm trying," I said. "But you've had awhile to absorb all this. It's all new to me, and my head keeps getting in the way."

"I know," Fin said. "I can really see that you're taking this seriously. Just don't take it so seriously that you forget to listen to your heart. You don't want to miss all the joy that is meant for you. Enjoy the journey and give yourself a break. This is a new way of thinking, so take time to experiment with it. Don't just take my word for it. Do it because it feels right for you. Now I think we both better be getting home."

And with that Fin was heading off humming to himself.

I smiled as I watched him walk away and wondered to myself, "How did I wind up spending my beach vacation with this odd little fellow?"

Of course, the word "synchronicity" floated through my head as I turned and headed back to the bungalow. And I thanked the universe silently for bringing me out to the beach late at night to see something even better than anything I had planned to do today.

DAY 6

The next morning I awoke refreshed from a deep sleep. I thought of the sea turtle I had seen the night before and instantly remembered to set my intention for the day.

"Today will be filled with the joy of life, bringing me inner peace to help me send kindness to all those I meet. All this or something better," I said. Then I noticed I was smiling. Whether it was remembering my experience with the sea turtle or setting my intention, I couldn't tell you. But it was a real genuine smile, and it felt good on my face.

I enjoyed a simple breakfast of fruit and yogurt and began painting the master bedroom. As I worked my mind wandered, as it often does when I do repetitive tasks, and I thought about what Fin had said regarding my heart telling me to do something that my mind was talking me out of. What could it be? Later I thought I would make a list of things that it might be and then see if Fin could help me discern which one it was.

Although it was morning, it was already warm enough that the paint dried fast, making it easy to get two coats of paint on the walls before 10:30 a.m.

I pulled off the painter's tape and moved the furniture back into place marveling at how a little bit of work could make such a difference. The room no longer looked tired. It looked warm and inviting. I stood in the doorway and looked around the room.

Now it looked like it did in my memories, happy and cheerful and waiting for life to happen.

I was about to sit down to write my list of what my heart could be telling me to do, but then decided that since it was still early, I could prep the next room for painting and still make it to the beach for the afternoon.

I thought I'd paint the living/dining room next, so I started pulling the furniture to the middle of the room. I had just pulled a picture off the wall from over the dining table when I was stopped in my tracks. There, taped to the wall behind the picture was a drawing of a beach scene I had done when I was thirteen or fourteen years old. On the bottom right hand corner of the drawing my aunt had written, "This wall reserved for Jack's mural."

Suddenly it all came back to me like it was yesterday. I had spent most of my time at the beach that summer drawing and painting. I had been getting pretty good at it too. So my aunt took one of my drawings of sunrise at the beach and asked me to paint it on her dining room wall. At the time I was thrilled and asked when we could start. She said we could go to the art supply store the next day, and she taped that drawing to the wall and wrote, "This wall is reserved for Jack's mural."

That evening Mrs. Vargas had come over to borrow a cup of something, and when she saw the drawing on the wall, she said, "Anita, have you lost your mind? He's just a kid. What if he does a horrible job? You're going to be stuck with it."

"But he's really very good," my aunt said patiently. She was always very patient with Mrs. Vargas.

"Look at those colors swirling around! I'd get sick trying to eat under that. I certainly wouldn't want that on my wall!" she said looking at the drawing.

"Well, I do. Now be quiet, or Jack will hear you," said my aunt.

But it was too late. I had already heard. And no matter what my aunt said, all I could remember was Mrs. Vargas's criticism of my art and that it wasn't good enough to go up on the wall. And so I told my aunt I'd rather spend the rest of my summer playing on the beach and that I might do it later.

My aunt asked if I had heard Mrs. Vargas, and I denied that I had. But I think she knew. And she said, "Well, Jack, this is just going to hang here until you paint that mural for me."

And it was still hanging thirty years later.

I used to enjoy painting and drawing, but I hadn't done it in years. I sat quietly for a couple of minutes wondering if I should start painting again. Just for fun. But I kept thinking of reasons why I shouldn't.

Then I remembered what Fin had said about synchronicity telling me to do something my heart wanted me to do, but my mind was talking me out of. He did say it would pop out at me, and here it was hanging on the wall.

I finished prepping the room for painting and left the drawing on the wall where my aunt had taped it. Then I got my beach chair and headed for the beach. This was too strange. I wanted to talk to Fin about it.

When I got to the beach, it was crowded with cars and people. So I walked a little way up the beach looking for Fin. I didn't see him anywhere, so I set up my chair and headed out to the water. The waves were larger than I was used to, but I thought I would try bodysurfing.

The first wave gave me a very rough ride twisting my body back and forth. I thought I must be doing something wrong and went out to try again. The next wave slammed me into the ocean's floor with such force that I scraped my arm.

Feeling less than enthusiastic about this experience, I decided to head back to the shore to nurse my scrape. As I sat there, I saw teenagers with boogie boards riding the waves and enjoying themselves immensely.

"I guess I'm just meant to sit here and think," I told myself. And so I did.

As I thought, I found myself sketching the drawing of the sunrise in the sand and making a mental list of supplies I would need to paint a mural. Then I'd dismiss the idea with thoughts of the cost of paints or the size of the project. I didn't have any idea how much paint I would even need. No, the whole idea was just crazy. I thought, "I'm too old to start painting again."

I put the idea out of my head and lay down to nap in the sun.

I awoke to a "wahoo!" and knew Fin must be nearby.

Looking out toward the water, I saw him swimming back out to catch a wave. They were still big, but he seemed to be riding them easily enough. I instantly sank into a funk. Why was everything so hard?

I sat and watched Fin ride the waves, and finally he walked over and sat down next to me.

"Why don't you come on in? The waves are strong but amazing," he said.

"Already been in," I said, holding up my arm so that he could see the scrape.

"Yeow! I've had those before. Make sure you put some antibiotic on it when you get home," he said. Then added, "So are you ready to try again?"

"I don't quite have the skill you have, Fin," I said testily.

"Not yet," Fin said, "but you've got the talent. You just need to develop it a little more."

"That seems to be the story of my life," I said and then told him about the drawing I found on the dining room wall.

"Jack, feeling that you should be better at bodysurfing, painting, or anything else is just the incredible possibilities for your future calling to you in the present. The mural is no different than bodysurfing. You may not feel comfortable riding the big waves yet, but as you keep practicing on the smaller ones, you're increasing your skills so that you will be able to enjoy riding the bigger ones. So instead of making your debut with a wall mural, why not start out on some small canvases and work your way up?"

"I know you're right, but I keep thinking—"

"That's your problem Jack," Fin interrupted. "You keep thinking. Listen to what you're feeling. What is your heart telling you to do?"

"I feel that I should try painting and try again at the bigger waves. But my mind keeps telling me that I'm not good enough."

"Well, that's your ego talking out of fear. How does it make you feel?" Fin asked.

"Lousy."

"And that's how acting, or not acting, because of ego-based emotions makes you feel. You're just listening to your kleishas, and with this painting thing, your kleishas have had years and years to build up, and they don't seem to be making you very happy. So choose something else."

"Like what?" I asked still feeling sorry for myself.

"Like action. You can't bodysurf or paint in your mind. You have to physically do it. By experiencing how your body moves with the wave or how your brush colors the canvas. So begin paying less attention to your mind dramas and worries and more attention to what the feelings in your heart and gut are telling you."

"But it's easier said than done," I argued.

"I know," Fin agreed. "I've been there. One of my synchronicity moments came when I was sitting, fueling my mind dramas and letting them stifle my life. I was stuck in traffic behind a huge red pickup truck, and on the back window of the truck were the words 'No Fear!'

"It may not sound like much to you. But to me it was an epiphany. Those words came to me at exactly the right time to help me realize that it was fear that was paralyzing my life and keeping me stuck where I was. From that moment on, whenever I feel myself worrying about how I could ever do this or that, or what people will think if I follow my heart, or even if it is just an unpleasant thing that needs to be done, like booking a dentist's appointment, I remember 'no fear!' and whatever it is goes to the top of my to-do list. What I found is that I could spend days worrying about doing something that might take less than half an hour to actually do."

I thought of how I'd put off doing so many things in my life. Was I really spending most of my life in my head thinking and not doing? Had I wasted my whole life?

I voiced these concerns to Fin.

"Here you go labeling again. Remember, you are exactly where you need to be at all times. You had to do what you did in order to get to this point in your life, so don't look at it as wasting your life, but learning from your life experiences. Always lessons, never losses!"

"You're right," I agreed. "Several years ago I would have never been able to open my mind to what you're telling me right now. Let alone begin to understand it."

"That's right. You were exactly where you needed to be then, so you can be exactly where you need to be today, so the universe can guide you to your greatest good. And remember, when bodysurfing, or anything else, give it your all. There's nothing like the feeling that you've done your best, and it leaves you with a feeling of no regrets. Now how about getting off your duff and back out into the waves?"

Who could say no to that?

So we got up and sand danced our way out to the cool ocean and swam out to the breaking waves.

At first it was difficult trying to catch the larger waves, but just like with the smaller waves, each failed attempt taught me something new. If a wave was too intense, I'd just duck under the water and let the wave's energy rush right over me. Finally I caught one that carried me all the way to the beach. Before I knew what happened, I yelled "wahoo!" as I stood up and ran back out into the ocean. When I got to where Fin was standing, he laughed and said, "Well done!"

"Thanks! It was a great wave," I said.

"And a better response," Fin added. "I see you're getting back your childish enthusiasm for life. Now if you can do it with waves that beat you up a little earlier today, you can certainly do it with your art. Don't let Mrs. Vargas or anyone else convince you to dim the light the universe put inside you, because when you do that, the whole world gets darker."

I laughed, "You're right. But it's been a long time since I painted. What if I don't have the talent anymore."

"Try it and find out, instead of just worrying about it. The worst that can happen is that you try it and see that you no longer enjoy it. So then it's done, and you don't have to worry about it anymore. The best that can happen is you just might find out that you really enjoy it, and it brings pleasure into your life."

"But what if, as an adult, I see that Mrs. Vargas was right and that I'm not very good?"

"It's no different than what you just did by celebrating the last ride with a 'wahoo!' Don't worry about looking cool. If people are passing negative judgments about you just because you are playing in the ocean or enjoying painting—it says more about them than it does about you.

"Just like you bodysurf for enjoyment, create for the joy of creating. It is a great form of meditation and helps bring all things back into perspective. It can help remind you of the potential you have to make your life and the world more beautiful."

And with that Fin jumped into a wave and rode it onto shore.

I followed and met him back on the beach.

"Fin, back there you said creating is a form of meditating. What do you mean?" I asked.

"When we create, it's like when we ride a wave. We're in the moment. No kleishas, no regrets—just living in the moment and experiencing it all. Meditation is like that, if you can just concentrate on your breath and let go of all thoughts and concerns. I find it easier to meditate through creating though. I lose track of time, and when I'm done, I feel fresh and relaxed. But a key to meditating through creativity is to set your intention at the beginning to let your creativity express itself without judgment from you."

"You mean just do whatever without any controls?" I asked wondering what his creations looked like.

"I mean create for the joy of it. Paint because it feels good. Not because you are creating a masterpiece. Thinking of it as a masterpiece in the making only puts pressure on you to live up to the standards of those who determine what is or isn't a masterpiece. And haven't you done that enough with Mrs. Vargas's comments about your art?"

"What should I paint?" I asked.

"Well, if you're looking at painting a mural of a sunrise, then I would suggest practicing painting sunrises," Fin said logically.

That evening after I had showered I decided to treat myself to dinner out and then go to the art store to get some paints, brushes, and canvases.

I dined at a great local dive that hadn't changed since I was a kid. The fried clams, coleslaw, and sweet tea were still as good as I remembered. Then for the first time in too many years I went off to buy art supplies. I lucked into a sale on acrylic paints and brushes (which I took as a sign that I was on the right path) and excitedly headed home, planning to get up with the sunrise and paint what I saw.

DAY 7

That night I had a restless sleep, waking up every hour or so to make sure that for some strange reason the alarm didn't go off and I'd missed the sunrise. Finally I got out of bed and excitedly went out with my canvas, paints, and brushes to sit at the cement table and watch the sunrise. Then out of nowhere I thought, "What if Mrs. Vargas sees me?"

My plans changed in an instant, and I took my supplies back into the house and walked out with my digital camera ready to take some pictures of the sunrise to use for reference.

(The "no fear" approach might have to be done in steps, and Mrs. Vargas was a formidable obstacle to me.) It was a beautiful morning, and the sun turned the clouds a lovely pink and purple before peeking above them to brighten the morning sky.

As I was sitting there I remembered that I needed to set my intention for the day. So I took a relaxing breath as I thought about what I wanted and said, "Today will be filled with the joy of life, bringing me courage and inner peace to help me to *create beauty* and send kindness to all those I meet. All this or something better."

It seemed like it was a little long, and I was afraid of it beginning to sound like a speech from a beauty pageant contestant asking for world peace. But then I noticed that was just my ego talking because, really, what's wrong with wanting world peace?

I checked the pictures in the camera and was satisfied that I had the photos I needed, so I went back inside. After breakfast I sat down at the table with a canvas and a brush and began to paint what I had seen. At first it was very stiff, and the colors and clouds looked fake and contrived. But then I remembered I was supposed to create for the joy of it. So I told myself that this was just practice, and I needed to play with the paints and brushes to see how they worked together. I painted and blended and then did it all again. It was really fun to see what worked and what didn't. When I looked up, I was amazed to see it was noon.

I hadn't planned on painting this long. I hadn't even started painting the living room walls. But Fin was right. I had lost track of time, and I had really enjoyed the experience.

I decided to give myself the day off from wall painting and made a quick sandwich and headed to the beach, excited to tell Fin about my first adult foray into painting.

I saw his chair and umbrella on the beach, set mine up next to his, then ran down to the water. I swam out past the waves and found Fin just floating in the water with his eyes closed and a smile on his face.

"Hello, Jack," he said without even opening his eyes.

How did he do this stuff?

"Hey, Fin. Am I disturbing you?" I asked. He looked so peaceful I didn't want to interrupt.

"Nope. I'm just feeling the energy of the waves as they go by. Very calming. You should try it."

I did try, but as usual, my feet sank. I had never been able to float without kicking my legs. My feet always sank. So I leaned back and kicked my legs and felt the sun on my face.

All of a sudden a fish jumped over me.

"Time to get out," Fin said.

"But I just got here," I protested.

"Trust me," Fin said and started swimming back to shore with me close behind.

When we got back on shore, I asked, "What was that about? It was just a little fish."

"Here comes a big lesson from that little fish," Fin said.

"Okay, I'm ready," I said, settling back into my beach chair.

"Always watch the little guys. If they aren't happy, something's wrong. And something must be wrong to make a fish jump out of the water like that. Either he's been hooked by a fisherman, or there's a big fish or shark after it. Since I don't see a fisherman, I'm thinking it could be sharks."

Just then the beach patrol truck went by announcing from their PA system to "get out of the water immediately. There's big fish chasing little fish, if you know what we mean."

"That's beach patrol talk for shark," Fin said.

There were only a few people in the water, and they got out very quickly. Then we all sat on the beach and looked at the water for any telltale fins cutting the surface.

"You see, Jack," Fin continued, "I've used the little-guy approach in business for years. It's how I keep my employees happy and business running smoothly."

"What's the little-guy approach?" I asked taking the bait.

"It's looking out for the little guys. By watching the fish I can tell if there's a shark in the water. By watching how my employees act, I can tell if there's a manager who is abusing his or her power over them."

"You run a company?" I asked amazed. I thought he lived at the beach.

"Sure do. But in order to live the life I want to live, I need to know that all my employees are happy. And that's how I choose companies to do business with. If the employees are happy, then they believe in what they are doing. And a company that is made up of people who believe in what they are doing is going to give excellent service."

"Why is that?" I asked.

"Well, let's go back to your boss who managed by fear. When you were producing results for him, were you happy?"

"No."

"Were you more interested in serving your clients or attaining results to show your boss you could handle the pressure?" Fin asked.

"In the results for my boss," I answered.

"Exactly. And that's why I look at a company's employees before deciding to do business with the company. Management by fear is just another term for ego-driven management. And you know what happens when you operate from ego-oriented feelings?"

"A lot of negative energy," I said.

"Exactly. And who needs to bring more of that into their life or their work life?'

"But how do you keep your employees motivated?" I asked. "I've worked for several companies and always felt they pushed us to make more profits so that we had jobs."

"Well, instead of pushing people with the fear of losing their jobs, how about informing them about how their lives make a difference to the company and to the clients. Helping them understand how the company helps the client and where they fit into the process of helping others. From sales, to the custodial team, to management, everyone has a role to play, and that role must be important, or the company wouldn't be paying that person a salary. So you see, that salary tells me that this person is important to the company, and so I treat them accordingly. A salary isn't paid instead of respect. They should both be paid simultaneously."

"I bet you're a good boss," I said. "Do you bring all the things you've been teaching me to the workplace?'

"You bet. What's the use of knowing how to make life better if you don't bring it to the place you spend most of your waking hours?"

"For you I think that means the beach," I said laughing.

"Right now it does. I've set up a good foundation with my staff and trust them to run things for the good of everyone. So I can spend time here. But enough talk about work."

Just then we saw another fish jump, and a fin cut across the water quickly in pursuit.

"Damn sharks," I said.

"Sharks just do what they were created to do. There's no need to hate them. In fact, they've remained virtually the same for millions of years because they do what they were created to do perfectly. We humans have changed and changed, but sharks remain the same, and did you know they don't get cancer? Somewhere in their DNA is the answer to the problem of cancer. I have a healthy respect for sharks, and am always on the lookout for signs of their presence in business or in the water."

Only Fin could give a life lesson on tolerance with a shark!

"I was hoping to get in some wave time today," I said.

"Well, I'd give it awhile," Fin replied. "Now that we know there are sharks in the area, and we know they're unpredictable and can bite, realize that when you jump into their environment, it is your choice. So don't blame sharks for doing what they do."

"Shark neutrality," I laughed.

"Exactly!" Fin said. "So how's the painting going."

"Gees, I can't believe I didn't tell you. I followed your advice and got some paints last night, and this morning I painted for hours. You were right, it was like time disappeared, and once I pushed the fear thoughts out of my head, I actually enjoyed myself. I even started to get the hang of painting clouds. It was not only relaxing, but it was also fun. Thanks for encouraging me," I said.

"It looks like that new chapter of your life is going to be an illustrated one," Fin laughed.

"It just may be at that," I replied.

We sat and watched the surf as the waves diminished until the ocean was almost as smooth as glass. Then I saw something I had never seen before. It looked like a giant bird kite propelling itself out of the water.

"What was that?" I asked Fin.

"Looks like a manta ray," he replied. "The sharks must still be around for him to be jumping out of the water like that."

"Is that a ray like in a stingray? He was huge."

"He's related to the stingray, but he has no stinger. They are pretty amazing creatures. You could learn a lot from a manta ray," he said smiling and looking at me from the corner of his eyes to see if I'd bite the hook he was dangling in front of me.

Of course I did.

"Okay," I said laughing. "What can you learn from a manta ray?"

"Glad you asked," Fin laughed back. "The manta ray moves gracefully like she is flying through the water. It looks effortless because she rides the water's current efficiently, moving her fins to maximize the energy of each wave. She rests, just gliding, in the water when the water's energy is pushing against her. So instead of struggling against the current, she floats with it, but when the energy of the next wave begins to pull her in the direction she wants to go, she combines her efforts with it to get her to where she is going faster."

"So," I added, "you're saying that it's okay to have downtime?"

"Sure! Everyone needs downtime to rest and rejuvenate so that when the next wave comes, they can ride it for all it's worth. You see, Jack, this time you are taking to reevaluate your life is a great use of your time and energy so that when the right wave comes along, you can use its energy to reach your highest good."

"It's really just like waiting for the right wave," I said generally pleased with myself that I was understanding these concepts.

"Exactly! Remember life brings what you need most. So when the surf is calm. Maybe you need time for reflection, or need to learn patience, or need to learn to be in the moment, or just need to rest so you'll have the energy to catch the next wave with enthusiasm and be able to ride it toward your highest good."

The beach patrol was still keeping us out of the water, and the sun was getting hotter, so I decided to call it a day and go back to the bungalow to paint some more. When I told Fin, he asked, "With a roller or with artist's brushes?"

"I think with artist's brushes," I said. "I just thought of a different idea to get the clouds to look more realistic, and I want to try it out. I'll see you tomorrow. Hopefully the shark will be gone by then."

"You never know," Fin said. "You've been coming to a different beach every day, so why should tomorrow be any different?"

"Isn't this Daytona Beach?" I asked feeling another lesson on the horizon.

"Yes. But it changes every moment of every day, even as we just sit here it's different. When the wave washes onshore, it brings sand and seaweed and other things that it leaves on the shore. Then it takes away other pieces of sand, broken shells, and garbage lying on the shore, leaving the shore different and changing the makeup of the wave. After each exchange of wave and shore, both parties are changed. If all this is happening at the beach, imagine what is happening in your life and the lives of people around you. Wanting anything to stay the same is just setting yourself up for disappointment or disillusionment. Instead, enjoy the moment, and whatever that brings, knowing that change is inevitable and that life would stagnate without it."

"Well, I have to admit since coming to Daytona change has certainly been in the air. A few days ago I would never have guessed that I'd be leaving the beach to go work on painting clouds," I replied as I mulled over how I had allowed my life to stagnate by keeping any kind of change at arm's length. This day at the beach had been full of lessons that would keep my mind occupied for quite a while.

"Have fun," Fin said.

I started packing up my things and saw a plastic bag blow by. By the time it entered into my mind to try to catch it, Fin was out of his chair and running after it down the beach singing to himself.

It was hot inside the bungalow when I returned, so I showered and turned on both the ceiling and oscillating fans, hoping the afternoon breezes would kick in soon.

I went over to the table where I had left my paintings to dry and was surprised to see that each of them had some good qualities. I liked the palm tree in one and clouds in the other. I grabbed a cold bottle of water from the fridge and sat down with my paints and a fresh canvas to see if my idea about painting the clouds would work. It did, and I spent the rest of the afternoon painting and enjoying just being in the moment. I found that by experimenting with the paints, I lost the fear of perfect performance and instead was fascinated with all the possibilities. "Kind of like life," I thought to myself and laughed. I think Fin was beginning to rub off on me.

After hours of painting, I cleaned my art supplies and pulled out the leftover shrimp and salad, then went to eat in the breeze cooling off the sunporch. As I was enjoying the shrimp, I heard a cough and looked up to see Mrs. Vargas standing at the door to the sunporch with her hair in rollers tied up in a bright-red-and-hot-pink scarf.

"Hi, Jack," she called. "Can I come in?"

"Sure, come on in," I replied, hoping that I could keep her on the sunporch and away from my paintings in the dining room. I was just getting my courage back to paint, and I didn't need any obstacles thrown in my way. "Have a seat," I said, pointing to the other rattan chair on the porch.

"Thanks," she said, snubbing her cigarette out on the step before she came in.

"It's so hot in the house I'm just enjoying the breeze out here," I said, hoping to keep her outside. "I'd offer you something to eat, but I don't think you'd like it."

She looked at my plate and wrinkled her nose in agreement. "Disgusting," she said under her breath.

I just smiled to myself, realizing it's just her opinion.

"But if you don't mind, I'll get myself one of them bottled waters," she said.

I insisted that she sit down and that I would get it for her. (Phew, quick save.)

I got rid of my plate and brought out two cold waters and handed her one of them.

"I see you're fixing up the place a little," she said.

"Yeah, the contractor told me the painter had a broken leg, so I thought I could do this myself and save my uncle some money."

"You gonna have it ready for the Hibiscus Lane Luau?" she asked.

"What's that?" I asked.

"It's a huge block party where everyone goes house to house for appetizers and drinks and winds up at the Henderson's house for dancing and swimming."

"When is it?" I asked, thinking about the pressure this might put on my vacation schedule.

"Two weeks from tonight," She said.

"Well, I haven't been invited by the Hendersons," I said trying to get out of it. "I don't even know who they are."

"They're the crabs that live at the end of the street in that big pink Spanish-style house. We all get together twice a year. Once for the luau and once for a New Year's party. It was during the New Year's party that you lit them firecrackers and got Styrofoam all over my yard," she reminded me.

Now I knew who the Hendersons were. Far from being crabs they were really nice. They'd let my brother and I go swimming in their pool when we were kids. Wow! Things really did stay the same around here.

"I'm hoping to have the place ready by then. I can't stay here too long. I have to get back to my life," I said.

"Good. Then I'll tell Charlie Henderson to put this place on the map."

"Let me ask my uncle if it's okay," I said. "He may not want me to."

"Well, while you're talking to him, why don't you see if he wants to come down for the party and see his old neighbors. It might be his last chance, we're not getting any younger," she laughed and then coughed.

"Once I got the place fixed up, I was going to see if he would come down and enjoy it. This party just gives me a definite timeline," I said more to myself than to Mrs. Vargas.

"Well, don't dawdle on letting me know about you being on the map. We need to get this thing moving so we can send out the invitations."

"I'll call him tonight and let you know tomorrow," I promised. "If we do participate, what do we need to do?"

"Well, first, you have to make sure your place is company ready and then provide an appetizer or beverage for the guests as they arrive. They'll stay just long enough to eat the food and then move on to the next house. There's about twenty of us, so it don't take long to go through a bunch of appetizers."

"Did my aunt and uncle do the luaus before?"

"If they were in town, they did. Your aunt made this great fruit punch with pineapple sherbet and ginger ale. I told her she was a fool for serving it because people could spill it on her furniture or carpets. But she didn't care. She said this place was a place to enjoy life, not worry about it. Hmmph."

"That sounds like her," I laughed, remembering how much my aunt enjoyed people.

"And your uncle let her do whatever she wanted. He adored her."

"That he did." I smiled. "They were great together, and we loved coming to spend the summer with them."

"Well, they looked forward to seeing your family a heck of a lot more than I did," she said.

It was hard for me to tell if she was trying to be funny, disagreeable, or just honest. So I decided to try Fin's advice and act out of love.

"I know I probably wasn't the quietest neighbor for you, but I hope I didn't interrupt your life too much. And I'm really sorry about the firecrackers."

She just sat there for a second. Not knowing what to do next. Then she said, as if to brush it off, "Don't think anything else about it. It was a long time ago, and you were just a kid."

(Whoa! What had just happened?)

"Thanks," I said. "And thanks for including us in the luau. I think Uncle Doug will like that."

She gestured her hand like it was nothing and then stood up.

"Well, I gotta get going and find out who else is participating," she said, and with that she was out the door.

After she left I sat on the sunporch for a while pondering Fin's advice about acting out of love. Could it really make a drastic difference? My experience with Mrs. Vargas was a good test of this theory. In fact, I was beginning to see Mrs. V as a test study.

As I sat there thinking, the sky changed colors as the sun set, and the night sky reminded me that I needed to call my uncle and let him know about the luau and see if he wanted to come to Daytona. I hadn't approached the subject of him coming to Daytona yet, but I hoped that this would give him another good reason to come back to his bungalow on the beach where we'd shared so many good times.

As I dialed his number a thought came to me: "What if he doesn't want to come back to the bungalow?"

But as the phone rang the first time, I remembered the manta ray I had seen earlier that day and remembered her lesson of going with the flow instead of struggling with the current to get my own way. It would be nice to have him come back, but even if he never saw the work I was doing on his place, it was enough for me to know that I had done it for him.

He answered after the fifth ring, and after exchanging pleasantries I gave him a brief update of the painting project telling him I thought he would like the colors I had chosen and completely leaving out my idea to paint the wall mural. I wanted it to be a surprise.

Then I broached the subject of Mrs. Vargas's visit, and the luau.

He laughed as he reminisced about the fun they'd had at the block parties. "You know," he said, "those were the only times I think I ever saw Gladys Vargas's hair out of curlers!"

"Well," I said, "that sounds like as good a reason as any for you to come down and enjoy the beach for a few days."

At first, he was apprehensive about coming down. He didn't want to drive by himself on the highway. But I assured him that since Jacksonville was only a couple of hours each way, I would be glad to drive over and pick him up.

I could sense his argument softening a little.

"Come on," I urged. "We could have a great time, and wouldn't it be nice to see all your friends again?"

"Well . . . ," he paused.

"Come on, if it's important enough for Mrs. Vargas to do her hair, surely you can drive a couple of hours. I can take you home the next day if you want."

"Well, sport, if you're sure it's okay. I'd love to see the old place again."

And with that, it was settled. I'd drive up the day before the luau and pick him up. Once he got to Daytona, he could decide when he wanted to go back.

After I hung up, I smiled to myself. It was going to be nice to give my uncle one last vacation in his bungalow.

Later, as I was lying in bed, I thought to myself, "This day did not go as I had planned, but it certainly turned out better than I had hoped. In fact, it was all that and something better."

DAY 8

The next day I was up early and watched the sunrise from the cement table in the backyard while I said, "Today will be filled with the joy of life, bringing me courage and inner peace to help me to create beauty and send kindness to all those I meet. All this or something better."

Once again I noticed I was smiling and felt certain that it was because I knew good things were going to happen. Was setting my intention actually connecting me with the universe, or was it just putting me in a good frame of mind to start the day? Either way, I was enjoying my time at the beach and decided to continue setting my intention each day.

The sky was full of dark clouds, and the sunrise was mostly gray and purple with small shimmers of silver sunlight shining through occasionally. As I sipped my coffee, I watched the colors change and the way the edges of the clouds were defined by the colors of the clouds behind them. I was really enjoying rediscovering who I am and discovering that the new me was seeing the world in a new way. I wanted to talk to Fin about this, and so I hurriedly finished breakfast so that I could paint the living room. Now that I had a definite end to the project, I wanted to get the walls painted so that I could get to the mural.

I did the trim work first and then painted in the rest with the roller. (It amazes me how much time it takes to paint the trim as opposed to rolling the vast space of the rest of the wall.) I was putting on a second coat when I heard a knock at the door. Looking out the window I saw that it was Mrs. Vargas under rollers and a head scarf of purple and pink daisies. I quickly hid the canvases I had worked on and opened the door.

"Well, did you talk to your uncle?" she asked in her usual abrupt manner.

"I did." I smiled. "And he's coming to Daytona for the luau."

"That's nice," she said in a noncommittal tone of voice. "But that's not why I'm here. Did he say whether or not his house would be part of the open house? That's what I need for my map."

"Oh yeah, go ahead and put this place on the map," I said a little taken aback by her attitude. Then I remembered Fin's advice of responding with love. So I added, "Thanks for asking us to be a part of the luau. I know my uncle is looking forward to seeing the old gang again. I really appreciate your letting us know about it."

Mrs. Vargas looked at me for a second. Smiled and said, "Well, he still is part of this neighborhood."

"I know," I said. "And I appreciate your kindness in keeping him connected."

"I'm not as bad as everyone thinks I am," she said with a slight smile. And then she gave me a look that could freeze fire and added, "But don't let that get around."

And before I could respond, she marched off the porch and across the yard to her periwinkle bungalow.

I smiled to myself as I realized that underneath those loud scarves, rollers, and intimidating attitude was a person who was (like all of us) basically good at heart, even if she was a little scary.

After finishing the second coat of paint, I hurriedly cleaned up, grabbed my gear, and headed off to the beach.

The sun was already hot, and the sand burned my feet as it edged over the tops of my flip-flops. I found a spot with few people around and set up my chair and towel, then sand danced to the water to cool off. I heard a few people laugh, but that just made me smile knowing that I had made someone laugh by my actions. The waves were smaller than I would have preferred, but I still was able to enjoy quite a few rides.

As I was getting out of the water, I heard a teenage girl tell a friend. "Call Greenpeace, a whale just beached itself."

Her friend giggled, and I turned to see who said it and what she was talking about. I saw the teenage girls but didn't see a whale. Then it dawned on me. They were laughing at me.

Instantly I looked down at my stomach. I was a few pounds overweight but nothing I would compare to a whale. At that moment, the joy of the bodysurfing was gone, and I went back to my beach chair thinking some very unloving thoughts about the two teenagers.

I immediately put on my shirt and sat there as my thoughts went from insecurity about my weight to anger at the girls, to anger at myself for putting on weight, to anger at anything and anyone I could blame. But the bottom line is I felt a lot of anger.

It was in the middle of this anger that Fin walked up.

"Whoa! What happened?" he asked.

At first I was too embarrassed to talk about it, but before long I was telling Fin about what had happened and how it made me feel.

"That would explain the shirt," he said.

I looked down at the shirt or, to be exact, my stomach covered by the shirt and nodded.

"Jack, don't you know that just because someone labels you as something doesn't make it true?" Fin asked with compassion in his voice.

"I know. But she's right. I am overweight."

"So is most of America," Fin said. "But I certainly wouldn't compare your physique with that of a whale. It's a perfectly good physique. And haven't we established that there's more to each of us than meets the eye?"

"Well, I think I'd like a little less of me meeting the eye," I said

"Most days I feel like I did when I was twenty-five and then I look in the mirror and see this bald old guy staring back at me, and I think, 'Oh right, that's part of me too.'"

"What's part of you?" I asked.

"My age, my being hair challenged—all of it. Including being happy most of the time and feeling like I'm twenty-five. It's all a part of the crazy dichotomy that is Fin. I know some people only see an odd little old man when they look at me. But that is lack of vision on their part. So if someone makes a crack about how you look or dress or wear your hair, just remember it says a lot more about them than it does about you."

"What do you mean?"

"When someone makes an unkind remark about someone else, it is usually out of an ego-driven desire to take the attention off of what they think are their own shortcomings or kleishas. So instead of taking their comment seriously, think of it as an ego-driven camouflage for the person speaking.

"Remember what it was like to be a teenager?" he asked.

"Ugh! I wouldn't want to go back to those days for anything. I was gawky and very uncomfortable with who I was, or was becoming," I answered.

Fin laughed and said, "I think most teenagers feel like that. Our teen years are a time for change, and change makes us humans uncomfortable. And when the ego is uncomfortable, it lashes out at others to make it feel better."

"So you're saying I should respond with loving kindness?" I asked, remembering how it had worked on Mrs. Vargas.

"I don't really think you need to respond to that at all. Just consider that it was a comment made to camouflage the insecurities of the person speaking, and don't take it personally. Just because she has offered it to you doesn't mean you have to accept it. By not taking ownership of the remark, you're giving it back to the speaker or letting it fall onto the sand, but you're not taking it with you and carrying it around."

"That makes sense," I said after a few moments. "But it still has made me self-conscious, because it's true."

"Well, if it bothers you, do something about it," Fin said.

"I have been losing weight," I added. "At least I think I have. I don't have access to a scale, but the waistband in my swimming suit doesn't feel as tight as it did last week."

"Good for you, Jack!" Fin said sincerely.

"Thanks," I replied.

"Remember, you are exactly where you are supposed to be at this moment, so that you can become all that the universe knows that you can be. So don't worry about what other people think. Now, how about some bodysurfing?"

I was feeling better about things and started to get up to join Fin when he said, "Hold on a minute," and sat back down.

"What's wrong?" I asked.

"Were you going to go bodysurfing in that shirt?" he asked.

I nodded yes.

"This is exactly what I was just talking about. You've taken ownership of that girl's comment, and now it's placed like a burden firmly on your shoulders as represented by that shirt. Don't be afraid to take off your shirt. You weren't yesterday," he said. "It was just a thoughtless comment. I can guarantee she's not thinking about you anymore because she's too busy worrying about what other people are saying about her. The irony is that everyone is so busy worrying about what other people are thinking about them to give her more than a passing thought. You see, our egos make us think that everybody is examining us 24-7, but the truth is that everybody's ego is so busy making him or her feel less than adequate so they have very little time to think about anyone else. Get out of your head and into life!"

"All right . . . ," I said grudgingly.

"Besides," Fin added, "when you bodysurf in a shirt, the extra fabric will catch like a sail and slow you down in a wave just like worrying about what other people think will slow you down in achieving your highest good."

"I knew there'd be a life lesson in there somewhere," I laughed as I took off my shirt.

"Come on," Fin said as he sand danced to the water.

For a moment I hesitated not wanting to draw more criticism to myself. But seeing Fin made me laugh, and then I realized I could be in the moment and enjoy it, or worry about what other people might think, and miss the joy of life trying to please others. So off I went arms in Egyptian hieroglyphic position oohing and ahhing all the way.

As I was swimming out, Fin went sailing past me in a wave, and moments later I heard a "wahoo!" I smiled to myself and thought, "I'm glad this is where I'm supposed to be right now, because it is a good place to be."

The waves were sporadic, but Fin and I managed to catch enough waves that we barely had time to speak. I'd hear his "wahoo!" and smile knowing he was having as much fun as I was.

It was hard to believe that my life could change so much in the course of two weeks and now here I was unemployed, bodysurfing in Daytona with my own beach guru and thinking about painting a wall mural. As I was pondering all this, Fin popped up beside me.

"It's a great day to be alive!" he laughed.

"You've got that right," I laughed back.

"You know," Fin said, "when I stand here and stare out at the vastness of the ocean, I feel so alive and connected to the universe and everything in it."

"Well, I'm hoping to be not so connected to the shark we saw swimming here yesterday," I added, only half joking.

"Ahhh, that was yesterday, and as we've already discussed, the beach is constantly changing, and so is the wildlife that swims in her waters. Which is one more reason to embrace change. Imagine if every day we had to stay out of the water because that same shark was feeding along the shallow waters of the beach. We wouldn't be able to enjoy a day like today. And since we have no guarantee what tomorrow will bring, I think we just need to enjoy this wave and not worry about yesterday's sharks or tomorrow's unknown."

And with that we both jumped into the wave. As I rode the wave, I worried that I might bump into Fin and ruin the ride for both of us, but we managed to avoid each other (or I should say Fin managed to avoid me), and we both washed up a few feet away from the two teenage girls I'd seen earlier. Not wanting to hear anything else unpleasant about my appearance, I turned and headed back into the water, but Fin said hello before joining me.

"See," I heard one of the girls say. "I told you guys would be all over me in this bikini."

I looked at Fin, and he looked at me, and we both smiled.

"What was I saying about self-absorption?" Fin grinned.

"Point taken," I said. "She didn't even seem to notice that I was the same guy she was making fun of earlier."

"Probably didn't," Fin said, "we were just a convenient prop the ego could use to boost its power over her. You know, so many people spend so much time listening to their ego and the advertisers telling them what their bodies should look like that they neglect to work on their inner selves. And it's the strength that comes from within that gets us though the difficult parts of our journey."

"So are you saying I don't need to take care of my body?" I asked.

"Not at all!" Fin exclaimed. "Your body is your spirit's computer system throughout your life. So just like how you maintain your computer to keep it running the programs you need or enjoy, you should also maintain your body so that you can do things like a jog on the beach or bodysurfing. But you should also spend time rediscovering who you are inside and developing the wisdom and strengths that will help sustain you in times when you feel brokenhearted or unhappy. Nothing from the outside world can help with that, no matter how big your muscles are."

"What about when someone offers a kind word or helpful advice?" I asked.

"Those can be helpful in the very short term. But then the moment is gone, and we're left still coping with whatever made us feel down to begin with. It's up to us to strengthen our inner wisdom and let it guide us and comfort us and help us along the way."

"How will I know when to tune into that inner wisdom?" I asked.

"Ahhhhhhh," Fin laughed. "That is the question. Earlier in my life I only tuned into my inner wisdom after I'd exhausted every possible outer influence first."

"That sounds a lot like me," I said and then stopped myself. "At least the old me. I've been trying to listen to my inner voice more the past few days, but it's hard to hear sometimes."

"It'll get easier to hear the more you rely on it," Fin said knowingly. "It's just like learning how to discern which wave to ride, stand quietly and listen to your gut."

And with that Fin jumped into another wave, and I quickly followed.

After a few more waves we retreated to our beach chairs to rest, and I told Fin about the luau and my uncle coming down to visit.

"That's a nice thing you're doing, Jack," he said. "I'm impressed that you are taking time out of your holiday to serve others. But don't use it as a distraction from working on what you really came to Daytona to do. You need to continue to try to rediscover what you want out of life."

I was a little taken aback by this. "I thought it's a good thing to help others."

"It is good to help others. But it's also good to follow where our path leads us and to know who we are and what we believe. All I'm saying is that sometimes it's much easier to help someone else with his dreams or goals than to discover and work on our own. Synchronicity has led you here, and you're very definitely where you're supposed to be. Just remember to live in the moment and not just for another deadline."

I laughed self-consciously because I was already making schedules and trying to figure out how to get everything done and still have beach time.

When I told Fin this, he nodded. "It's only natural. I know you love your uncle. And what you are doing for him is great. But at the same time I feel pretty sure that your uncle would feel bad if you completely gave up this time of self-discovery so you could paint his house. Painting his house may be part of your journey, but it isn't the whole journey, neither is bodysurfing or artwork. They are all just parts of this impermanent time of your life."

Thinking of this time in my life as impermanent made me feel rather sad, and Fin must have seen it on my face.

"Impermanence isn't a bad thing. Would you want to go back to where you were two weeks ago?"

"No," I said adamantly.

"And who's to say that in two weeks or two years you'll want to come back to this moment and time. That's the beauty of impermanence, we're always progressing in our journey. And speaking of journeying, I've got to be on my way."

And with that, Fin packed up his beach gear and was heading down the beach whistling.

I stayed a few minutes longer, and as I was packing up my chair and towel, the two teenage girls walked by me. Sticking to my determination to respond with loving kindness I said, "Have a great day."

The girls giggled, and then one said to the other, "See, I told you he liked me better than you."

I just smiled to myself and marveled at how strange the ego is.

When I returned to the bungalow, I saw a hot pink piece of copy paper sticking out of the screen door. It was an invitation to the luau with a map of Hibiscus Lane and the houses that would be providing refreshments. I saw my uncle's bungalow marked on the map and decided to get back to work on the interior painting. I still had the kitchen, the guest room, and the sunporch to paint, plus the whole outside of the house and a mural. Good Lord, what was I thinking?

With a new sense of urgency, I began prepping the kitchen for painting. I figured that although this room had the least amount of wall space, that would mean that it would take longer to paint since most of it would have to be done with a brush, even the cabinets.

I had worked several hours when I noticed that it was dark outside, but the painting was going smoothly, and so I decided to forgo dinner for a couple of pieces of fruit and keep on painting. It looked like I only had a couple of hours of painting left, so I just kept brushing away. But what had deceptively looked like a couple of hours had turned into almost five. Finally the kitchen was painted, and I breathed a sigh of relief as I headed toward a shower and my bed, tired but happy with my accomplishment.

As I lay in bed I thought about the day. It had not been exactly full of joy, but I had been able to enjoy it by understanding that nothing is permanent. (Even feelings or, thankfully, painting the kitchen.)

DAY 9

The next morning I awoke with the heat of the sun beaming through the window. I had missed the sunrise (by about two hours) and was starving. I walked into the newly painted kitchen and was surprised how bright and cheerful the turquoise kitchen walls and white cabinets looked in the daylight. I grabbed a bottle of water and a cup of yogurt and went out to the sunporch to enjoy the morning breeze. This room was going to be my next project, and I surveyed it with a wary eye. Since two walls of it were jalousie windows, it wasn't a lot of wall space, but there were some cracks in the walls that would need to be patched before I could begin to paint. Another trip to the hardware store was added to my agenda following breakfast.

As I enjoyed my breakfast, I remembered to set my intention for the day and said, "Today will be filled with the joy of life, bringing me courage and inner peace to help me create beauty and send kindness to all those I meet. All this or something better."

I grabbed my trusty pad and pencil and began making a list of what I would need to patch the walls, and a list of questions to ask about the process. I also needed a few groceries, so I decided to combine my errands into one trip.

When I arrived at the hardware store, I looked for someone to help me get the right supplies and answer my questions about using the patching material. She was a woman in her midtwenties with black hair and multiple piercings. At first I was intimidated by her appearance, but she was very helpful and made me feel like it would be no problem, even for a novice like me.

I asked if the twenty-four-hour drying time was an approximation or the maximum time needed for the patching compound to dry before I could paint, and she said, "It's kinda like life. When the time is right, you'll know it because it will just feel right. Not sticky or tacky, just right. If you rush it, you may just have to start all over again."

I looked at her, smiled, and said, "Thanks for your help and the good advice."

Was there something in the water that made everyone a philosopher around here? Or was it just the laid-back lifestyle of coastal living?

Feeling reassured, I then set out to the garden section to look for a few plants to fill in the neglected flowerbeds. I was looking at the pale blue flowers of a plumbago when I noticed a familiar-looking woman in the next aisle. It was Mrs. Stevens who lived across the street and two doors down from my uncle's bungalow. She was wearing a bright pink T-shirt that accentuated how frail and pale she looked. Her red hair had faded to an apricot color, and her green eyes were fixed cautiously downward on the plants, so she didn't notice me as she leaned on her shopping cart, slowly making her way down the aisle. At first I was relieved, because I wanted to get my tasks done so that I could work on some cloud painting and still get to the beach. But then I noticed that she wasn't aware that something had fallen out of her purse.

"Excuse me. You dropped something," I said.

She looked up with a start but didn't recognize me. "Oh thanks," she said and turned around to look at the paper on the ground. But instead of bending down to pick it up, she just looked at it. Then she shuffled over to a nearby shelf and began to lean down on it.

This looked like a bad idea that could bring the shelf down on top of her, so I offered to pick it up for her.

Relief flooded her face, and she thanked me.

As I handed her the paper I said, "Aren't you Mrs. Stevens from Hibiscus Lane?"

She looked startled.

"I'm Jack, Anita and Doug's nephew from down the street. I'm helping my uncle fix the place up while I stay here a few weeks."

"I was so sorry to hear about your aunt," she said. "She was a lovely person, and we were battling cancer at the same time."

"I hope you are feeling better now," I said, trying not to think of how my aunt's battle with cancer had ended.

"Well, they say I'm cancer-free, but I've never quite recovered from the chemotherapy. It's left my feet numb and my balance a little off, so I fall easily if I'm not holding on to something. But other than that, I'm fine," she said smiling. "I'm mighty grateful to you for picking that paper up. Otherwise, I might just be sprawled out in the middle of the aisle."

"Glad to help, Mrs. Stevens," I replied.

"Please call me Velma," she said as she steadied herself with the cart. "Is your uncle going to be here for the luau?"

I told her that he was and asked if her house would be part of the festivities.

"Lord, yes!" she said, shaking her head and smiling. "I just can't say no to Gladys Vargas, she scares me."

I laughed, "She certainly has that effect on a number of people. But I think her bark is worse than her bite."

"Honey, her bark is enough for me. The whole time we were talking about the luau she was looking at my overgrown flower beds in the backyard. Then she just grunted and walked on out."

"That sounds like her."

"Before I got sick, I used to be out in those flower beds all the time. But now it seems everything just takes so long to do that I run out of time before I can get into the backyard."

"I think anyone who goes to the luau will certainly understand if your flower beds are not what they used to be," I said, trying to be supportive.

"But I'll know," she said, and then added, "and so will Gladys Vargas. Well, my grandchildren are coming in town next week, and I'm hoping that they will be able to help me plant and weed. I'm looking around now to see what type of plants are available. I'll come back next week and pick them up when my grandchildren can help me."

I was relieved that she had someone to help her. We said our good-byes, and I was about to check out when I remembered that I wanted to pick up a few plants for the flower beds. As I went back into the garden center, I saw Mrs. Stevens almost fall over as she picked up a potted hibiscus and put it into her shopping cart. At first, I wanted to run right over and help her, but then I remembered that she said that she would be plant shopping next week. I didn't want to pry, so I decided my plant shopping could wait for another day and headed over to the cashier, hoping Mrs. Stevens would be all right and wondering if I was doing the right thing.

As I was driving out of the parking lot, I passed the garden center and saw Mrs. Stevens with several other plants in her cart. "How is she going to get them out of her car?" I wondered to myself as I drove out of the lot.

After arriving home I quickly began patching the cracks in the walls. Since the compound would take twenty-four hours to dry, I decided to work on my cloud technique some more. If I continued this progress on the different aspects of the picture, I hoped to be able to begin painting the mural the following week. I practiced loading the paint on my brush so that I could paint a mixture of colors with one stroke. It sounds easier than it was, and I almost gave up several times in frustration. But then I would remind myself that perhaps this was the time I needed to practice patience and perseverance. I kept painting and reloading the brush until I understood how to hold the brush and move with one fluid motion to get the effect I was hoping for.

When I looked up at the clock, it was almost 3:00 p.m. Where had the time gone?

I looked outside and saw that it was a beautiful day, so I cleaned up my brushes and then headed to the beach.

On the way I passed Mrs. Stevens's house. Her little blue car was parked in the carport, and I saw plants sitting in the backseat of the car. I debated whether I should do anything, rationalizing that she might have a dozen good reasons why the plants were still in her car, but then I stopped all the chatter in my head and asked, "What do I feel is the right thing to do?"

I was ringing her doorbell in less than a minute. When she came to the door, I said, "Hi! I see you had some luck at the garden center. Would you like me to get them out of the car for you?"

She looked a little surprised as she held on to the screen door decorated with a scene of an alligator and palm trees, but then said, "Oh, I don't want to bother you. I'll just do it later."

"It's no bother at all," I said. "It'll only take a few minutes."

"Well, if you're sure. Just take them out of the car and put them in the back of the carport. I'll water them there until I can get them into the ground."

I went to the carport, saw her car was unlocked, and started unloading the plants. There were two yellow and one red hibiscus, three pots of beach daisies, and a four-foot banana plant. I didn't even want to think about how she got that in her car.

"The soil seems kind of dry, would you like me to water those for you?" I asked.

Once again, relief flooded her face, and she said, "If you're sure you don't mind. The hose is around back."

"No problem, Mrs. Stevens."

"Please call me Velma," she insisted.

I went in the back and saw the flower beds she had talked about earlier. There were a few dead plants in them, but mostly they just needed a little pruning and weeding to make them look as good as new. I hoped her grandchildren would help her, but decided to keep an eye on the plants on the carport as I went to and from the beach each day, just in case.

When I came around the side of the house with the hose, I saw Velma staring at her flower beds looking a little confused.

"Are you all right?" I asked.

"Yes," she replied. "It's just that the yard doesn't look as bad as I thought it did last week. Could it be that just the plants are growing quicker with all this rain and making the yard look nicer? I could've sworn that I had more weeds in my yard."

"I guess it could," I said, thinking she must be having a senior moment and trying to brush it off nonchalantly.

I finished watering the plants, said good-bye to Velma, and headed off to the beach looking forward to cooling off in the ocean.

I looked around for Fin but didn't see him, so I hurriedly staked my claim to a small section of the beach and sand danced into the water.

The waves were small, but the current pulling at my feet and back out to sea was very strong. I tried to stand to catch a wave, but the current was so strong that it kept pulling me off balance. Then a lifeguard blew his whistle. I looked around and saw he was motioning for me to go back to shore. I had just started to walk back to shore when my feet were swept out from underneath me, and I was pulled under the water.

My body was tumbled over and over as I struggled to get back up to the surface. I held my breath wondering what was happening to me. My mind raced with a mixture of confusion and the fear of what would happen next. Finally the current weakened, and I floated up to the surface gasping for air. More scared than anything else, and with my heart beating ninety miles an hour, I looked toward shore and saw I was about fifty feet farther out than I was before. The lifeguard was heading toward me, so I motioned that I was okay and swam toward shore, embarrassed and more than a little surprised at what had happened. As I got to the lifeguard, he asked if I was okay. I told him I was and asked exactly what had happened.

"That was a rip current," he said. "We've been having a lot of trouble with those today. Are you sure you're all right?"

I assured him I was fine and ambled off to my beach chair to regain my breath and my dignity. I'd never been singled out by a lifeguard before, and all the stares from the people on the beach were a little embarrassing.

Part of me just wanted to crawl into a hole, but the other part of me was just happy to be alive and be able to feel the sun on my face again. It all happened so quickly. It's amazing how life can turn on a dime.

I was thinking about all this when Fin walked by with his bucket and garbage grabber.

"Hey, Jack!" he said as he walked up to me.

"Have a seat," I said, offering him my towel. My hand shook a little, and he noticed it.

"What's wrong, buddy?" he asked.

And so I told him about what happened with the rip current.

"Man," he said visibly shaken. "I should've warned you about those."

"You told me they were like gratitude," I said a little more accusingly than I meant to.

"No," Fin corrected me gently. "I said gratitude was like that little gentle current that pulls at your feet to give you that extra energy on your ride. I've always thought of that as an undercurrent, although that could be considered a rip current, I guess. But what I think of as a rip current is this strong current of water running back out to sea from shore. It's nothing like gratitude, a real strong rip current is more like karma."

"Karma!" I exclaimed not really sure I was in the mood for a lesson at the moment.

"Yeah, karma. You know what karma is?" he asked.

Part of me wanted to blurt out an answer to end the discussion, but then I realized I really wasn't sure what karma was. So I shook my head.

"Well, remember how we discussed that for every action there is an equal and opposite reaction?"

I nodded.

"Well, karma is the result of our previous actions. Just like a rip current is the result of big waves rapidly coming into shore over the ocean's uneven floor.

"You see, when the waves come to shore quickly, they bring an excess of water that has to drain back into the ocean somehow. So the water flows back to the sea beneath the waves and through the lowest point of the ocean's floor. You see how those waves are breaking to our right and to our left?" Fin asked, pointing out to a still place in the ocean with waves breaking on either side.

"Yes," I replied.

"Now look directly in front of us and watch. No waves are breaking there. They are just flowing over that spot."

"Right," I replied watching the waves flow closer to shore in that area before they crested and crashed down.

"That shows you that the ocean's floor is lower there because the waves aren't breaking at that point like they are on either side of this area." Fin continued, "So the water flowing back to sea is going to take the path of least resistance and drain back to sea through that low area. When you get a lot of water trying to flow through this one small area, there can be a pretty strong current running back to sea. That's a rip current."

"Why don't they warn you about them?" I asked.

"They do," Fin replied. "Just listen to the surf report on the radio or television."

I laughed, "You know, I haven't watched television for over a week now."

"Good for you," Fin said. "Although getting the weather and surf report off one of the local news casts is a good idea."

Just then a beach patrol pickup truck went by warning all swimmers to stay close to shore due to strong rip currents.

"They've also been warning swimmers about the rip currents over their PA system all day," Fin added.

"I had just gotten here when I went in the water, so I didn't hear any announcements," I said, still wanting to blame someone for not letting me know about the rip currents.

"You should always be respectful of going into the sea and remember that everything has its risks."

"But I've been saying my intentions each morning for the joy of life," I protested. "That certainly wasn't joy I felt out there today."

"True," Fin replied thoughtfully. "But setting your intention doesn't mean that you will live without challenges. Sometimes the greatest growth of the human spirit comes from the challenges we meet in our life. And out of that growth can come more peace and contentment, and from these can come joy. It's not like a magic wand where you say 'hocus-pocus' and get your wishes. Each of us is here to learn certain things, and synchronicity is here to help us get that education and take us to our highest good. And sometimes our highest good is learning a healthy respect for the things that can harm us, or others."

"What happened to your 'no fear' philosophy?" I asked teasingly.

"Fear and respect are very different things. Fear, real or imagined, can paralyze your life or keep you from doing something you want to or should do. For me, respect means that although I may have concerns, I'm still going to live life to the fullest and just show a healthy respect for the things that concern me while I enjoy my life around them."

"Like swimming in the ocean when there could be sharks or rip currents?" I asked.

"Or like driving a car when there could be a drunk driver or taking a chance on something I really want to do even though there is a chance I could fail. Remember, everything is neutral. It's how we respond that makes it seem good or bad."

"Okay," I said. "I get that everything's neutral and the sea's rip currents are just a natural way for beach drainage and not a direct attack on me. But explain that whole karma thing to me."

"Well, science teaches us that for every action, there is direct and opposite reaction. So for everything we do, there is a reaction. Just like the big waves rushing into shore cause a lot of extra water to drain back to sea causing a rip current, our actions also have a direct effect on our surroundings and the people in them. For example, say I told you a lie and you found out about it. Would you be willing to readily trust me the next time I told you something?"

"Probably not," I said.

"So you see the lie is the wave that comes crashing to shore, and the rip current is the reaction of distrusting what I say," Fin explained.

"I didn't think karma was so immediate," I said.

"It can be, or it can take years. Let me ask you this: which wave would be stronger and bigger? A wave that begins its journey to shore in the middle of the Atlantic Ocean or one that is formed in the middle of a pond?"

"The ocean wave."

"Good. Why?'

"Because since a wave is energy, it has farther to grow in strength and size," I guessed, hoping that I was right.

"Exactly! Well done," said Fin. "You see, when we do or say something we expend energy, so we are sending energy out into the world."

"That makes sense," I agreed.

"And if for every action there is a reaction, then it makes sense that if the reaction happens quickly, it's more like a wave in a pond than one in the ocean. So if I tell you a lie and you call me on it, I have a chance to explain why I told you the lie. It could be that I meant to deceive you out of malice, or I could have deceived you to keep from hurting your feelings, or it could be that I meant well but was misinformed. By being confronted with my deception, I can explain my rationale. That can definitely have an impact on your reaction. But if I say something that isn't true and you discover it later and feel betrayed, I could easily be written off as a liar, and that would not only strain our friendship, but also keep you from putting any further trust in me. And if you told others that I wasn't to be trusted, it could cause an even larger impact on my reputation and friendships."

"So the longer karma waits, the stronger its punch?" I asked.

"Exactly!" Fin said.

"I know a few people who are going to get quite a wallop someday," I laughed and then caught myself. "I guess I shouldn't be laughing at their misfortune."

"Always lessons, never losses," Fin said. "Karma is just a natural flow of energy, just like waves and rip currents. Since the universe is guiding us to our greater good, I think that karma is like a second chance at the lesson but from a different angle."

"Huh?" I said confused.

"If you believe that the universe wants you to succeed, and is guiding you to your highest good, then karma is just the universe's way of using your actions to help you learn the lesson from another perspective. Say, I do you a favor," Fin said.

"You're constantly doing me a favor by helping me understand all this," I said. And then added, "I'll never be able to repay you for all you've done for me."

"I don't want you to repay me. This is given without expecting anything in return. I do this as a way to help others experience my love of life and all that is in it. Loving and helping others make my life wonderful. This is my gift to give, and I give it freely. I'm grateful to you for receiving it so willingly."

"It's my pleasure. I count you as a trusted friend," I said, knowing that the words only scratched the surface of my gratitude.

"You see, that's how karma works," Fin said.

"Huh?' I said again. "I must've missed something."

"I do something for you that you appreciate, and you react with friendship and trust."

"But I thought karma only worked on bad things," I said.

"No, karma is nothing but energy coming around to teach us our lesson from another point of view so that we can grow to our highest good. Karma shows us when and how our actions are appreciated as well as when and how they're not."

"So my life is full of karma?" I asked.

"Sure, from the people you trust as your closest friends to your boss who managed by fear and caused you to dislike him."

"So is karma responsible for me losing my job?" I asked, wondering what I could've done to deserve that.

"It could be. I don't know everything you've done in the past or what lessons the universe wants you to learn. It could also just have been a way for your old employer to cut their bottom line. Or it could just be a wake-up call that life is meant to be lived, not just worked through. The important thing to remember is that we need to learn from what we are encountering and grow to be all that the universe knows we can be. Sometimes we might know exactly the cause of what has happened: like telling lies and having no one trust you. You go from being someone who is trusted to someone in need of being trusted. So since you didn't get the trust lesson when you were given trust, you are now learning its value from the vantage point of needing to earn trust."

"That makes sense," I said.

"Other times it could just be synchronicity guiding you to your greatest self," Fin added.

"Isn't that the same thing?"

"Very Good!" Fin replied. "You see, in order to become the person the universe knows you can become, you need to learn certain things. Thinking of karmic lessons as synchronistic signs to your greater self instead of punishment is the right attitude to have. By realizing that life is an amazing journey filled with lots of adventures and scenic changes along the way, it takes the stress out of most of the changes. The point is to learn from your experiences. That's why they're occurring. What's important to remember is that karma is not fatalistic. The quicker we learn our lessons, the quicker we can move on to our greater good. If you end up in another job with another angry boss, it may be that you still have a lesson to learn regarding how you deal with that type of person.

"Oh, and live in the present. Don't spend too much time looking for your past karmic indiscretions. React properly in the present."

"So like with Mrs. Vargas." I said, thinking out loud. "I blew up some firecrackers years ago and she remembered me doing it, and has held a negative opinion of me for not respecting her yard. That negative opinion either stayed the same or grew since she'd had no interaction with me since that experience, even though I've grown and changed. So when she saw me 30 years later, my past actions caused her to react negatively toward my being in her neighborhood."

"I'm sure that had a lot to do with it," Fin said. "Plus as we discussed before, she doesn't like change. You could have been someone she had never met before, and she still may have become angry that things were changing again."

"But when I reacted kindly to her negative statements, it stopped her from making more negative remarks, and she even forgave me," I remembered.

"That's learning from your experiences. You see, through something that could have had you sending more negative energy into the world, you chose to react with kindness and stopped the flow of negativity in this situation. Mrs. Vargas may not like change, but you've certainly done your best to show her that not all change is negative."

Just then the beach patrol truck went by again telling people to stay out of the water. "You care to join me as I finish my walk?" Fin asked. "It doesn't look like we're going to get to bodysurf today."

We got up and walked to cooler sand where the surf was just lapping the shore.

As we walked, I wondered if karma was a system of rewards and punishments designed to keep us in line.

"Well, some people believe that. But I think that karma provides us another chance at learning a lesson that will help us get to our greatest good. It's like the other day when I was floating in the water but you had to kick your feet to stay afloat. Each of us is different. So given the same circumstance, we may need to act in different ways in order to keep afloat. For me it was keeping my head back, chest out, and letting the air in my lungs raise me to the surface. For you a little extra effort was needed. We're both getting a similar experience just in different ways. And as any teacher will tell you, not all students learn the same way. So I may have less trouble rising to the water's surface, but more trouble diving down to the ocean's floor, and you may be the opposite. Either way, we are getting the lessons we are supposed to receive. Not to reward or punish us but to guide us to our highest good."

"But don't you think that there are people who should be punished?" I asked.

"I think we usually do a pretty good job of punishing ourselves," he said. "We all have free will. So if someone breaks the law, he or she shouldn't be surprised if they have to pay the consequences. They made the choice to break the law."

"But what if the law is wrong or unjust?" I asked.

"Don't get me wrong. I don't think all laws are right or just. There are people throughout history who challenged the law in order to show it was unfair. Gandhi, Martin Luther King, and Nelson Mandella come to mind. They knew that the law was created by humans, and humans make mistakes. They also knew that they could be punished if they broke the law. However, these people became great leaders because they didn't respond to the unjust with violence. They responded with love and a purpose for the greater good of others. Adversity comes to each of us. It's how we react to adversity that makes us great or makes us bitter. Remember, always lessons, never losses."

"I think I've heard that before," I laughed.

"I'm sure I'll say it again too," Fin laughed. "I keep saying it to remind myself as well as you."

By this time we had gotten back to my beach chair, and so as Fin went on his way, I decided to pack up my gear and head back to the bungalow.

I was still a little shaky as I made my way back to the bungalow. I appreciated the warmth of the sun on my shoulders and the cool breeze at my back. I guess the adrenaline was still racing through my body because everything seemed very vivid. Having been caught in a rip current was unsettling, and it had me thinking how grateful I was to be alive.

When I got back to the bungalow I pulled a cold bottled water out of the fridge and plopped down on one of the lounge chairs on the sunporch. The jalousie windows were open, and I turned on the ceiling fan to help stir the air.

As I sat there I pondered life and how what I had thought was so definite was now so questionable. In the past several weeks everything I had believed in or had thought was important was changing. It was a little unsettling, like having my feet swept out from underneath me by the rip current.

But I had survived the rip current, and I would survive having my feet swept out from underneath me in my career as well. In fact, since that had happened I was talking to people I would never have met and learning new things I never would have learned if I had been stuck in my little office twelve hours a day. True, I needed to make a living doing something, but shouldn't I also be enjoying life while I do it?

I sat there feeling the sea breeze come in the jalousie windows and cool the porch, enjoying the moment and the fact that I was becoming a student of life. I may not have come to it voluntarily, but I was learning that life is about more than an office and a title. Life is short and needs to be lived to the best of our ability, and that means learning lessons and accepting changes as part of the grand scheme of it all. Before last week I hadn't thought the universe cared a lick about me any more than I had cared about the ants scurrying about the parched ground in the backyard. But if the universe really did care enough about the sea turtle to guide her to the place where she hatched in order to lay her eggs, and it cares enough about me to get me off the work treadmill so that I could experience my highest good, then surely I needed to put forth the effort to continue the journey and not fall back into my old way of thinking or living.

Second chances, karma, whatever they are called, are gifts to start over, and this is what I planned to do. Although all of Fin's ideas were helping me realize this, it was the very unpleasant experiences of losing my job and being held under by the rip current that were the swift kick in the butt I needed to see that I needed to stop existing and start living again.

I smiled to myself as I thought, "Maybe there is something in the water here, even I'm becoming philosophical."

Since I couldn't begin the painting on the sunporch walls until the patching compound dried, I decided to paint the bathroom. It was small, which meant no easy rolling but more tedious trim painting.

I taped off the bathroom that was small and muggy and began painting the tropical splendor color on the walls. Its bright hue showed how faded the paint on the walls had become, and I thought, "Kind of like my life, before and after this adventure."

"Definitely something in the water," I laughed.

It was just before 9:00 p.m. when I finished, and I went out on the sunporch to cool off. It had just turned dark, so I left the lights off as I looked out at the palms rustling gently in the breezes.

I was congratulating myself on a job well done and thinking I should grab a bite for dinner when I saw a shadow go across the backyard. It almost looked like a bear stooped over and walking on two feet. I strained my eyes to see more, but it was gone quickly, and all I heard was the rustling of the palms.

"Maybe it was just my imagination, whoever heard of a beach bear? Beach bunnies, yes!" I smiled to myself. "But not beach bears."

I sat there silently for few minutes and didn't see anything else, so I dismissed it and wandered off to the revived and cheerful kitchen to get a cup of yogurt and make a salad.

I went back outside and sat in the dark while I looked for signs of whatever it was, but all was silent and seemed right with the world. I started to doze off and roused myself enough to take my plate to the kitchen and then climb into bed exhausted and happy to be alive.

DAY 10

The next morning I was up before the sun and sat at the cement picnic table watching the colors in the sky change from dark to light. Since I had been working on painting a sunrise, I was amazed at how I noticed so much more detail. Instead of seeing the whole, I was experiencing the uniqueness of each sunrise. Yes, the whole was spectacular, but what made it beautiful was its many parts. "Just like life," I thought. "There is something definitely in the water," I laughed to myself.

I then set my intention, "Today will be filled with the joy of life, bringing me courage and inner peace to help me create beauty, and send kindness to all those I meet. All this or something better." I was feeling very comfortable with this phrase now. It seemed like it was the right phrase for me, at least for that moment.

When it was light enough to see, I went carefully toward the back of the yard to look for any evidence that a bear or something had been crossing the yard. But the sod was thick, even if it was brown, and I didn't notice anything except that it needed to be watered. So I was out with a hose when I noticed Mrs. Vargas coming across the yard with her hair tied up in a big yellow-blue-and-orange paisley scarf.

"Why are you watering your grass?" she asked.

"It's looking a bit brown," I replied.

"But it's going to rain for the next two days," she said. "You're just wasting water and time."

"I really need to start watching the weather report," I said more to myself than to her.

She told me the channel of a local station that gave the weather every few minutes and the surf report every half hour and was getting ready to leave when I heard myself say, "Are there any bears in Daytona?"

She burst out laughing, "Bears? Jack, I think you've been sniffing too many paint fumes. Does this look like a forest to you?"

I laughed self-consciously and told her what I thought I had seen the night before.

"Well, it sure wasn't any bear," she said a little warily. "You sure you saw it?"

"I think I am. But yesterday was filled with a lot of excitement, so maybe it was just my imagination."

"I've lived here nearly fifty years, and I've never heard of a bear round these parts."

"You don't think it was a prowler?" I asked suddenly aware that maybe it wasn't a bear or my imagination.

"If there's a prowler around here, I'd know it. I'm a light sleeper, and I know everything that goes on in this neighborhood. So don't you worry about that. It might have just been a big dog or something."

I laughed and said, "Okay," even though I knew that if I had seen something, it surely wasn't a dog.

"Now you stop watering your yard," Mrs. Vargas said firmly. "You're just wasting water since it's going to rain, and you're wasting perfectly good beach time too, since you'll be stuck indoors once this tropical storm comes ashore."

"Tropical storm! Should I be worried?" I asked. (She had certainly gotten my attention.)

"Nah. It's just going to be a lot of rain and some wind. Not so great weather to be outside."

"When will it come ashore?" I asked.

"Later this afternoon. And it will water your uncle's yard just fine and with the nitrogen-rich water that only rain can bring. The yard will be bright green by the time the storm is over."

And with that she was off to her bungalow shaking her head and muttering something to herself.

I went inside and for the first time in a week turned on the television. I found the channel Mrs. V had told me about and watched the weather report. Sure enough, a tropical storm was moving toward us with minimal winds and lots of rain, so I decided to enjoy the beach time I had before the storm arrived. The surf report said that rip currents were a danger at the Volusia County beaches, so I decided to just enjoy the beach and the breeze and stay in ankle-deep water.

I grabbed my gear and was at the beach in minutes.

I staked out my waterfront real estate for the day and decided to walk along the beach. The waves were big and pounding the shore, and as I walked I found a variety of unusual things washed up along the with ocean's foam. I now understood why Fin carried his garbage grabber because there were some things I was not willing to pick up. But I did pick up a fair share of things and take them to the blue garbage cans located on poles about every hundred yards along the beach. Things like a shoe covered in barnacles, a child's plastic boat, a deflated plastic raft, and a tire. Not an inner tube but a tire! How did that get there? I wondered.

I walked down to a wonderful dive of a restaurant that served great mahimahi and washed my hands several times before sitting down and ordering. The meal was delicious washed down with cold water and some iced tea. And as I watched from my table, the waves seemed to be getting larger.

I was heading back toward my beach gear when I saw a news van parked on the beach and wandered over to see what was going on.

There I saw a reporter putting on a nylon windbreaker too large for him and position himself so that the wind made it flutter like a flag. Then he started his broadcast about the coming tropical storm and the high winds and large surf. I looked around and thought to myself, "Yes, the surf was rough, but it really wasn't much windier than a usual afternoon sea breeze."

Was I just inexperienced with such things at the beach? Or was he making this out to be much worse than it was actually going to be?

I waited until after his camera was off and asked him if the tropical storm had changed since this morning.

"It's a bit stronger. Better get ready to hunker down," he said casually and then walked off to chat with the cameraman.

I decided that I must not be taking this seriously enough and headed back to pack up my beach gear and get ready to "hunker down" as the reporter had so seriously stated several times during his time on camera.

When I approached my chair, I saw that Fin was sitting meditation style on a beach towel smiling, with his eyes closed and his face pointing up to the sun.

I approached quietly not wanting to disturb him, but as I got within fifteen feet of him, he said, "Hey, Jack, I was wondering where you were."

"Lunch," I laughed. (How does he do that?)

"Hope you enjoyed it," he said with his eyes still closed.

"I did," I said. "But now I have to go get ready to hunker down for the approaching storm."

"It sounds like you've been listening to the news reporters up and down the beach," Fin said smiling.

"Yeah," I replied. "And the reporter I saw made it sound like it was going to be an awful storm. I might even drive back to Orlando until it's over."

"Well, that's your choice," Fin said. "It's always wise to be respectful of nature."

"What are you going to do?" I asked.

"Well, it's a tropical storm, which means a lot or rain and wind but nothing major, so I'm just going to do some things inside until it is over," Fin replied calmly.

"You seem awfully calm about all of this," I said.

"You must have been too, or you wouldn't have come down to the beach, gone for a walk, and eaten lunch," Fin replied turning to look at me. "What changed?"

"I saw a news reporter giving his report of how conditions are worsening at the beach," I said, feeling a little foolish as we both sat chatting in the sun.

"They are worsening compared to what they have been, but think back to what the reporter said," Fin said calmly.

I closed my eyes and thought of how the reporter spoke about the impending storm and the tone of voice he used to show he was serious.

"Now tell me what you know about the tropical storms. How much rain are they predicting?'

"About three inches," I said.

"And what are the winds supposed to be?" Fin asked.

"Gusts of up to sixty miles an hour," I answered.

"Is that much different than a typical summer thunderstorm?" Fin asked.

"Well, it's a little stronger, and it's going to last a couple of days," I said defensively.

"Right. But it's not much stronger than a usual thunderstorm. Last week we had a thunderstorm with wind gusts of eighty miles an hour."

"Right," I agreed thinking about some of the blinding Florida rainstorms I've driven through.

"So what made you begin to worry about this tropical storm?"

"Well, a few years ago my home was damaged by three hurricanes in less than two months," I said, remembering how Hurricanes Charley, Francis, and Jeanne came almost every two weeks.

"But those were hurricanes," Fin said logically, "this is a tropical storm. By living in Florida you know that. So what scared you?"

I thought about it for a moment, and then it occurred to me, "The way the reporter was talking about hunkering down and his delivery was just like what I had watched during all three hurricanes."

"So you're buying into a fear-based mentality?" Fin questioned.

"I thought you said it was good to be respectful of nature?" I argued.

"It is," Fin agreed. "But it's also good to think for yourself. You have the facts, don't let someone else's take on something make you stop thinking for yourself."

"What do you mean?" I asked.

"Obviously you weren't too worried about the tropical storm when you decided to spend the day at the beach."

I nodded.

"Or when you ate a leisurely lunch."

I nodded again.

"But when you saw the reporter treating the tropical storm with the same severity as he would a category 5 hurricane, you began to panic."

He was right. "Is this about neutrality again?" I asked.

"You catch on quick," Fin said. "You see, the media knows that we live in a fear-based society. Last night I even saw a promo for the news that said, 'Robbery turns fatal in a local neighborhood. Was it yours? Details at eleven.'

"What kind of reporting is that but fear-based? We'll scare people into watching our program. Unfortunately it works because we are afraid of losing our jobs, of the economy, of terrorists, of poisonous paint on children's toys, the list goes on and on. And in order to capitalize on this, the news keeps us on pins and needles about what dangers lurk around every corner."

"But isn't it important to be informed?" I asked.

"Yes, it's important to be informed so that you can make informed decisions. Not parrot back what a reporter has said. Take the facts and realize that a thing is just a thing and act accordingly. If your life is in danger, by all means take the proper precautions, but don't spend your life living in fear. That's not living, that's just buying into someone else's agenda."

"Who's agenda?" I asked.

"Whoever is benefiting from the fear," Fin said.

"Remember your management-by-fear boss?"

"Yeah," I said hesitantly, not exactly seeing where this was going.

"He controlled you by fear, right?"

"Yes," I agreed.

"So if you were to rush back home right now, what were you going to do?"

"I'm not sure," I replied honestly.

"Would it have involved watching the news constantly?" Fin asked.

"Definitely," I said, the lightbulb slowly coming on inside my fear-based brain.

"That's what I mean. When you're well informed, you should think for yourself. Not subscribe to letting someone else tell you what to think or how to act."

I nodded again.

"Now if there were a hurricane coming," Fin continued, "I would be the first one to be getting off the beach and onto the mainland. Not only for my safety, but also for the safety of the rescue crews who have to answer the 911 calls of people too stubborn to leave after all the facts say it's too dangerous to stay. But since we're talking some rain and heavy wind gusts, I'm not going to spend the next two days glued in front of a television to bolster the ratings of the newscasts. I'm just planning to keep updated on the weather and still enjoy my time spent indoors."

I agreed, and Fin looked at me very solemnly and said, "What I just said goes for everything I've told you."

"What?" I asked.

"When I tell you something, don't just take my word for it. Examine it. See if it feels right for you, and then if it does feel right, include it into your life. Don't just put it into your life because you're afraid of missing out on something or not fitting into the group mentality. Do it because if feels right for you, then trust your gut—"

"Jump in and enjoy the ride!" I chimed in laughing.

He laughed too.

I assured him that I was examining what he said and trying things out to see if they worked in my life. So far everything seemed to be pointing me to a happier life, so I was sticking with what I was learning.

"It won't hurt my feelings if something doesn't feel right for you," he said. "We're different people living different lives, so some things I do are bound to feel uncomfortable to you. I'm just sharing what I've learned that has made my journey so incredible."

"And I appreciate it," I assured him. "I do have a question," I added. "Were you just meditating when you were sitting there before I got back?"

"Busted," Fin smiled back.

"I thought you said you liked to meditate by creating," I said.

"I do," Fin said. "But I don't limit myself to just one kind of meditation experience. There are a number of ways to meditate.

Personally, I try to experience the power of the universe wherever I am. Worship isn't just sitting in a building while someone gives a lecture. That may give you inspiration, but to really connect with the universe is to immerse yourself into life, hear life's energy, and remember that the joy of life comes from a higher power that is amazing, loves you unconditionally and wants you to be happy."

"But on the beach? With all the people?" I asked hesitantly.

"Sure. Why not? All this is just a part of the rhythm of life. So I close my eyes and hear children laughing and waves crashing and feel the breeze blow grains of sand against my skin. It's all a part of why I live at the beach."

"But how do you keep your concentration? Shouldn't you be saying om or something?" I asked, afraid that I was showing my ignorance about the subject.

"I could say, 'ommmmmmmm,'" Fin agreed. "But I was meditating on how good life is at this moment, so I was enjoying the moment, and that includes the laughter and squeals of children and the cawing of the seagulls. Which, by the way, is another sign that the tropical system won't be too bad."

"Huh? Are you getting messages from beyond now?" I teased. (Although with Fin I wasn't sure if it was teasing.)

"No, just from the birds," Fin laughed.

"So the birds talk to you when you're meditating?" I asked skeptically.

"Yes," Fin said, "and that seagull over there told me he doesn't like your swimming suit."

I recognized the joviality in his voice and said, "All right, O beach guru, please explain. And by the way, that is just his opinion and doesn't make it so. My swimming suit is neutral."

Fin laughed and said, "Well said. If this were going to be a really bad storm, the birds would know it and leave for safer conditions."

"How?" I asked amazed.

"They are equipped for survival, and one of their survival tools is to know when to get out of the way of an advancing storm," Fin said.

I remembered my grandmother looking at the birds flying around in a rainstorm and saying, "It's going to keep raining for a while, the birds are out getting their feathers all wet. I sure hope those feathers don't shrink up on 'em."

When I told Fin this, he laughed and said, "Exactly! You see the birds are a part of the rhythm of life, just like the waves and those children playing over there and you and I. So by paying attention to the rhythm of life, you'll be more connected to what's going on around you and can make wiser decisions as to where synchronicity is guiding you."

We sat in silence for a while as I pondered this. Then another thought flashed in my head and I asked, "Are there any bears on Daytona Beach?"

Instead of laughing at me, Fin looked lost in thought for a minute and then said, "I can't recall ever hearing of any. Why?"

He sat quietly as I told him of my experience from the night before.

"Well, it seems to me that you have a mystery on your hands." He smiled. "Just remember, things aren't always as they appear. But if you sit quietly and listen, you just might get the clues you'll need to solve it. However, to be safe, you may want to lock your doors before going to sleep."

"What happened to not living in fear?" I asked.

"I'm not saying to be afraid. I'm just saying that since you think you saw something or someone walk across your backyard in the night, you may just want to exert a little caution. No different than checking the surf report before you go to the beach."

"Point taken," I said. "And then thought of how Mrs. Vargas had told me that this was a neighborhood where they didn't need to lock their doors. Were things changing a little too much in this quiet neighborhood, or was my imagination running away with me?"

I expressed my concern about this to Fin. This time he laughed and said, "From what you've told me of Mrs. Vargas, she'll know if there is something sinister going on in the neighborhood, and if she knows, so will everybody else, so I wouldn't worry about it."

He was right, I told myself as I looked out to the darkening horizon.

"Well, it looks like the storm is getting closer, so I'm going to head on back home," Fin said. "I'll see you in a couple of days. Will you start your mural while you have all this time to spend inside?"

"I don't know if I'm quite ready. There are things I'm happy with and other things I'm not quite ready to paint," I reasoned aloud.

"Well, why not give it a try? Postponing is just another form of worry." Fin smiled.

And with that he was heading down the beach humming a tune for all to hear.

I had been back home about an hour when the rain started. At first it was a soft drizzle. But then it increased and decreased throughout the day. Nothing serious, just a lot of rain.

"I might as well get started on painting the sunporch," I thought to myself and got out the yellow paint that was for the exterior of the house since technically they used to be exterior walls before it was made into a sunporch.

I tested the compound and saw that it was dry, so I began to paint around the ceiling and other trim work first. The stucco walls were coarser, and so it took more strokes to get the paint evenly on the walls. (Does any home-improvement project go as expected?) Fortunately in a closet I had found an old roller for stucco surfaces and used it to roll the cheerful yellow paint on the walls. In the course of a few hours, the walls were covered with their first coat. The paint was taking a long time to dry in the humid air, so I wrapped the roller in a plastic bag and stuck it in the refrigerator. This was a trick I learned when I helped a friend paint her house. It keeps the paint from drying on the roller so you don't have to wash the roller as often.

"Okay," I thought to myself, "now what's next?"

I saw the canvases on the dining room floor and looked them over again. I definitely liked the cloud technique on one of them and the way the waves looked on another. I had a palm tree that I liked the look of, but it wasn't quite there yet, so I decided to keep playing with paint techniques to get the fronds looking real. I was painting queen palms like the ones in the backyard. I had been trying to paint them with just a few strokes, but their fronds went in every direction, so I decided to study just one frond and look at the elements that combined to create its stately appearance.

What I found was each frond had hundreds of leaflets hanging in two rows and pointing in every direction. So I decided to paint the arc of the frond and one row of leaflets, then paint the second row over the first to give it depth. It worked! It was a little out of proportion, but the effect is what I had been looking for. I had just needed to take the time to pay attention to what I was doing and watch what had unfolded.

It was difficult mastering this technique, and I was surprised when I looked up at the clock and saw that it was already 8:30 p.m. I went into the kitchen to cook dinner and turned on the television to the local twenty-four-hour news station to check on the weather. It looked like it would continue to rain for the next day or so.

I turned off the TV and brought my dinner out to the sunporch to listen to the wind and the rustle of the palms as I ate.

To me there is something almost hypnotic about a rainstorm. The air seems heavier and comforting as it wraps around me, stirring occasionally with the wind. When I was a kid, sleeping out on my aunt and uncle's sunporch, my aunt told me that the sound of the palm fronds blowing was the rustle of the wings of angels watching over me as I slept. I hadn't thought of this in years, but that night I listened to the palms blowing and felt safe and connected to a universe that is looking out for me.

DAY 11

I awoke around 7:00 a.m. and found myself lying on the lounge chair in the sunporch. It was still raining. "I must have dozed off," I thought to myself as I stretched and yawned. I picked up the dishes from the night before and took them to the kitchen looking at the canvases as I passed them.

"Not bad," I said congratulating myself as I saw the way the palm was looking.

I turned on the TV to get the latest on the tropical system. It had weakened but was still going to be affecting our weather pattern for the next twenty-four hours. "Looks like I can get a lot done on the bungalow," I thought to myself while turning off the TV.

As I fixed breakfast, I set my intention, "Today will be filled with the joy of life, bringing me courage and inner peace to help me create beauty, and send kindness to all those I meet. All this or something better."

After breakfast, I checked the paint on the sunporch walls, and it was dry, so I pulled the roller out of the refrigerator and painted the second coat of yellow on the walls. It certainly brightened up the sunporch even on such a gloomy-looking day.

I cleaned out the roller for later use on the exterior of the house and decided to paint the walls of my bedroom. I pulled the drawers out of the old oak dresser to make it easier to move away from the wall. In the bottom drawer I found an old folder filled with drawings I had done while staying with my aunt and uncle: sunrises, dolphins, sharks (what boy isn't fascinated by sharks?), and pelicans (I've always thought pelicans looked so prehistoric). These drawings were good, even after all these years, and I had forgotten all about them. It was a surprise to see how easily the memories came back to me of how I had drawn them and what inspired them, the pelican especially. We called him Terry because I thought he looked like a pterodactyl. And he would always land in the backyard of the bungalow when we were cooking on the grill. He'd sit in the yard waiting, and my uncle, being a softy for anything hungry, would always throw him some fish before he grilled it. He felt that giving any bird something cooked might throw off its digestive track since it wasn't designed to eat cooked food.

I had forgotten all about Terry and the barbecues in the backyard and wondered if the grill was still in the closet of the carport. I wandered outside and opened the closet (left unlocked of course), and there it was. "I think I'll grill out when the weather gets better," I thought to myself. I also found some tiki torches and citronella oil for the torches. "Grilled mahimahi will be a nice way to celebrate getting the inside of the house painted," I thought to myself.

Then I went back inside and began painting the guest bedroom. Because it was small, the trim took longer than the rolling. But thanks to the ceiling fan helping the drying process, I had both coats on the walls before noon.

I stopped and looked around the house. I had painted all the interior walls. "Now what?" I asked myself, and then I looked up to see the large unpainted wall with my drawing taped to it looming before me. I wasn't planning on painting the mural until next week. "I need more practice!" I told myself, a little unnerved about the thought of actually painting the mural. It was one thing to think of it as something in the future but another to think of it as something I could be doing right now. All my work on the interior was done. Then I remembered Fin saying, "Procrastination is just another form of worry." And what was worry but another form of fear. So using the "no fear" philosophy guess what should move to the top of my list.

"I'll think about it after lunch," I told myself and grabbed a cup of yogurt and a banana with a bottle of water, and took them to the sunporch. I watched the rain fall from the roof onto the flower beds around the house. Well, it was too wet to garden, and I'd finished all the other painting. Maybe I could go out to the art store and at least pick up the paint I would need to paint the mural. I looked at the tubes I had used covering the canvases and guessed about how much of the different colors I would need to paint the wall.

Then I studied the drawing I had done thirty years ago. It was actually pretty good. It seemed to be missing something, but I wasn't sure what it needed. The sky was vibrant with color, and the ocean sparkled under the rising sun. The queen palm on the right framed the one side nicely. But it needed something on the lower left-hand side to balance it off just a little.

I pondered this for a few minutes, showered, and headed off to the art store.

When I got back, I opened the door, and there again loomed the blank wall. Fin's "no fear" policy popped into my head again, and that meant that whenever he started worrying or fretting about something, he put it to the top of his to-do list. At the moment I was trying to keep the mural at the bottom of my to-do list, but if I was trying to change my life, then I had to change how I lived it, so I decided to start the mural.

A thousand doubts rushed into my head, and Mrs. Vargas's comments from thirty years ago dominated them. But if everything is neutral, then this mural would be too, and I would just have to paint it in all its glorious neutrality to see if I still found it neutral or really liked it. My aunt seemed to really like my drawing, and so did my uncle. So why was I drawn to Mrs. V's negative opinion? Was it that hard for me to believe that I could create something beautiful? I liked the drawing I had done and the practice paintings. So why was it difficult for me to believe I could do something bigger? Was it the size? Or was it that this couldn't be hidden and so my work would be out there for all to see?

This was a dilemma, but then I tried to quiet my mind and my fear of being judged and listen to what I was feeling. Besides the worrying about what others would think (which of course was based in fear), I still felt it was the right thing to do. So I pulled the table and chairs away from the wall, laid down my drop cloth, and instantly got painter's block.

More questions and doubts ran through my head. But the major one was, "Where should I start?" The same question ran through my head when I had decided to paint my uncle's bungalow, and the answer was one room at a time. So to use that same analogy in the mural, I should paint one element at a time. Starting with the background that happened to be the sky and clouds (which I was pretty good at) and the sparkling water (which I had also been able to show on canvas.)

Plus, as I had learned, it was only paint, and I could always paint over it. But if I was just getting this bungalow ready for my uncle to sell, why should I bother? The new owner might just paint over it. "Nothing is forever, even mistakes. Learn from them and move on. Just enjoy the moment and create for the joy of it," I told myself.

I stared at the blank wall some more as I prepared my palette with the various colors I would need for the sky and then got intimidated again.

What was intimidating me? It was the blankness of the wall and all the possibilities it held. So I took a deep breath, dipped my brush in the paint, and made the first streak of color across the wall.

It felt good, really good.

And without further delay, I dropped the fear and became involved in creating something out of love. Love for two people who were always there for me and showed me how special they thought I was, even when I wouldn't listen.

Hours went by, and I felt I was lost in the painted sky as I touched up the background of this cloud or used lighter paint to show sunlight. Each detail drew me in further. When I stopped, it was seven hours later, and my shoulders ached, but my mind was clear. No fear, only wonder and contentment.

I stepped back and looked, surprised I had done so much, and yet knowing I had done it to the best of my ability. Before me was a vibrant sunrise filled with fluffy, swirling clouds and shimmering waves.

I had painted the sea and sky and felt good about it. Tomorrow I would tackle the palm tree, but for now the base of the painting was finished, and I knew I would sleep well.

DAY 12

I slept amazingly well. I credited it to the mixture of exhaustion and getting something started that I had been worrying about. I awoke to some thunder, and as I wandered toward the kitchen, I looked at the mural and smiled. It looked pretty good already. The clouds had depth, and the water did look like it was catching the first light of the day. I thought to myself, "I really am creating beauty! Just like I'm saying when I set my intention."

With such inspiration, I quickly set my intention again. "Today will be filled with the joy of life, bringing me courage and inner peace to help me create beauty, and send kindness to all those I meet. All this or something better."

I grabbed a cup of yogurt and some toast and brewed some coffee, then headed out to the sunporch to enjoy the patter of the rain, but there was no rain. Only thunder in the distance and the dampness that hangs in the air during a Florida storm. Then I saw a mockingbird land by a puddle on the cement table outside, take a drink of water, and fly off.

"Does that mean it's going to rain longer or that there is a lull in the storm?" I asked myself as I headed to the television to check on the weather, only to find that I was wrong on both counts. The system had moved by quicker than they had thought, and so hot, humid weather was our forecast.

I went back out to the sunporch to finish breakfast and chuckled to myself as I remembered how worried I had been about the storm. I'm glad I didn't spend my time driving back to my house or "hunkering down" in front of the television.

I heard more tweeting and watched a female cardinal hop onto the cement table and take a drink of water. The thunder rumbled from a farther distance away, and for the first time I can remember I just sat and listened to the rhythm of life with no thoughts but that of gratitude for being a part of it all. This lasted for less than a minute before my mental to-do list reminded me that I had a week to finish painting the outside of the house and the mural, plus plant some drought-tolerant bushes in the flower beds. In order to get all this done, and still have beach time, I needed to get a move on. I tried to get back to that moment of peaceful calm and gratitude, but it was gone, and my brain was telling me that "time was a-wasting."

It was early, and I could already start to feel the heat and humidity, so I thought I would at least paint the palm tree's lower layer of leaves on the fronds on the wall before heading out to the beach. The palm's trunk went quite easily since I had already established the light source (sun) and knew where the highlights and shadows must go. I then carefully placed seven fronds on the painting. Each one arched as if it were being blown by a gentle morning breeze.

By the time I had finished the base of the last palm frond, it was almost 1:00 p.m., I was coated in sweat, and my neck and shoulders were starting to ache again.

I quickly showered, made a sandwich, and headed off to the beach. The waves were smaller, and quite a few people were already in the water. The sand was packed down and still damp from the rain making it easy to walk on. I claimed my section of beach real estate for the day and walked off to the lifeguard stand to ask if there was a danger of rip currents. He told me that he hadn't been told of any, so I quickly ran into the water to cool off.

The waves were about three feet, and although they were smaller than I usually liked to bodysurf, I enjoyed them, and the relative safety of no strong rip current. I was standing just past where the waves were breaking, looking out to the vastness of the horizon and resting a little when Fin popped up next to me.

"I see you survived the storm," he said to me with a sardonic twinkle in his eye.

"Yeah. And I got a lot done," I replied. "How about you?"

"I got a lot of things done too," Fin said.

Just then a flock of pelicans flew majestically overhead, and one pelican came crashing down beak first into the water twenty feet away from us.

"It never ceases to amaze me how graceful those birds can be in the air and how painful it looks when they dive for food," I said.

"They really are amazing creatures," Fin agreed. "They were on the endangered species list. But are coming back. I love seeing them flying around here."

"I always thought they looked prehistoric," I confided.

Fin laughed, "They certainly do. I'm not sure how long they've been around, but I do know they have a lot to teach us."

Fin looked over at me smiling ear to ear.

"I was wondering when I was going to learn something today," I laughed. "Please enlighten me."

"Nobody can enlighten you but yourself," Fin laughed good-naturedly, "but I can tell you what the Native Americans felt they could learn from the pelican."

"Native Americans?" I exclaimed, surprised at the turn this conversation was taking, and then surprised at the fact that I was still surprised by anything Fin said.

"Yes, you see, the Native Americans really paid attention to the energy of life and its synchronicity, although they didn't call it that. However, they understood their connection to the universe and all its creatures. They learned from each creature the traits that made it powerful and studied how its habits could bring harmony into their lives and the life of their tribes. You've seen photos of the animals on totem poles?"

I nodded.

"Well, each of those animals has a meaning and symbolizes traits or actions important to why the totem pole was created. The pelican symbolizes the proper use of abundance by eating when it is hungry but not hoarding food or killing what it cannot eat. They also represent control of ego."

"You mean by flying so gracefully and then crashing so ridiculously into the water to feed?" I asked smiling.

"That, and the way a pelican doesn't fight the others in its group for food. Each one hunts on its own, even when he is flying in a flock. The others in the flock don't try to take the food from him because they know there is plenty to go around, so they don't try to exert their will over another member of their flock to steal the food out of the mouth of their fellow pelican."

"But don't all animals know that there is plenty to go around?" I asked. "Isn't that instinct?"

"You'd think so," Fin said, looking out to the infinite sea and then turning to look at the beach. "But look at that flock of seagulls over there," he said, pointing to a group of gulls swooping down on one seagull that had what looked like a dead and rotting fish in its mouth.

"They do seem to eat anything," I said.

"Yes," Fin agreed. "But look at what they're doing."

I watched as the birds dove and tried to take the fish out of the seagull's mouth. The seagull took flight, and the birds attacked him, one after another. Finally a second gull stole the fish, and then a third gull knocked the fish out of the second gull's mouth. They watched it fall into the sea and then flew back to shore still cawing at each other.

"I've been in corporate meetings like that," I laughed.

"Unfortunately, we human beings can be a lot like that from time to time," Fin said.

"So can seagulls teach us anything positive?" I asked.

"Of course, all creatures have more positive traits than negative ones. For example, some sailors believed that seagulls were spiritual messengers telling them that land was near. Personally, whenever I'm feeling troubled by something and I see any bird in the sky, it reminds me to take a step back and get a bird's-eye view of the whole situation and not just the limited view I can get from standing, moping, or wallowing in just one place. It reminds me once again that there is more than one point of view to any situation."

"Neutrality again. Right?" I asked.

"Right," Fin laughed.

"Does everything lead back to neutrality?" I asked.

"I think as humans we need to remember that there is more than one point of view, and that nobody has all the answers," Fin said.

"Well, you seem to have a fair share of them," I said, trying to compliment him.

"I really don't," Fin protested. "There was a time when I thought I had all the answers, but then synchronicity led me to the point where I am today, where I have more questions than answers." Then he smiled and said, "And I wouldn't change it for the world. I enjoy being a student of life and learning from everything."

Just then a great wave rose up, and I jumped in and rode it to shore calling out a loud and happy "wahooo!" as I got up. In reply, I heard Fin laughing where I had left him, and I jumped back in to spend the rest of the afternoon enjoying the water, sun, and some great rides.

After several hours, Fin and I returned to our beach chairs. As we sat silently watching the world go by and hearing the crash of the waves and the energy of life, I was reminded of my fleeting moment of meditation and gratitude on the sunporch. I told Fin about it and asked, "Was that meditation?"

"Yes! Well done!" he said, holding up his hand for a high five.

I high-fived him, but was still uncertain. "It seemed so short," I said. "And I couldn't get it back after it ended. I'm not very good at it."

"But you did it," Fin insisted. "So just like painting, you know you can do it, now it just takes practice. In fact, I've heard meditation described as the time between thoughts. That could be ten minutes or two seconds. The point is you've experienced it."

"But so many things keep going through my head," I protested.

"Good for you for noticing," said Fin. "It must've really bothered you."

"Sure did," I agreed.

"Just like when you were trying to stand still in the water and the waves kept knocking you around?" Fin asked.

Then the light went on in my head as I remembered how the waves knocked me about as I was trying to stand still. "Exactly. So by trying not to have thoughts, I was noticing the thoughts about the future that were keeping me from being able to be still in the present?"

"Right!" Fin smiled. "And now that you recognized those thoughts, you know what was keeping you from enjoying your meditation longer."

"But how do you ignore them?" I asked. "They just kept coming."

"Ignoring them isn't the answer," Fin replied. "When I'm trying to meditate and thoughts keep coming into my head, I acknowledge them and say silently to them that I recognize that you are there and will think about you again in a few minutes when I can concentrate on you, but right now you are no more than a distraction from my connectivity to the universe."

"But what if what's coming into your head is part of your connection to the universe?" I protested. "Like my work on my uncle's house? I'm working on it to help him and put love out into the universe . . ." I stopped in midsentence, shocked at what I had just said.

"That sounded weird," I added.

"Did you mean it?" Fin asked.

I thought about it and then remembered to stop thinking and see how I felt about it. It felt right. Yes, I wanted to help my uncle, and yes, I felt by doing something for him I was able to put a positive energy out into the world.

Finally, I said, "Yes. I just never said anything like that before. It sounds so 1960s."

Fin laughed, "Jack, I think it's safe to say that putting more positive energy into the world is a good thing no matter what decade you're in. So getting back to your question about quieting even the thoughts that you may think connect you to the universe. Personally, I think that even those thoughts need to be silenced for a few minutes so that we can reconnect to the universe and recharge without anything draining our attention or energy. Although your ideas were to help your uncle, they were also draining you away from your connectivity to an infinite universe that wants you to succeed and pulling you into the more ego-based emotions of worry, deadlines, and what ifs. All I'm saying is realize that if those worries are valid, they will be there when you stop meditating and will pounce back into your brain. But if you've given yourself a little downtime, their urgency will be put back into perspective."

"That's the same way I feel after I've finished painting," I said. "Everything is in perspective."

"Same goes for bodysurfing or anything we love to do," Fin added.

He was right. When I was out enjoying the waves, I was concentrating on the energy of the ocean and feeling the connection to the energy of the universe as I rode the wave into shore.

"So bodysurfing is a form of meditation?" I asked, amazed.

"Anything can be if you allow it to connect you to the universe in a way that can revive your spirits and help put your worries into perspective," Fin answered.

"Isn't that just escapism?" I asked.

"I don't think so," Fin replied thoughtfully. "I think escapism is getting away from your worries or problems by using your imagination or watching television to distract you or make you forget your troubles. What we're talking about here is acknowledging your worries, putting them down while you recharge, all the while knowing that they will be there waiting for you when you finish recharging. It's not trying to escape them, but instead it's realizing they are there and equipping yourself to handle them appropriately by reconnecting to your source of power for mental clarity."

In a strange way this made sense to me. "So you're saying that if I'm trying to meditate, instead of blocking my worries, I need to acknowledge them and then ask them to wait until I recharge?"

"Interestingly put, but yes. It won't stop the chatter in your head completely, but it will certainly help you get on your way to being able to meditate. If nothing else, it can bring to mind what seems to be bothering you so that you can deal with it. Sometimes I have a great meditation and moments of true clarity. Other times my mind won't stop, and I become aware that there are some things that are bothering me so much I can't put them down for even a few minutes. But if I meditate the next day, I might find those things that seemed insurmountable the day before are not even bothering me anymore. We, like the beach, are constantly changing, and so are our thoughts and priorities. Realizing this can help take the pressure off from any of our thoughts."

We sat there silently as I pondered what Fin had said. He was right. What had bothered me when I was trying to meditate was no longer bothering me, or I would've been back at the bungalow planting bushes instead of sitting at the beach. Was the real issue that I didn't like to be inconvenienced by things that could keep me from what I wanted to do at any given moment?

I asked Fin about this, and he said, "You have just uncovered one of the main secrets of life. We worry so much about being inconvenienced that we inconvenience ourselves more by thinking and stressing about it than if we just handled it. It's just another form of fear. Fear of being inconvenienced."

"So I should handle it with the 'no fear' policy and just get on with it?"

"If you can, yes. But if you can't, just acknowledging that it's just fear of inconvenience that's worrying you. This can put things into perspective and help you to remember that life goes on."

"When you worked for your management-by-fear boss, what was the fear he held over you?" Fin queried.

"Loss of my job?" I answered.

"Why?"

"Because I need to earn money in order to live, and finding another job would be a hassle."

"So you survived the management-by-fear boss but then lost your job anyway . . ."

"Right?" I said, not seeing where this was going.

"And now you're on the beach bodysurfing and getting back into the rhythm of life."

"Well, when you put it like that, it doesn't sound so scary," I laughed.

"Yes. You've been inconvenienced, but look what has come out of it."

"Okay, okay! Point taken," I laughed. "What I'm seeing as an inconvenience could be synchronicity leading me on to my greatest good. It's neutrality once again."

Fin just smiled a big ear-to-ear grin and leaned back in his chair.

I smiled and did the same and let my body soak in the sun while I listened to the laughter of children, the waves, and the electronic song of the slushy truck as it made its way down the beach. All this reminded me that I was in step with the rhythm of life.

Later that afternoon as I walked back to the bungalow, I passed Mrs. Stevens house and saw that the car was gone, and the plants were still in her carport. I walked over to see if they needed water since they had been under shelter during the long rain. They did seem a little dry, so I watered them with the hose and headed back to my uncle's place, reminding myself to see if she needed any help in planting them.

After returning to the bungalow I checked the outside of the walls to see if they would be dry enough to start painting. They looked dry except down by the dirt, so I began to make plans to begin painting the outside of the house the next day. I then went inside tired and content. After a shower I was about to put on the Ella record and relax when I thought, "What if it draws Mrs. V over?" The mural was looking nice, but if she said something negative, it might ruin my momentum or even my ability to finish it.

"Whoa!" I thought to myself. "Why am I giving her that much power over me? She's just my uncle's neighbor and someone I may have had a dozen conversations with. Why would her opinion weigh so heavily on me?"

"Did I value her opinion so much over my own? No. Did I admire her so much that I wanted to be like her? no! Was I afraid of her? Well, not as much as a when I first got here."

But then it occurred to me that I was just afraid of being criticized. Period. Not just by Gladys Vargas, but by anybody.

I remembered one of my first conversations with Fin, when he told me that "we weren't put on this earth to be secure. We are put on this earth to make it a better place, which means laughing often, taking risks and helping others. That takes courage."

If that takes courage, then my current panic over Mrs. V seeing my art was nothing more than fear-based thinking. So I decided to stop operating out of fear and put on the Ella record. If she comes over, I'll deal with it, and if she doesn't come over, well, that was okay too.

"She's really not as bad as she likes to seem," I reminded myself as I walked over to the record player.

Soon the first notes of "Over the Rainbow" were playing, and my mind released its fears as I picked up a paintbrush and started painting the second layer of leaves on the palm fronds. I enjoyed loading the brush with different shades of greens and golden yellows and angling the brush to make a shaded effect going from light to dark on each leaf. By the time I had finished, it was 12:30 a.m., and I was exhausted, and my neck and shoulders ached again. So I washed my brushes and headed off to bed.

DAY 13

The next morning I overslept the sunrise by several hours, and I set my intention for the day before getting out of bed. After I fixed breakfast, I went out to see if the exterior walls were dry enough to paint. They looked and even felt dry to the touch at the bottom near the flower bed, so I decided that I would begin the prep work for painting.

Soon I was brushing the exterior walls with a broom to get the cobwebs out of the corners and loosening any dirt that may have been stuck to them. Then I pulled out one of the five-gallon drums of yellow paint, prepared my roller, and applied the first coat of paint onto the front of the house. It went on smoothly, and the stucco sucked up so much paint that it dried quickly. I made a game of seeing how close to the edge I could get with the roller without touching the roof overhang. I had gotten enough experience by that time that I was only about two inches away from the top. After I finished rolling the front, I wrapped the roller in a plastic bag, stuck it in the refrigerator next to my yogurt, and began the trim out on the front part of the house. It went fast since it was only a door, two windows, and the area close to the overhang. By 2:00 p.m. I had finished the first coat, and it looked so nice I continued the trim out on the sides of the house. I had just congratulated myself and was getting ready to clean up and head to the beach when the contractor pulled up in his green pickup truck. A small barrel-chested man got out of the truck, walked over to me smiling what looked like a strained and insincere smile.

"Hi. I'm the contractor. Are you Jack?"

"Yes, nice to meet you, Vincent?" I said, remembering his name from the many times I had wondered when he would call.

"Vinnie," he corrected. "It looks like I'll be here to start work the day after tomorrow."

My heart sank. Two more days! I was already beginning my third week, and he still hadn't done the first thing on my uncle's bungalow. I was beginning to get angry when I realized that I really couldn't control anything but my reaction to his schedule.

"Well, that sounds good to me," I replied steaming a little, even as I was trying to respond with love. "Do I need to do anything to get ready for you?"

"You probably want to get that painting finished," he said. "We'll be throwing the roofing shingles down, and you'll be in the way if you're still painting."

"What?" I thought to myself. "Finish the whole outside by tomorrow night?" Now I was really steaming, while reminding myself, "Respond with love, respond with love, respond with love!"

"I'll do my best," I said. And then I asked, "How long will it take to get the new roof on?"

"About two days if everything goes well," he said.

"And if it doesn't go well?" I asked.

"Longer," he said ominously.

"You'll also want to park your car in the street to keep from getting roofing nails in the tires while we're working, and wear shoes in the yard so you don't step on any nails. We'll do a sweep with magnets after we're through to be sure to get the nails out the yard."

I told him that there was a street party in seven days, and I was hoping to have the project finished by then.

He laughed and said, "Me too."

That didn't sound too reassuring, and I was beginning to get angry with his not wanting to commit himself, but I reminded myself to respond with love, or at least kindness. So I asked if I could get him a cold drink.

"Nah. Thanks though," he said, really smiling this time. "I just wanted to drop by and tell you my time schedule. I'll call you if anything changes."

He shook my hand and then headed back to his truck.

I waved as he drove off, and then my brain went into panic mode.

I had to finish the outside of the house by tomorrow night!

"Get organized," I told myself. I already have the first coat on the front of the house, and the sides are trimmed out so I can roll them today too. The back of the house was the sunporch, which I had already painted. So that just left doing a second coat of paint on the house tomorrow. It would probably mean that I would have to forego my beach time for the next couple of days. But then I would be finished with the house painting and could enjoy my final days on Daytona Beach.

As I went back to the refrigerator to get the roller, Fin's advice about not giving up my time of reflection just to meet deadlines came into my mind. Was I going to miss out on something? Was some great revelation going to happen at the beach today and I would miss it because I was just rushing the painting to meet someone else's schedule?

I looked at the white cement dolphin ornament that was mounted on the wall by the front door and remembered that Fin said that dolphins reminded him to take a deep breath to clear his mind. Well, one breath didn't quite do it, so I took another and then another. I did feel my body relaxing, and then I thought, "I'm exactly where I'm supposed to be."

So I went in and grabbed the roller and went back outside to begin rolling the side of the bungalow. It's a small house, so it only took a couple of hours to finish the first coat. Then I started painting the second coat on the front of the house. It went much faster than the first coat since the stucco wasn't sucking up so much paint this time. As I painted I reflected on how the contractor had irritated me and wondered, "Whatever happened to customer service?" After all, we were the customers, and yet he acted like we had to fit around his schedule. But then I thought, "Okay, that's one point of view. Now look at it from his point of view. Maybe he's trying to do a good job, and as you've observed, home-improvement projects don't always go as expected. So he's taking longer to make sure the job is done right."

"Maybe," I thought to myself. "There was that tropical system that knocked out a couple of days, and his painter is out of service until his leg heals. So that could throw him off schedule. But I'm really still on schedule because I'm finishing up the painting, so all he needs to do are the other things my uncle asked him to do."

This thought made me feel better, and I had finished the second coat of paint on the front of the house before it was time for dinner.

I hadn't eaten much that day and was hungry, but wasn't in the mood to cook. I walked down to the beach and found a great little restaurant with tables on a deck overlooking the ocean. I ordered the stuffed shrimp and a cold iced tea and sat there enjoying the taste of the food and the sound of the surf and the fact that someone else did the cooking and would do the cleanup.

As I sat there, I watched as people walked by enjoying the cooler twilight temperatures. Children scrambled in the sand laughing, and couples strolled hand in hand. "Life is good," I thought to myself as I enjoyed the rhythm of life at the beach.

I took a leisurely stroll along the beach, watching the moon's reflection shimmer along the water. The ocean seems so mysterious in the darkness. I walked for about an hour just enjoying the warm breeze and the sound of the waves crashing against the shore.

Upon returning to the bungalow I heard a noise like a grunt coming from the backyard. Carefully I moved to the side of the house and peered around the corner and saw the same bearlike shadow crossing the backyard and going over into the neighbor's yard.

My heart raced. I was going to find out what it was. I watched silently from the side of the house as the shadow crept slowly by. I went to creep around the corner and tripped on the metal paint tray I had left out to dry. The shadow jumped when it heard the clatter, and by the time I had gotten back up, it was gone.

I ran toward where I had seen it, but there was nothing there. I stood there straining my eyes in the darkness but didn't see anything. I was halfway into the neighbor's yard when a thought occurred to me, "If this is a bear or a burglar, they just might attack, and what do I have to defend myself but a set of keys?"

With that thought, I carefully returned to the bungalow wondering if I should call the police. After all, if it was a danger, shouldn't somebody say something? But if I said, "It looked like a bear," they would just laugh at me.

I went in the kitchen to get a drink of water when I saw the light go on in Mrs. Vargas's bungalow. "Did she hear something too? Was she okay? The shadow was moving in the opposite direction of her place, but it could have doubled back," I thought to myself.

I decided to go over and ask her.

I was knocking on her door before I realized I wasn't sure what time it was. However, Mrs. Vargas was quick to tell me. "For God's sake, Jack, it's eleven thirty! What's wrong? You scared me half to death."

She was wearing a dark blue scarf that matched her dark blue sweatpants and T-shirt. "Maybe all those bright colors she wore during the day were too bright to sleep in," I joked to myself.

I told her what I had seen and that I thought she might have seen something or been in danger.

Her response was less than enthusiastic. "Boy, you're just working too hard. Have you been out drinking?"

I assured her that I was not out drinking, and she assured me that there were no bears in Daytona Beach.

"Do you think I should call the cops and report a prowler?" I asked.

"A garden prowler who just likes to stroll through people's flower beds dressed as a bear at ungodly hours of the night?" she scoffed. "Look, I told you I'm a light sleeper, and if anything was lumbering around out there, I would have heard it."

"But something must have gotten you up?" I argued.

"Just thirst," she said. "Now go on back home and get some rest. I'll keep an ear out for bears or whatever."

I saw that arguing was pointless and dejectedly went back to my uncle's bungalow.

DAY 14

I slept fitfully and was awake with the dawn the next morning. Before I even got the coffee brewing, I was outside looking for some clue to the mystery prowler, but I couldn't find a thing except a couple of broken branches on a hibiscus plant. Hardly convincing evidence that bears were on the prowl.

I went back inside, made my coffee and toast, and carried everything out to the cement picnic table to eat. I was almost finished when Mrs. Vargas made a beeline over to me and said, "You're up early. I thought you'd be sleeping it off today, Jack."

I assured her I had not been drinking the night before, and she just laughed. "Whatever, Jack, whatever. Did you find any evidence of your bear?"

At the moment, responding with love was a bit difficult, and so I took a long sip of coffee before responding. "Nope," Was all I could muster.

I think she saw my irritation and said, "Well, I was raised in the woods near Lake Okeechobee and used to be good at tracking animals, let me take a look."

"Be my guest," I said as politely as I could.

She stared down at the ground and looked ridiculous with that huge scarf covered in peach and black swirls tied around her head. Her head looked so big it appeared as if she would topple over. It was as big as (and then it hit me) a bear's.

Seeing Mrs. Vargas humoring me actually answered my question. It was Mrs. Vargas who was prowling the yards in the middle of the night. But why? Was that her snooping hour? Although it seemed to me that every waking hour was her snooping hour. Obviously, I wasn't going to find out from her since she was putting on this charade. So I'd just have to figure it out myself.

Mrs. Vargas had gone past my neighbor's yard and into the next yard before she returned. "Sorry, Jack," she said. "I didn't see anything."

"Well, thanks for looking," I replied. "You were right before, it probably was just a big dog."

She looked up and smiled. "Yeah, probably," she agreed. But she also shot me a sideways look of caution at my sudden change of mind, before heading back to her bungalow.

I finished breakfast, cleaned the dishes, then remembered to set my intention with a little change in it. "Today will be filled with the joy and *mystery* of life, bringing me courage and inner peace to help me create beauty, and send kindness to all those I meet. All this or something better."

I smiled to myself and went outside to look at my handiwork on the front of the house. It looked good. The white trim looked shabby in contrast to the bright yellow walls, but I would be painting that soon enough. I pulled the roller out of the refrigerator and continued to roll the paint onto the house. By noon the house had two coats of yellow paint and was looking very bright and cheerful.

I grabbed a quick sandwich and began to paint the white trim that was around the edge of the roofline, the front door, the closet doors in the carport, the window sills, and the cement dolphin on the front wall.

As I painted, I tried to figure out what Mrs. Vargas was doing. I couldn't come up with anything. Was she just snooping? Was she having a romance with one of the neighbors? Was she sleepwalking? Was this any of my business?

I decided that it wasn't and redirected my mind to thinking about more enlightening things like, "I'm exactly where I need to be to become who the universe knows I can become."

I wondered who that would be. Just exactly who did the universe want me to become? I truly believed that I could become more than

I currently was. And looking back, I certainly had become a better person than I was three weeks ago. Even if I was unemployed now. I was learning to see other points of view besides my own. And I was understanding, at least at the basest level, the meaning of neutrality and how it applies to all things and experiences. I was even understanding how a policy of no fear could help lead me to the person I wanted to become. Heady concepts to be sure, and three weeks ago I wouldn't have even tried to understand them.

I pondered how it had all started with the loss of a job that I was unhappy with, followed by my courage to put off job hunting while I tried to figure out what I wanted out of life, then coming to Daytona, and learning how to bodysurf from a funny little senior citizen who loved life and all it has to offer.

"Life certainly has a strange flow sometimes," I laughed to myself. "But it gets you where you need to be."

As I pondered and painted, I was once again lost in thought and the rhythm of the brushstrokes. Time flew by, and it was 5:00 p.m. before I knew it, and I was done.

I stepped back to admire my handiwork. It had the happy look I remembered from my childhood. This was a place where the good things in life happened.

I walked around the house and found a few areas that needed to be touched up. Then I cleaned my brush and went to store the paint in the carport closet. When I opened the closet, I saw the old barbecue grill sitting there. Smiling, I pulled it out and thought, "Tonight I'm going to celebrate."

I also pulled out the tiki torches, filled them up with citronella oil, and set them up in the backyard.

I grabbed my trusty pad and pencil and made a list of what I would need to pick up in order to grill. Then I showered and headed off to the store.

Driving back to the cheerful little bungalow I had a very big sense of satisfaction that I had helped my uncle and done a darn good job doing it.

I unloaded the car, put the charcoal in the grill, and lit it. It ignited with a big *whoomph!*

Then I went inside to start marinating the grouper and fresh vegetables I had purchased. There's nothing like fresh fish and vegetables grilled over an open fire!

I was just getting ready to put the food on the grill when there was a knock at my door.

I looked out the kitchen window and saw that it was Velma from across the street.

I opened the door, and she held out a plate of homemade cookies and smiled. "I see you're getting ready for dinner, I just wanted to drop these off to thank you for everything you've been doing for me," she said.

"Please come in," I said, seeing how wobbly she was and remembering her fear of falling.

"Oh, I don't want to interrupt anything," she said hesitantly.

"No, please. Why don't you join me for dinner? There's plenty," I assured her.

It took a little more convincing, but finally she agreed to stay for dinner. We stepped into the living room, and she instantly exclaimed, "What a beautiful painting!"

Oops, I had forgotten about the mural. Now whether I was ready or not it was on display for another's critique.

"Thanks," I replied. "I'm still working on it, but I'm pretty happy with it. And it's been a lot of fun to do."

"Does your uncle know you're painting this?" she asked.

"No, it's a surprise." Then I told her the story of how I was going to paint it when I was younger and, without naming names, told of the neighbor who had discouraged me, and how my aunt had left my drawing hanging on the wall for thirty years until I found it.

She laughed and said, "I think it was well worth the wait. It's beautiful. I love the colors in the clouds especially."

I was a little embarrassed, although very pleased about this compliment. She sat in the living room while I went into the kitchen to cube the grouper and vegetables and put them on shish kebab skewers.

As I was heading outside to the grill, I said, "I'll be right back," not wanting her to have to walk more than necessary. But she insisted on joining me and sat at the picnic table and chatted with me while I grilled our dinner.

When it was ready, I took it inside, put it onto plates, and brought it out on a tray with two glasses of iced tea.

We sat and chatted about my visits to Hibiscus Lane when I was a child and how kind my aunt and uncle had always been. I asked how long she had lived here, and she told me over fifty years. She loved it here and said I would have to come and see her paintings.

"I didn't know you were a painter," I replied.

"Oh, heavens no," she laughed. "Not paintings I painted, but paintings I bought from these nice fellas that used to travel through here years ago. They were just passing through, but they painted such nice pictures of trees and the beach. When one of them would come around, I'd buy a painting if I could afford it. They weren't very much by today's standards, but back then $15 or $20 was a lot of money. My husband worked in construction, and I worked as a hairdresser, so we had enough for mortgage, groceries, and little extravagances from time to time. My husband would just shake his head and laugh and say, 'Velma, they got your number.' But I knew he liked the paintings, and he could see how much that money could help the traveling artist."

"Are you talking about the highway men?" I asked astonished.

"I think that's what they call them today," she said. "So you've heard of them?"

"They are huge in the Florida folk art circles. Their pictures can sell for thousands of dollars today. It looks like your good deed paid off." I smiled.

"Good karma," she laughed. "I believe that if you do something nice for someone, it'll come back to you sooner or later. That's why I brought you those cookies to thank you for all you've been doing in my yard."

"I haven't done that much," I assured her. "I'm just glad to help. By the way, do you want me to put those plants in the ground for you? It shouldn't take long, and I could do it tomorrow. I'm worried that they'll dry out if they stay out of the ground much longer."

"But you've already done so much, I hate to ask," she responded. (It seemed to me that she was making an awful fuss about me watering her plants a couple of times. But then maybe she didn't have anyone to help her. Or maybe she was just buttering me up to help her plant them. Either way, I was glad to help someone who seemed like a nice person.)

"I just found out that my grandchildren aren't coming for a couple more weeks," she added.

I told her I'd be at her place around 8:00 a.m. so that we could plant them before it got too hot. She was very grateful, and we ate her delicious cookies and sat out chatting like old friends until way past dark.

Finally, she had to leave, and I walked her back to her bungalow. She used my arm to steady and guide herself, since her eyesight was about as good as her balance.

When I got back to the bungalow, I cleaned the dishes and looked back at the mural one last time before I went to bed. It had passed its first inspection, although it was from a very nice person. Nevertheless, someone else had seen it, unfinished even, and still liked it.

I was smiling as I drifted off to sleep and dreamed of traveling the state and painting for a living. In the dream it was all painting, pleasant art lovers and sun, sand and surf without any of the critics and prejudices that could meet a vagabond painter. But isn't that what dreams are for? To show us the good things in life so that we have the courage to face the obstacles that block our way.

DAY 15

The next morning I was up early and enjoyed my breakfast watching the sunrise from the cement table in the backyard. It was a cloudy morning, so slivers of silver shone through the dark purple clouds. The pelicans were already flying, and it reminded me that I had cooked out the night before, and Terry, the pelican, had not come to mooch any food. I wondered if he was still alive. How long do pelicans live?

I was disappointed that he hadn't come, even though I hadn't thought about it at the time. I guess, in the back of my mind, I had hoped my uncle and I would have a cookout, and he would show up, and it would be like old times.

After breakfast, I went back inside and looked at the mural. I still liked it. There were things I might do differently the next time, but I liked how it looked. However, it was still missing something. I just wasn't sure what. I had all the elements that were in the original drawing only in much more detail. The palm fronds looked almost real. I was pleased that I was creating something beautiful. This reminded me of saying my intention. I still hadn't worked it into my daily routine yet. But I reminded myself that it takes twenty-one days for a habit to be set. I was still remembering to do it, just not always first thing in the morning.

"Today will be filled with the joy and mystery of life, bringing me courage and inner peace to help me create beauty, and send kindness to all those I meet. All this or something better."

I noticed a big grin cross my face as I said the word "mystery." Although it really was none of my business, I was curious about what Mrs. V was covering up. "Maybe she'd had an argument with one of the neighbors and was burying him piece by piece in different people's yards," I chuckled to myself.

I remembered the contractor was coming that morning, so I sat and waited, thinking he would want to start early since they would be up on a hot roof. And as I waited, I stared at the mural a little longer, hoping that I could figure out what was needed to complete the picture, but nothing came to mind. I wrote a note for the contractor, telling him where I would be, and headed over to Velma's to plant the bushes.

She was sitting in a chair on the carport waiting for me with a posthole digger and a shovel leaning against the wall next to her.

"Hey, Jack!" she called to me as I walked up her driveway.

"Hi, Velma!" I replied.

She was wearing a big straw hat that was tied under her chin and had a big smile on her face. It made me feel good that I could do something that would make someone smile so grandly.

"Let's get started," I said, grabbing the plants and carrying them, two at a time, to the backyard.

Velma steadied herself with the posthole diggers as she walked around to the back. "You know I just love flowers," she said. "I think they prove to me that God has a plan for everything and everyone."

"Gees!" I thought to myself. "Is everyone here a philosopher?" But instead of verbalizing those thoughts, I asked what she meant.

"I mean, if you look at a seed, it's this little tiny hard thing. Then you put it in dirt and cover it up. Add water and sometimes a healthy dose of manure, and from out of all that comes this lovely plant with blooms that add such beauty to the world. It looks nothing like it once did, and all that dirt and manure makes its transformation complete."

"I hadn't thought of it like that before," I said, liking the analogy of the seed being covered by dirt and crap and then being stuck out in the storm in order to become something beautiful.

"Well, when I was your age, I didn't either," Velma replied. "But then, when I went through my cancer, it just sort of hit me. I think when people meet hard times, they really have a chance to grow. So there I was going through chemo and seeing what other—pardon my expression—shit life had to throw on top of me, when I looked out to my garden and the thought hit me. I just sat there and laughed. 'Well,' I told myself, 'this is either gonna make you into a better person or kill you. And to tell the truth at that point either would have been just fine with me.

"But it didn't kill me, and now I have a whole new appreciation for life and for being able to do the smallest things. I also have a whole new appreciation for accepting the help of others. Before I was very independent, but now I realize that dependence isn't a weakness but a strength."

"Can you explain what you mean?" I said, puzzled by this idea.

"Well, I hope I can do the idea justice," she said shyly. "But as I was sitting in my house, too tired to do much of anything, I had a lot of time to think. At first I was very down on myself for being such a burden to others. Neighbors checked in on me, and volunteer organizations brought me meals so I wouldn't have to cook. All the while I was not only feeling sorry for myself, but also feeling like I was just a burden to everyone else. Then one day this friendly old man dropped off my dinner and saw that I was really feeling down. He asked what was the matter, and I told him everything about how I was feeling. My self-pity was so high that I just sobbed and sobbed to this poor man about all my troubles.

"He looked into my eyes and said, 'You don't know what a blessing you are in my life.' Then he told me of how his son had died, and how he mourned and felt sorry for himself being left without this wonderful man who had brightened his life so much. At first he was so overwhelmed by his grief that it permeated his entire being. Then one day he decided that he could either sit in that house and rot or go out and try to make life better, if not for himself at least for others. So he started volunteering at the center that brings meals to people who are homebound because

THE BODYSURFER'S GUIDE TO LIFE

of illness. What he found is that by helping others, he was able to get out of bed with a purpose in mind. Of course, he still missed his son, but life was continuing for him. So he thanked me for giving him a reason for getting out of bed in the morning.

"This took me by surprise. But then I remembered how I had always enjoyed helping others. It made me feel like I was a part of something bigger than my own little problems. But I was always on the side of giving and not receiving. Then it occurred to me: if there were no one to receive, I wouldn't have been able to give. It was a hard thing for me to admit that now I needed to be the one receiving, so that someone else could give. But there I was letting this man, and all the other volunteers, help me. It was humbling, but at the same time I saw it as a sort of blessing. I was seeing how what I did for others could help them and was learning it from the vantage point of needing help. Before the cancer, I had always helped people and might even have bragged about it. Like I was so nice and kind, and they were so needy, but I helped them because of my goodness. Then I was forced into a situation where life had me understand that I shouldn't be doing kind things to prove how good I am, but I should be helping people because we are all the same. They didn't want to suffer or need help any more than I did, but they received my sometimes very self-congratulatory help with much more grace than I received the help of others."

She looked off in the distance for a moment and then looked back to me. "You know, the other day when I told you Gladys Vargas scares me?'

I remembered it well and nodded.

"Well, I wasn't quite truthful. Don't get me wrong, she is a formidable force in the neighborhood. But what really disturbs me about seeing her now is remembering how rude I was to her when she tried to help me."

"I can't imagine you being rude," I said quickly.

"Oh, honey, I was. I was going through my treatments, and the yard was looking worse and worse, and I just couldn't get outside in the heat and do anything. I wasn't even thinking clearly. Sometimes just getting out of bed to answer the door would wear me out. Anyway, Gladys Vargas comes by and says she noticed that I hadn't been out in my yard lately, and she'd be glad to do some weeding and cleanup for me. At first I declined, but she is formidable, and soon she had worn me down.

"The next morning she was in my yard bright and early trimming my hibiscus bush. I rushed out as fast as I could. Horrified, I yelled, 'Stop! How can you even consider trimming my hibiscus at this time of year. I won't get any more blooms for months. How dare you do that without asking?'"

She said she was just trying to help, and I replied that her idea of help and mine were obviously not the same, and I'd appreciate it if she just left.

As she was telling all this, she looked down to the ground, and I could tell she was reliving one of her least-favorite moments.

"What did Mrs. Vargas do?" I asked.

"Well. She just stared at me for about a minute. Said, 'You got it, toots.' Then she picked up her garden tools and walked away."

"Wow!" I exclaimed. I couldn't imagine this soft-spoken woman getting the better of Mrs. V.

But then I thought, "Was she really getting the better of anything or anyone? Her ego-thinking was scaring away help she desperately needed and hurting someone who was trying to help her."

"I know. Not one of my proudest moments," she said, smiling an embarrassed smile.

"How are things between you and Mrs. V?" I asked.

"Cool to icy. We were neighbors but never very good friends. Now I try to be cordial, but she remains icy."

"Did you ever try to apologize?" I asked, wondering if that was even the right thing to say.

"I tried, but she cut me short and told me to never mention that day again. Then she glared at me and walked away," Velma said, with her hand touching her heart.

I could see Mrs. V saying that, but also knew her tough exterior covered a lot of kindness. I was about to tell Velma when I remembered Mrs. V telling me she wasn't as mean as people thought she was and then giving me the death glare before instructing me not to let that get around. I knew exactly the glare she must've given Velma, and "formidable" was a very good word to describe it.

"Now," Velma said, "I could really use the help in my yard, and yet my wanting everything my way kept me from getting it. That is, until you started helping me."

I was feeling like I was about to get suckered into a lot of yard work. So I once again protested that I only watered some plants and was planting them for her. That's all.

"But what about all the weeding?" Velma protested.

"Ummm," I said feeling a little awkward and selfish. "I only have a couple of days left, and I was planning on spending them at the beach. I'm sorry if I gave you the wrong impression."

Velma looked confused and said, "But you've already done all the weeding."

Now it was my turn to look confused. "No, I haven't."

"But I thought . . . ," she said and then stopped.

I looked at her flower beds, and they were all free of weeds. There were even the traces of where some weeds had been recently pulled.

"Wow! This asking for mystery in my life was working big time," I thought to myself.

Then the word "mystery" made me think of Mrs. V sneaking around in the middle of the night, and I asked, "Did it seem like you just woke up, and the flower bed was weeded?"

"Yes," she answered. "It was you, wasn't it?"

"No. But I think I know who your midnight helper is," I laughed. "But first, let me ask, have you ever seen Mrs. V wear dark colors?"

"Lord no!" she laughed. "For years I just thought she was color blind. It turns out she's not, she just likes bright colors. What does that have to do with anything?"

"Well, I think your helper is Mrs. V," I said, impressed more by Mrs. Vargas's wanting to help Velma than by my obviously astute powers of reason.

Then I told her of my seeing what I thought was a bear for several nights and then discovering it was Mrs. V who was sneaking around the neighborhood dressed in navy blue. I was a little ashamed of myself for thinking of her snooping around or having an illicit affair, while all the while she was helping people incognito.

"Does she know you think it's her?" she asked a little disbelieving.

"Are you kidding? No way am I going to tell her I've figured it out. She was trying to convince me that I was drinking. I don't think she'd take kindly to my saying, 'gotcha!'"

I was smiling, but Velma seemed disturbed. "Well, how do I repay her for her kindness?" she asked.

And then we both said in unison, "By accepting it," and laughed.

Planting the bushes and banana tree took less than an hour. Then we watered them thoroughly and sipped a glass of iced tea while enjoying the view of the garden. Afterward, I headed back to a bright yellow bungalow with no contractor in sight.

When I got inside I saw my cell phone light blinking. I had a voice mail from Vinnie telling me that he was delayed but would be there bright and early in the morning. Since he wasn't there in front of me, responding with love wasn't as big of an issue as labeling him "inept."

"There's nothing else I need to do here," I said to myself realizing that I would have to wait to plant the plants until the roofing was finished. So I watched the surf report while I packed up my beach gear and then headed to the beach, glad to have solved my mystery and feeling generally proud of myself.

I was on such a high that I was surprised at what happened next. I was thinking that I had the last laugh on the folks at work because here I was finding myself and enjoying life while they were caught up on the treadmill at work. And then *boom*, my mind thought, "Why are you congratulating yourself? At least they have jobs. You haven't even started to look."

"Huh, where did that come from?" I thought.

"What are people thinking about me? They're probably laughing at me right now, and I don't even know it because I'm too tied up in feeling groovy."

I could feel my good mood slipping away, and although I was struggling against it, it was pulling me under quick.

I decided to try to get it out of my mind by bodysurfing. But the thoughts still lingered as I rode wave after wave onto shore. I was about to get out of the water and sulk on the beach when Fin's shiny head popped up next to me.

"Whoa!" he said, "Are you in your kleishas again?"

"Yeah," I said, not wanting to admit what a failure I was at all this living life-to-its-fullest stuff.

"Work again?" he asked.

I nodded, not looking at him.

"You know," he said, "life is a lot like the water in the waves. It gets caught up in a cycle until it comes crashing down. Then it's free to wash back out into the great, big sea of possibilities. You just have to open yourself to the flow and rhythm of life. You've done it before, and done it well. This happens to everyone. So don't let it bother you. Instead, recognize how it feels and realize that the sort of thinking that brought it on causes these bad feelings. Then when you find yourself thinking life-destructive thoughts, remember how they made you feel the last time and realize that you can choose something else. It may not be easy at first. But just like responding with love, or bodysurfing, it gets easier with practice."

"I just wish everything didn't take so much practice," I said, still feeling sorry for myself.

We were silent for a minute, and then Fin said, "Don't be so down on yourself. Learning to roll with the energy of life takes practice, just like playing volleyball, or painting.

He had a point. (Again!) "But why is it so hard?"

"It isn't always hard, but we can get caught up in these cycles just like you got caught up in that rip current the other day. What happened when the rip current released you?"

"I floated up to the surface," I said, remembering how dizzy I was when I was finally out of the rip currents twirling energy.

"Exactly!" Fin smiled. "And just like that rip current, these challenging times in our lives can leave us feeling disoriented. But because the universe wants us to succeed, we naturally float up. Some faster than others, depending on how fast we learn to go with the flow and stop fighting the current."

"So are you saying I just need to keep holding my breath and keep hoping the universe will pull me up for air before I drown?" I asked incredulously. (Yes, my ego was intact, and I was ready for an argument.)

"No," Fin chuckled. "Although that was a good analogy."

"Thanks," I said already feeling my ego dropping its defenses.

"It's more like saying to yourself, 'Okay, I'm stuck in this cycle of energy that has pulled me off my feet and is making me spin out of control. I know I need to get out of this, but if I use up all my energy before the cycle weakens, I won't have any left to swim to shore. So you twirl with it, not because you are enjoying it, but because you are examining it waiting for the weakness that will be your opportunity to break free."

"You're saying that if I study the negative energy, I'm caught up in as a third-person observer, I can find the hole in the logic and break out of it?" I asked.

"Nicely said, Jack!" Fin smiled. "And by examining it and the circumstances that brought you into its energy, you can learn how to avoid the situation in the future. How did this all start?"

I told him I was only thinking how happy I was to be enjoying life while the poor saps at where I used to work were stuck in their cubicles.

"So you were feeling superior to the people you worked with?" Fin asked.

Then it hit me, I was acting out of ego and feeling cocky and not feeling kindness or love toward my ex-fellow coworkers. Some were my friends. "So my negative thoughts backfired on me? But how? Isn't the ego's job to make me feel better than everyone else?"

"Most often that is what the ego tries to do. But I know you well enough to know that you're a pretty compassionate person, and so your ego got you thinking, 'I'm soooooooo much better than they are,' and then beat you up for thinking you are better than your friends. The ego's goal is to gain control of you, so you'll listen more to ego than your gut feelings. The ego is a strategist and likes to try to bait you into ways it can control you."

"But why now?" I asked.

"Maybe because you were seeing what life could be like if you didn't let your ego control you, and so the ego wanted to yank your chain and remind you that it is in control."

"That's just sick!" I said. "So what should I do next time it happens?"

"Think back to the thoughts that brought you to your state of unhappiness and then recognize them for what they were. Ego-based thinking."

"What if the thinking is based in some other type of thinking?" I asked.

"The way I look at things, our actions are based in either ego or love. All the things that make us feel less than joyful are ego-based, like worrying about what others think or say, fear, jealousy, anger, and a whole slew of other negative emotions."

"Then what does love-based thinking do? And how do I get it?" I asked.

"I really don't call it thinking out of love. Instead I say acting out of love. Love is shown through our actions. We can think and say all sorts of things, but if our actions say otherwise, well, the old adage applies here. Actions do speak louder than words. To see if you're acting out of love, see how you're feeling at any given moment. If you're not feeling joy or something similar, then ask yourself, 'Why am I not feeling joy?' Trace your thoughts back, and you'll find an ego-based emotion at the root of it all."

This was a little confusing to me, so I asked for an example.

"Say, I'm sitting here angry because I was having such a nice day, and something negative about people I work with popped into my head."

(It sounded familiar already.)

"Now I'm sitting here brooding while I could be enjoying my day at the beach," Fin continued.

"So far I'm right there with ya," I said smiling.

"Good. Suddenly I realize I'm at the beach, and all I'm thinking about is what someone from my workplace did to me."

"I'm still with ya," I said.

"So I have two choices: I can sit there blaming them for ruining my day at the beach, or realize that I'm the one ruining my day at the beach by my reaction to what they did and ask myself, 'Why am I not feeling joy right now?'

"From there, I follow my thoughts back like so 'it's not my fault that my boss is a big, fat jerk. He's ruining my day . . .' Think about it. Question it. Is he ruining your day, or is your response to what he did ruining your day? He may not have treated you fairly, but that moment is over. Now it is your turn to respond to that treatment with more ego thinking, or getting out of your head, and all the justifications your ego is coming up with for you to feel lousy, and say, 'But it's my response to his actions that is making me feel lousy right now.' Then take back the power to control your moods that you've so freely doled out to others."

"How?" I asked, feeling like this was out of my control.

"By saying to yourself, 'Okay, my boss let me go even though I've worked hard for the company. I tried to do my best, but it seems like we are going in different directions now. I may not approve of what was done, but by dwelling on it I'm letting those actions have power over my current life. He chose to let go of the power he had as my boss, why do I still want to give it to him?'"

"You're right!" I exclaimed excitedly. "I was still trying to make him responsible for my life. He let that power go, and I was still trying to hand it back to him. How stupid am I?"

"Not stupid, human," Fin laughed. "Don't beat yourself up. We all do this, all the time, because it is easier for us to blame someone else instead of taking responsibility for our own feelings or actions."

Fin was right. It was easier for me to blame them than take responsibility for my own happiness. Because, really, I hadn't been happy there for a long time and should have left, but instead I just blamed them for my unhappiness and made the job worse by saying things like, "Work is a four-letter word," or "That's why they call it work."

"You see, Jack, your grudge against your boss is like a big rock. You're out here treading water, and you're holding this big old rock in your hands, and you're blaming it for wearing you down when you have the choice to let it go and stop wearing yourself out."

"But that's easier said than done," I protested.

"I know, but the first step is just acknowledging that you're the one carrying this big old rock with you. After that, you can figure out what's best for you. But my bet is on releasing it and being more buoyant."

I laughed and said, "Okay here goes," as I mimed dropping a large boulder into the water while I brought my knee up to make a splash.

Fin laughed too, "Good imagery."

"Now every time you start to feel that boulder weighing you down, remember how you dropped it in the ocean and then ask yourself why you picked it back up."

Then a big wave came, and Fin was off enjoying the ride while I just stood there and laughed. I felt great again, and made a vow to myself to not give the power of my emotions away so easily. Then, feeling lighter than I had all day, I jumped into a wave and enjoyed the ride.

After a few more rides we both went back on shore, sat in our beach chairs, and I promptly fell asleep. When I awoke, Fin was gone, so I decided to pack up my gear and head on home. As I was putting on my shirt, I found a note in the pocket that read, "Rest is important—nothing cleanses the soul like a nap in the sun after a great session of riding the waves. Fin."

I just laughed and headed for home, knowing I was exactly where I was supposed to be.

When I arrived back to the bungalow, I sat and stared at the mural. I still couldn't figure out what it needed, so I decided to just try painting different things on the remaining canvases to see if ideas sprang to mind. But after spending all day in the sun and the surf, I didn't have a chance to paint because right after dinner I fell into a very peaceful sleep.

DAY 16

The next morning I woke up before sunrise, full of energy. I put on the coffee and then went out to the sunporch to set my intention and try meditating. Setting my intention was the easy part.

I had just closed my eyes when a million thoughts came into my head. It was something like this: "Okay, my eyes are closed. Mmmm, I smell the coffee. Isn't caffeine great? Quiet my mind. Oh, maybe I'll have some toast with breakfast. Did I buy jelly? Stop thinking for just five minutes, brain! Didn't that sound like I was thinking backward? Shouldn't it have been, "Okay, brain, stop thinking for just five minutes." Or something like that? "quiet! No more food thoughts. Okay. There. Just breathe and count your breaths—one, two three . . . You know you only have a few days left to finish the mural. You have to pick up Uncle Doug in a few days. What do you think you should put there? How about—stop it! Okay, brain, just one minute. Just give me one minute of silence. Then think all you want. That should be easy, I'll count it out to sixty . . ."

Well, you get the idea. I never paid attention before to how fast my brain worked, but I got a very good impression of its capacity for thinking randomly and at great speed that morning. I was a little discouraged but remembered that Fin said it took practice. (Like everything else.)

After another couple of minutes of mind babble, and maybe three seconds of silence (which could've just been transition from one idea to another), I got up and made breakfast. As I sat at the cement table in the backyard, I watched the sunrise and the pelicans begin their day. It was so peaceful that I was completely caught up in its beauty, unaware of anything but the moment. No mind babble, just peace. I'm not sure how long it went on. But as soon as I realized what was happening, the mind babble continued. "Whoa! See, I did it. Wow that was cool, and I wasn't even trying. Maybe I was trying too hard. Okay, let's try it again." Silence. "Whoa! I did it again. Yeah, but not for more than three seconds. Try again. And again." Silence. "How's that . . . oops . . ."

So I realized that I could quiet my brain when I wasn't thinking about it. That gave me hope because I knew it could be quiet. Now all I had to do was figure out how to clear my thoughts while I was trying to meditate. I seemed to do better with my eyes open instead of closed.

I turned and looked at the purslane planted next to the table. It has beautiful yellow blooms that open in the morning and close in the late afternoon. One of the buds looked like it would open soon. I stared at the veining in the petals and the color gradients from bright yellow to pale. I thought I saw it moving, but it seemed so imperceptible that maybe it was my imagination. I continued to staring, breathing deeply, and enjoying its beauty.

The next thing I knew the flower was half opened! I didn't remember seeing it open that much, and I didn't remember anything really except feeling very peaceful. "I just did it again," I thought. Maybe I needed a visual in order to let myself go into a peaceful state.

Now I was excited. I could hardly wait to tell Fin about this.

Just then, I saw Vinnie's green pickup pull up in front of the house. I walked over to greet him. He looked tired, but he smiled and said, "Good morning."

"It's great to see you!" I said, and really meant it.

"You'll want to move your car out to the road so it doesn't get hit by any debris or pick up any nails in your tires," he said.

"Right, I forgot," I said and ran inside to grab my keys.

When I got back outside, Vinnie was leaning a ladder against the house and climbing up to take a look at the roof.

"What's the verdict?" I asked.

Vinnie told me it should take about two to three days if everything went well.

I reminded him about the luau and asked if the yard could be checked for nails before the luau, even if the roofing wasn't done. He assured me that would be no problem. So I put my mind at ease, realizing that I could only control my response to things. The roof may not be finished, but people would be able to walk around in the yard without getting a nail in their foot.

"It's going to get kind of loud here," he said.

And, just at that moment, I heard the deep base vibration of a car stereo as it parked in front of the bungalow. Out of a new white truck popped two sleepy-eyed men in their twenties.

"See what I mean?" Vinnie laughed.

"Please don't play the radio too loud," I said. "I have a neighbor who doesn't like change around here."

"I know Mrs. Vargas." He smiled. "I've done work for her before. Don't worry."

I asked him if there was anything he needed me to do, besides move my car. He told me, no and then said that they would be taking off the old shingles that day and, hopefully, putting on the new shingles the next day.

"Today will be loud," he said smiling. "But tomorrow you'll definitely want to find someplace else to be. We'll be hammering in the new shingles, and it can give anyone a headache."

I laughed and thanked him for the warning. Then I showed him where the bathroom was, packed up my beach gear and cell phone (in case he needed to get in touch with me), and headed off for a day at the beach.

It was still early when I arrived at the beach. I staked my daily claim to a small section of beach and decided to go for a walk. It was already warm, and before long I was sweating and feeling the heat of the sun. As I walked I began to worry about what would happen after I left Daytona. I was picking up my uncle in just a couple of days, and yes, it was easy to think that the universe was working with me while I was at the beach, but what about when I got back to the real world? The world with deadlines, stress, and expectations. What would people think about me being out of work for so long and not even looking for a job? What if I don't get a job in the field that my education and experience are in? Will I have to start at the bottom? Was I just lazy or hedonistic? Here I was hanging out at the beach while people were having real problems. Hell, even I was having real problems, but I was ignoring them. Thinking positive thoughts instead of addressing the issue of being unemployed. After everything I'd been learning here shouldn't I be putting those ideas into action, instead of just being a beach bum? In other words, my kleishas came rolling in, wave after wave.

I was overburdened by these feelings once again. But at least I was recognizing the thoughts and the negative effect they were having on me. So I jumped in the water to cool off. It felt great! There's nothing like a face full of saltwater to clear your head.

I floated in the water for quite a while, enjoying the cooling sensation of the water on my body and warmth of the sun on my face. Until three weeks ago, it had been years since I had done anything like this. And now, it was a natural occurrence. While floating I felt my apprehensions drift away.

I was staring out to the horizon when I saw a fin roll past me about thirty feet away. Then more fins began to roll into sight. Dolphins! I was in the water with dolphins and actually seeing them. Just then, a dolphin rolled up and blew air out of its blowhole not more than fifteen feet away from me. "Breathe," I told myself. And I took several deep breaths as I watched the dolphins swim by.

I was still in the water watching the dolphins swim farther and farther away when a shiny tan head popped up next to me.

"Hi, Jack!" Fin said.

I was startled out of my peaceful state and looked over, embarrassed at being so jumpy.

"Sorry, Jack, I didn't mean to startle you." Fin grinned.

"Not your fault," I laughed embarrassedly. "I was just lost in thought while I watched the dolphins swim by. That was pretty cool!"

"Did you remember to take a few deep breaths?" he asked.

"I sure did," I said. Then I told him about what had been bothering me before I had jumped in the water, and my doubts about whether I would ever get the hang of being in sync with the universe."

"It sounds like not only your kleishas were joining you on your walk, but that your ego was also trying to twist what you've been learning and turn it against you." Fin smiled.

"I'm just not good at this living-life-to-the-fullest thing. I have a very low guilt threshold," I said, feeling like a failure.

Fin laughed, "Well, if you keep saying things like that, how do you expect to change your life? Whenever we make a statement saying, 'I am this,' or 'I am that,' we are reinforcing thought patterns and belief systems. So saying I am this negative thing is really a self-defeating action, reinforcing a negative belief system. Instead, say 'I am currently feeling this way, but I know that no feeling is final. I want to know how to change this thought into something more positive, because I know the universe wants me to succeed.'"

Now I felt really discouraged and must've looked it because Fin said, "Don't be discouraged. Humans have been beating themselves up with teachings that were meant to enlighten them for thousands of years. You're in very good company."

"What?" I asked.

"Sure! We have been given a number of teachings meant to show us how to live a more enjoyable life by great teachers throughout the years, and yet we humans seem to take those teachings and turn them into something to feel guilty about."

"Example, please?" I asked, very curious about this.

"Okay, Christ told us to not judge. Right?"

"Right," I replied.

"So how many people have you seen who don't like someone because they are judgmental and we aren't supposed to do that? For example, 'You're prejudiced against me, so I hate you for your prejudice, because prejudice is evil.' Or someone who thinks himself a bad person for judging his sister and thinks that he shouldn't, but he can't help it. So it must be proof that he's a bad person?

"You see, the lesson of not to judge others was meant as a way of teaching people that there are many views of the same thing . . ."

"You mean neutrality?" I asked.

"Exactly!" Fin smiled.

"Okay. How about another example?"

"Sure. Buddhist philosophy is based on the four noble truths that show people are more alike than different: (1) no one wants to suffer, (2) what truly causes suffering, (3) everyone wants to be happy, (4) what truly causes happiness. You with me so far?"

I nodded.

"So when I started studying Buddhist philosophy, I loved the idea that these four simple principles could link everyone in the world because they were true to everyone. But then I started to get angry with the people who weren't open to this thinking, or who were practicing a different set of ideas to try to make them happy and obviously failing miserably. 'It serves them right!' I'd think as their attempts at being happy always caused them pain. In fact, I was often glad when they failed.

"So I had turned these teachings, given to help people understand that human beings have more similarities than differences, into a way to categorize, judge and feel superior to the very people I was supposed to feel connected to."

"In other words, you were using the teaching in such a way that you achieved the exact opposite of what the lesson was intended to teach?" I asked.

"Exactly! But I wasn't finished with distorting it, because then I turned it on myself and thought, 'I think I'm so great, and yet I'm doing what the teachings are saying not to do. I'm not finding unity and happiness, I'm finding separation and unhappiness through the use of these teachings. I'm a failure!'"

"I can relate," I said.

"So can everyone on this planet," Fin said. "It's a part of human nature to do this to ourselves, and others."

"I still don't get why the ego beats us down so much," I stated.

"To protect us," Fin replied.

"What?" I exclaimed.

"Well, its logic is that it's protecting us by keeping us feeling like we aren't capable of doing certain things, or striving for certain goals, so that we don't attempt something and fail. Because failure would be a blow to the ego, and that's not what the ego wants, so instead it keeps us locked in a box of self-doubt, too afraid to venture outside its safety to where our dreams can become a reality."

"That is messed up," I said, shaking my head.

"Humans are definitely an interesting species," Fin laughed.

"So how did you stop this thinking process?" I asked.

"Forgiveness," Fin replied.

"Excuse me?"

"Exactly! Excusing me, and everyone, including yourself. Real forgiveness. First, I had to forgive other people, because if they were really trying to find happiness in ways that were making them unhappy, it's sad for them, but no reason to make me hate them. In fact, I should feel compassion for them. And I needed to see that I was doing the same thing in a different way, and that we really were much more similar than I would have liked to admit. But then I realized that if I forgave them, then I would also have to forgive myself. Because if it's okay for them to be human, then it must also be okay for me to be human. Not an easy task when all the what ifs and mind dramas kick in."

"So forgiveness is a major key in living life to the fullest?" I asked as we were getting out of the water.

"Right. You see, we spend so much time replaying things that have happened in the past saying, 'I should have said this, and that would teach them,' that we end up chaining ourselves to these events long after they could have been forgiven and left in the past," Fin said as we walked back toward my beach chair.

"Forgiveness is like the ocean's waves that come to smooth the shore crushed by our feet, giving us a clean slate upon which to continue our journey," Fin continued.

"I've always found it hard to just forgive and forget," I said, feeling bad about myself.

"Don't turn this into something to beat yourself up with. And I'm not saying to forget. I think we can learn valuable lessons about ourselves, and our lives, if we remember the trials we've had and the strengths we've gained from them. All I'm saying is drop the blame and remember that you're exactly where you're supposed to be to take the next step toward who the universe knows you can become. At any given point in your life, you can stop and change directions. The choice is yours. Give yourself some slack, you've only been working at this for a couple of weeks," Fin said smiling and patted me on the back.

"Okay," I laughed feeling better about not getting everything right in the first month of trying to become a better me.

By the time we got back to my beach chair, the beach had gotten crowded. Not far from my chair sat an elderly man in a wheelchair with very fat wheels. With him were two elementary school-aged children.

"There's my friend Tom," Fin exclaimed. "I told him I'd teach his grandkids how to bodysurf. Wanna help me?"

"Sure," I said, impressed that someone in a wheelchair could find a way to get out to the beach.

Tom waved as he saw us approaching. "Hey, Fin! These are my grandkids, Anne and Bryan."

"I'm Jack," I said introducing myself. "Fin said I could help teach the kids to bodysurf if it's all right with you."

"Well, if you're a friend of Fin's, it's okay with me." Tom smiled.

Fin went right into action talking to the kids and becoming their friend within a matter of minutes. Bryan was the bolder of the two, ready to conquer the world, while Anne seemed to listen and process everything more carefully.

"Are you ready to go bodysurfing?" Fin asked.

"I want a boogie board!" Bryan said.

Tom looked embarrassed, and Fin smiled at him and looked down at Bryan and said, "Life isn't about getting everything you want, it's about doing your best with what you're given. You have great waves—you don't need a boogie board. Just jump in and give it your best effort. Anyone can have fun with a boogie board, what I'm going to teach you is part of the secret bond of bodysurfers and can help you enjoy the rest of your life. But I can't teach it to you if you're just going to boogie board."

"I want to learn it!" Anne chimed in.

"He was asking me!" Bryan protested.

"Hold on!" Fin said very seriously. "Before I teach you the secrets of bodysurfing, you have to take the bodysurfers' oath. Are you ready?"

Both children nodded seriously.

"Do you solemnly swear to use the secrets of bodysurfing to enjoy life more? And do you solemnly swear to keep from hurting yourself or anyone else while riding the energy in the awesome ocean on the most awesome of waves?"

"I do," They both said very seriously.

I smiled, and Fin looked at me very seriously too and said, "I didn't hear you, Jack."

"Oops, sorry! I do!"

"Do you solemnly swear to realize that there are an abundance of awesome waves out there, and to understand that not every wave's awesomeness is meant just for you? And that there is enough awesomeness to go around, but when the right wave offers its awesomeness to you, do you promise to jump in and enjoy the ride of you life?" Fin asked.

"I do!" we all chimed in.

"Good. Now I'll teach you the secret bond of the bodysurfers' handshake, and we can all go for the ride of our lives," Fin said and then began an intricate and very confusing handshake that somehow involved a move that he said was "the sacred surfing swim of mother turtle" but looked more like the funky chicken. "Now everyone into the water!"

The waves were still small, but large enough to get a gentle ride, so the four of us headed toward the water, while Tom leaned back in his chair and smiled.

It was hard for me to put into words how to jump into the waves at just the right time, so Fin would teach them a quick lesson, and then each of us would take a kid and help them catch a wave. At first I was very frustrated that they weren't catching on. But then I remembered it was only a few weeks ago that I was right where they were. So I thought back to what had helped me to learn, and soon I was sharing Fin's wisdom with my own spin to each of the kids.

Within half an hour, both Anne and Bryan were jumping into waves like old pros. Fin and I laughed as Bryan washed up to shore with a big "wahoo!" and Tom clapped from his wheelchair.

"Helping others enjoy the experience is worth the pay off of seeing their joy and hearing their laughter. Don't you agree, Jack?"

I nodded as I caught Anne who was diving back toward me in the surf.

After a while longer, the children were as tired as were we, so the four of us headed back to shore where Tom was smiling ear to ear. "How was it?" he asked.

"Awesome!" came the reply from all four of us, representing three generations bound by the bodysurfers' oath. (People really were more alike than different.)

Tom laughed and said that they'd better be getting back home before Grandma called the beach patrol.

"Can we do this again tomorrow?" Anne asked.

Tom looked at Fin, who looked at me, and I said, "That'd be *awesome!*"

"Awesome!" They said in unison as we wheeled Tom's beach-tired wheelchair through the sand to his van.

By this time it was midafternoon, and I realized I hadn't eaten lunch. I pulled out the peanut butter sandwich I had packed in my knapsack and offered half to Fin.

"Thanks! I forgot to pack a lunch," he said, gratefully accepting my meager gift.

"My pleasure!" I said, glad to be able to share something with this guy who was teaching me so much.

"This has been a great day!" Fin said.

I agreed enthusiastically.

"What are your plans for the rest of the day?" he asked.

"You're looking at it," I laughed.

"Good plan." He smiled.

I explained that the contractor was finally at my uncle's house, and I was avoiding the noise by being at the beach. I thought I'd go back to the bungalow around 4:00 p.m. to check on the progress.

"Good plan," he repeated.

I sat back and smiled. Yes, it was a good plan. And as I sat there I was grateful for the joy and peace that comes from knowing all is right with the world.

As I was enjoying the moment, I remembered the problem I was having quieting my brain when I was trying to meditate, and mentioned this to Fin.

He laughed, "It's amazing how fast our brains work, isn't it? I remember when I first started meditating, the more I concentrated on meditating the more thoughts ran into my head."

"That's exactly it!" I said and then told him about how I got lost in the moment watching the sunrise or the flower open.

"Good for you, Jack! That's a very good way to quiet the mind, just like doing something you love, like creating or bodysurfing."

"Maybe I'm just an open-eyed-meditation kind of guy," I said.

"You could be at that. But don't close the door on sitting quietly with your eyes closed either."

"But the thoughts just keep pouring in that way," I said.

"Well, maybe you need to control the thoughts. Sometimes I sit with my eyes closed and just send out gratitude for all the wonderful things in my life. I list them one at a time saying things like, 'I am so grateful to be able to enjoy swimming in the ocean.' Or, 'I am grateful for my sense of humor.' You know, anything that pops into my head. It makes me feel very good to realize all the good things that are in my life."

"Kind of a 'count your blessings' meditation?" I asked.

"Kind of, but instead of just ticking them off a list, I say by memory, I feel the joy that each experience brings me as I think of my gratitude for it."

"Do you do it every day?" I asked.

"I probably should, because I always have so many things and people to be grateful for. But some days I'm able to just sit quietly and meditate, and other days I just use the smile meditation."

"The what?' I asked. (Why was I surprised at anything this man said?)

"It's a meditation where I tie my breathing into my thoughts. So when I breathe in, I connect to the infinite love of the universe. And when I breathe out, I smile, sending out love into the world. I continually repeat these thoughts with each breath. Sometimes, I lose complete track of time, and other times certain people pop into my head, and I send out love to those specific people or groups of people."

"Don't you get bored saying the same thing over and over?"

"Who gets bored from smiling?" he laughed.

He had a point.

"Plus, the purpose of meditation isn't entertainment, it's to get to a deeper understanding of yourself, and your connectivity to the universe and everything in it. If I was feeling entertained, I would also probably feel distracted. Instead, I'm looking for a stronger understanding of why I am here," Fin said.

"And why are you here?" I asked interested in what he would say.

"I think I'm here to learn to love unconditionally and to help others do the same." Fin smiled.

"Is that why I'm here too?" I asked.

"Could be. Only you and the universe know for sure."

"Well, the universe may know, but I sure don't."

"You may not know it here," he said touching his head. "But you know it here," he said touching his chest above his heart. "Just listen and as you grow through life, it'll become clear."

"More practice?" I said, rolling my eyes in mock exasperation.

"Yep. They say practice makes perfect, and isn't that what you want your life to be?" He smiled.

"But if I do all these things you've told me to do every day, I won't have time to actually live life," I said with a real concern.

"So integrate what works into your life on a rotation basis. Be aware of your feelings and where you are in your life journey and then see what you can add to make the journey more enjoyable, and more enlightening. We're constantly changing, and our spiritual practices should be too. If we're just doing the same thing because it is comfortable, it may not be helping. Life isn't meant to be comfortable, but if you push past your levels of comfort to where you can experience growth, you'll certainly enjoy life a lot more in the long run. Just like you did when you learned how to bodysurf. It wasn't easy at first, and you felt foolish at times, but you kept with it, and now enjoy it not only physically, but as a way to stay in the moment and find peace."

"In fact, I could use a little bodysurfing meditation right now," I laughed.

"Let's go," Fin laughed as we both sand danced across the hot sand and into the water.

The waves were amazing, and we enjoyed ride after ride completely lost in the joy of the moment.

When we got back to our beach chairs, I found that Vinnie had left a voice message on my cell phone telling me that all went as expected, and the next day they would start nailing the shingles to the roof.

"Everything okay?" Fin asked.

I leaned back, smiled, and said, "Life is good!"

About an hour later, I made my way back to my beach home. Walking down the street I could see the bungalow's new black tar paper roof contrasting with the bright yellow of the freshly painted walls. "It looks like things are going to go smoothly after all." I smiled to myself.

After dinner I decided to go for a stroll on the beach. The sun was just setting over the mainland, and I was enjoying the afterglow of colors painted in the sky. My shirt and shorts billowed in the sea breeze as I walked along the sand cooled by the gentle waves. I wandered, enjoying the night and watching as the stars began to appear in the sky. I was lost in thought when I realized that I had walked further than I had intended and began the long walk back to the bungalow.

As I walked along the beach, the moon began to rise over the horizon. It was just a slight crescent with both ends pointing up and looking like a Cheshire cat smile. I smiled back and walked along the beach enjoying an evening watched over by such good humor.

I was about halfway back to the bungalow when I saw a red light on the beach. Wondering if it was Fin, I wandered toward the light, and sure enough, there he sat with his red flashlight fixed on a sunken patch of sand surrounded by four poles wrapped with some orange safety ribbon. He turned and whispered loudly, "Hey, Jack, just checking on this turtle nest."

"So that's what that is," I thought to myself. I had seen them up and down the beach and should have realized what they were, but I'd been so absorbed in what I was doing that I had never given them a second thought.

"Are they going to hatch tonight?" I asked hopefully.

"Could be. The incubation period is between forty-five and seventy days, and according to the markings on this pole, it's been sixty-eight days so far," Fin said, pointing to one of the four poles that had a date and a few other numbers written on it.

"Can I join you?" I asked, hoping that I might see sea turtles hatch.

"Sure, pull up some sand and have a seat," he laughed.

I plopped down on the sand and looked at where Fin was pointing his light.

"You see where those holes are?" he asked as he moved his flashlight to a couple of holes dug just within the ribboned-off square.

"Are those where the turtles come out?" I asked, staring intently at the holes for any movement.

"Nah. Those are crab holes. The crabs dig their holes there and wait for the turtles to hatch. When they do, the crab nips the muscles behind the flippers of the baby turtles so that it can't pull itself to the sea and then the crab drags it into his hole for dinner."

That thought made me angry, and I said, "Let's fill in the holes."

"When I first found out what the crabs do, I wanted to fill in their holes too." Fin smiled. "But then I realized that the crab is just doing what he is created to do and doesn't deserve to die just for being a crab. By the way, same goes for people."

"Looking at it from that point of view, you have a point," I answered. "But I'm not sure I could just sit here and watch the crab do that to a baby sea turtle."

"Would you be able to watch if a sea turtle was about to eat a crab?" Fin asked.

"Yeah, but that's different," I said.

"Why? Because a baby turtle is cuter than a crab?"

I had to think about that for a while before I answered. "That could be a big part of it," I answered. "Plus, I eat crab but not turtle, so I think that may have desensitized me to the notion of eating crab."

"How do you think the crab nourishes its body so that you can nourish yours with crab meat?"

He had a point. Why was I so ready to kill the crab to save a turtle? Was it the notion that sea turtles are endangered? Or just that crabs are ugly and turtles are pretty cool?

"You know, there is a whole food chain out there before it gets to our tables," Fin said.

"You're right," I agreed grudgingly.

"But," Fin added, "crabs are also very skittish, so just the fact that we are here might keep it hidden in its hole."

I liked the thought and decided I'd stick it out. "Do you think this nest will hatch tonight?"

"Should. The beach patrol has been raking the area in front of the nest for the past week. See this little indentation?" he asked, moving the flashlight beam along a small indentation in the sand.

I nodded.

"That wasn't there this morning. Which could mean that there's movement in the nest, and they're just waiting for the moon to rise a bit higher so that they can follow its reflection to the water.

"Why don't the turtles hatch during the day?" I asked

"It's an instinct thing. If they hatched during the day, they wouldn't stand a chance. The seagulls would be on them in a second," Fin explained.

I thought of how seagulls swarm at anything and grimaced at the thought of the turtles struggling toward the water only to be picked off en masse.

"The more I learn about sea turtles, the more I'm amazed by them," I said.

"They are pretty amazing creatures," Fin agreed. "Humans could learn a lot from baby sea turtles."

"I thought that might be the case," I laughed. "Please go on."

Fin laughed and said, "Well, since you insist."

"That indentation I just showed you could mean that one of the turtles has hatched and is waiting for the right moment to start the trip to the water. The rest of the nest is waiting for a signal from her, and when she starts to move her flippers, the others in the nest start to move theirs too. This shifts the sand down and pushes the turtles up to the surface of the nest where their race to the sea begins. It's a community effort to get all the turtles out of the nest. If each one had to do it on their own, the ones toward the bottom of the nest might never see the light of the moon. But since they work together for the good of the entire nest, they each have a greater chance of survival."

"So you're saying that if we humans took a cue from these reptiles and worked for the good of the entire human race, the world would be a better place," I said. "Isn't that a little idealistic? You're the one telling me about the strength of the ego and its hold over people."

"Idealistic, sure, but Martin Luther King said, 'We have made of this world a neighborhood and yet we have not had the ethical commitment to make of it a brotherhood . . . . We must all learn to live together as brothers or we will all perish together as fools.'"

We both sat and pondered this as we sat and watched the turtle nest and the luminescent moon smiling among the stars.

I'm not quite sure if I was lost in thought or dozing a little when I heard Fin whisper, "Did you see that?"

I perked up immediately and focused my attention to where the red flashlight beam was pointed. I could see the sand move a little. It seemed to shift just a bit and then stop.

Then it did it again, and I found myself holding my breath in anticipation of what was about to happen.

Then it did it again. And again.

Then suddenly the sand started to shift quickly, and a small turtle about three inches long rose up out of the sand followed by two, no three, no ten, no a whole bunch of turtles. I saw one of the crabs come out of its hole and Fin said, "Stand up."

I did and the crab darted back in its hole.

"Just keep moving, and the crabs should stay in their holes," Fin said.

The turtles seemed confused as to which way to go, and Fin jumped up and turned on a flashlight. "I brought this along just in case the moon didn't cast much of a reflection into the water," he said.

Instantly, the turtles started heading for the flashlight as Fin headed for the water. I held the red flashlight on the turtle nest and watched as the last of the turtles emerged from the sand. Every time I saw a crab start to come out of a hole, I would move and the crab would dart back inside.

The tide was low, and it took the small turtles about ten minutes for the first of the hatchlings to reach the water. When I saw that no more turtles were coming out of the nest, I carefully made my way behind the last of the turtles, looking for crabs that may try to dart out and grab a snack.

It was amazing to see these little creatures that were designed to swim pull themselves across so much sand to get to the water. One seemed to be struggling, and I started to bend down to pick it up and help it and Fin yelled, "Don't touch them. They have to crawl down to the water by themselves so that they can get their bearings of where to come back to lay their eggs. Plus their journey on the sand stretches their muscles and gets them warmed for when they start their lives in the water. They are exactly where they are supposed to be to help them through the next part of their journey. Just like you and I."

So I watched as the turtles struggled and pulled their way toward the surf. As I followed up with the last of the turtles, I was able to watch them crawl into the surf and be washed out to sea.

"Bon voyage, my friends," Fin called out as the surf swallowed the last little turtle.

It was an amazing experience, and I told Fin so.

Fin agreed.

"You know," Fin added, "it's humbling to see how these reptiles follow their instincts and go to the light reflected on the water where they will spend the rest of their lives. Transforming from their life on land to a life where they will hopefully thrive in the sea. I wonder how much more abundant human lives would be if we just followed the instincts the universe designed into each of us instead of listening to our egos."

I hesitated a moment and then said, "You know I read somewhere that only one in one thousand sea turtles makes it to maturity."

"But think of how vulnerable they were on land," Fin replied. "Their instincts took them to where they had a much greater possibility to thrive."

"With a little help from you and a flashlight." I added, playing devil's advocate.

"We all need help to find our way sometimes, even if our instincts are trying to guide us." Fin smiled. (Though I couldn't see him, I could hear it in his voice.) "Don't you agree?"

"You're right," I agreed, thinking of how my life had changed, thanks to Fin and his guidance sans flashlight. "But what if we weren't here to scare the crabs and guide them with a flashlight?"

"But we were," Fin added. "Coincidence or . . ."

And then we both said, "Synchronicity!" and laughed.

"The point is," he continued, "to do what you were created to do, and not let your ego or other's expectations get in the way. You've just witnessed an amazing feat by baby reptiles. Imagine what amazing feats you are capable of if you get out of your own way and follow where the universe guides you."

I smiled to myself and then realized that I was actually smiling at life, with Fin and a great big smiling moon. Even on a night as dark as this, life at the beach could certainly be enlightening.

"We'd better get some sleep, it's almost one thirty," Fin said. And with that he wandered off humming to himself, and I walked back to the bungalow, thinking of the amazing scene that had just played out before me and thanking the universe for that moment of synchronicity.

DAY 17

The next morning I woke up to my cell phone ringing. It was Vinnie telling me that something had come up with one of his children and that he wouldn't be able to work on the bungalow that day.

I was groggy and mumbled something about when to expect him, and he replied that it should be the following day, but he'd keep me posted.

Too tired to argue and definitely too tired to try to turn my thoughts to loving kindness, I mumbled, "Please do." And then hung up.

About an hour later, I finally got out of bed grumbling about the unpredictability of construction crews and stubbed my toe on the corner of the bed. I hopped to the kitchen to get the coffee going, spilled the water as I was putting it in the coffeemaker, and then showered as I fumed about my schedule being interrupted once again by Vinnie.

By the time I was through with my shower, some of my frustration had dissipated. I walked out back to the cement table to enjoy my coffee and a bowl of fresh fruit. It wasn't until I was almost through with breakfast that I remembered to set my intention. "Today will be filled with the joy of life, bringing me inner peace to help me create beauty and send kindness to all those I meet. Even Vinnie, although I guess I won't be seeing him today. All this or something better."

Well, my rather unkind thoughts of Vinnie and crew hadn't really brought the joy of life to me. And I certainly wasn't sending kindness to them. So what was I doing wrong? I pondered this a few minutes and then thought that I was dwelling on the fact that he hadn't finished the job instead of the fact that in just one day he and his crew had done a great job in tearing off the old shingles and putting up the new tar paper on the roof. He obviously knew what he was doing, and he was letting me know if he wasn't going to come. So he was being responsible. And should I be upset that he put caring for his children as a priority over work? Part of me wanted to say, "yes!" but really, since I didn't know what was wrong with the child, I had no idea of what to think. So I decided to not worry about it and trust that Vinnie is a professional and would act accordingly. "I'm right where I'm supposed to be to get where I'm supposed to go," I mused to myself as I sipped my coffee and watched the pelicans fly toward the beach.

I was feeling better about things as I walked inside to wash the dishes. I went into the dining room to look at the mural. It just needed something in the lower left corner in the sand. What was it? Nothing came to me, and I decided that it would come to me exactly when it was supposed to. Although I was hoping it would come to me before my uncle arrived. I really wanted him to see the mural finished. It was almost done, but I wanted it to be complete.

I picked up my list of things to do and realized I still needed to buy a throw rug to cover the cracks in the terrazzo floor in the living room. So I carefully walked around the debris in the yard to the car and headed off to shop.

As I drove out of the neighborhood, I saw Velma holding on to the porch railing as she watered the plants in the front of her home. She waved, and I waved back and called out, "Looking good!"

She laughed and waved again.

"Life is good," I found myself thinking again. "No, it's not going exactly the way I would have planned it, but it is good."

I was halfway to the store when I caught myself grinning from ear to ear. I couldn't remember what I was thinking of, or if I was thinking of anything in particular. I was just smiling! That made me laugh, and I smiled all the way to the store.

Once inside the carpet department of the home-improvement store, I was amazed at all the choices for indoor/outdoor rugs. I found a set of two rugs with a border of palm trees on sale for less than any of the other single carpets. It was a great deal, so I bought the set not knowing what I would do with the second rug.

As I was heading toward the checkout line, I saw that the decorative strings of lights were on sale. I chose some with plastic tiki shades to string along the back of the bungalow for the luau.

On the way back I congratulated myself on all the things I'd been able to check off my list. The only thing left to do was plant some flowers and shrubs around the garden beds. I couldn't do that until after the roof was complete, or the plants would be trampled and broken.

I pulled up to the bright yellow bungalow and was pulling the carpets out of the car when Mrs. V walked up.

"Is Vinnie going to get this mess cleaned up in time for the luau?" she asked.

"He said he would," I replied.

"Shouldn't he be here today?" she asked.

"He should've been here, but something came up with his kid," I answered.

"Which one?" she asked.

"I don't know. Does it matter?"

"It sure does!" she said sternly. "If it's Louise, that means she must be really sick, 'cause she's always so healthy. But if it's Ricky, I hope it means he must be feeling better and they're taking a beach day."

"What?" I exclaimed.

"Yeah, Ricky's got one of them blood diseases and is sick a lot of the time. But every once in a while when the weather is as beautiful as it is today, if Ricky is feeling well enough, Vince takes him out to the beach. That kid is so sick so much of the time that when he's feeling well enough to get out, they go to the beach so he can play and enjoy things like other kids his age."

Suddenly I wasn't fuming about Vinnie anymore. In fact, in my mind I was congratulating him for having his priorities straight.

"Well, I hope he's planning on having this mess cleaned up before the luau," she repeated.

"If he doesn't, I will," I promised as I watched her light a cigarette and walk back to her periwinkle blue home.

I hauled the rugs to the sunporch to unwrap them. I took the larger of the two and put it in the living room. It looked great and actually made the room look bigger. But what was I going to do with the second one?

I turned around to go back out to the sunporch to move the second rug and realized it was exactly where it was supposed to be. So I picked up the wrappings and smiled to myself as I mentally checked another thing off my list.

It was late morning when I remembered that I'd promised to meet Fin to take Tom's grandchildren bodysurfing. I hurriedly applied a healthy dose of sunscreen and headed off to the beach. Once there, I saw that Tom was already watching Fin and the kids in the water.

"Hi," I said as I approached Tom. "It looks like Fin has things under control."

"As much as anyone can with those two kids," Tom laughed.

I laughed too, and we chatted for a few minutes about how lucky Tom was to be able to have his grandchildren spend part of the summer with him and his wife at the beach. I told him about my childhood memories of summer at the beach with my aunt and uncle and that those are some of my best memories.

"Hey, Jack, it's about time you got here!" I heard Fin yell over the waves.

"I think that's my cue," I laughed.

Tom agreed, and I headed for the water where Bryan was riding a wave right onto the shore. He got up and shouted "wahoo!' while I applauded, and then we both ran into the surf.

It was fun watching Anne and Bryan enjoy the waves with the enthusiasm only a child (or Fin) can have. After a while we were all exhausted and headed onto the beach, where we sand danced to our towels giggling and laughing the whole way.

"Grandma's made enough lunch for everyone," Tom said, pointing over to the van.

Fin and I walked over and pulled a large cooler filled with all sorts of goodies out of the trunk.

We laughed and chatted about all sorts of things. Then Fin held up his finger with tiny pieces of sand stuck on it.

"You see these tiny grains of sand?" he asked.

We nodded.

"Each one of these was part of something much bigger, but that something was hard and rigid, so instead of bending with the waves, it stood strong, and the waves wore it down and broke it apart. Now it is tiny pieces of sand.

"Yesterday you proved that you are able to go with the flow and ride the waves of life. You are now official bodysurfers. So always remember that although things that are rigid may seem not to change, it is only an illusion. For with each wave of energy the hard are worn down, while those who go with the flow may move and bend, but they can also celebrate the energy of life while their surroundings shift and change."

The kids looked very solemn as if they had been given a very special lesson (although I'm not sure if the lesson wasn't really for me. But then, I guess that any good lesson transcends age.)

"You mean this sand was once something besides sand?" Anne asked.

"Yes." Fin smiled.

"Like shells?" she asked.

"And rocks," Bryan added.

"And the stony entrance to a pirate's cave," Fin added.

"And a seaside castle," I said.

"And stones from a sunken city," Tom added.

And for the next ten minutes we all added to the conversation the things that we thought could've been broken down to make up the beach we were sitting on. The suggestions got sillier and sillier until Fin broke up the conversation with a, "Who wants to go bodysurfing?"

Followed by a resounding chorus of, "I do!"

"But first, you have to finish your lunch," Tom said.

Bryan gobbled the last of his sandwich down, and Anne said she would finish hers on the way to the waves.

As we got into the water, Fin and Bryan dove right in, while I waited in the shallower water as Anne munched on her sandwich. Then along came a big wave and knocked her over. She got up looking started and holding the remains of her sandwich, a very limp-looking piece of bread.

"I think you just made some hungry fish very happy," I said.

"You really think so?" she asked.

"Sure do," I said

"Then they can have this too," she said, dropping the dissolving bread into the water.

Then we both dove out toward the waves and a fun afternoon of bodysurfing.

In a little while Anne got very tired and headed back to sit with Tom onshore while Fin, Bryan, and I played in the waves until Tom called to us that it was time for them to be getting back home.

After Tom and the kids had packed up and headed home, Fin and I sat on the beach enjoying the combination of the warm sun on our skin cooled by the sea breeze.

"You know," Fin said with a smile, "our lunch today was a lot like the lessons of life. Don't you think so?'

I confessed that I hadn't really thought about it and asked him to explain.

"Well, if you insist." He smiled.

"Oh, I do! I do!" I laughed.

"Our lunch today was given to us to nurture our bodies, just like life's lessons and teachings are given to nurture our lives. So today while you and I and Bryan took ours and internalized it, by eating it, Anne took hers and held on to it, but didn't make it a part of herself. So when faced with the ever-changing energy of life, we could use the energy it gave us to move with the waves, while she tried to be rigid to protect what she was holding on to. Of course, she was knocked around and lost what she was trying to protect. She bounced back well, and with a good attitude, but got tired easily because she had tried to protect what was given to her instead of nourishing herself with it."

"So you're saying that I shouldn't hold on to all the lessons you've been teaching me?" I asked incredulously.

"No!" Fin said. "Instead, make them a part of who you are. Then instead of trying to protect your beliefs when life's energy changes around you, your beliefs will help you move with the energy of life. And who knows, you might just be able to jump in and . . ."

"Enjoy the ride of your life!" we both said together.

"But isn't holding on to your beliefs important?" I asked.

"How many people do you know that will argue and fight over what they think is right?" he asked.

"Quite a few," I said as their faces swirled in my mind.

"So if you are trying to argue that your opinion is right, does that mean that there is a chance that you opinion is wrong?"

"I guess," I said trying to see where this was going.

"But if you know something is right, for example, that your parents love you. Do you have to argue the point?"

"No."

"Why?"

"Because I know they love me, but I can't explain how. I could say they are good parents and have always been there for me and helped me. But that doesn't necessarily define love."

"But still you know in your heart that they love you?'

"Yes."

"So if I tried to argue that they didn't, what would you say?" Fin asked.

"That I know that they do, and I don't feel I have to prove it to anyone," I said a little defensively.

"Exactly! Fin said. "And if that is true for love, it is true for everything else I've told you too."

I nodded trying to get a healthy grasp on this concept.

"You see, if someone tries to talk you out of something that is working well in you life you can say to them, 'It seems to be working well for me.' But if someone challenges a belief that you are just holding, but have never put to the test, then you can either admit that they may be right because you haven't really had the need to test it, or argue that your belief is right, even if you don't know if it is or not. A lot of wars have been started this way."

"So, like you said a few days ago, I need to put what I'm learning to the test to see if it is right for me, and if it is, then I should let it become a part of me and the way I live in the world."

"Well said," Fin replied. "Now if you'll excuse me, I have to go help a friend." And in a moment he was heading down the beach whistling.

I stayed on the beach a little while longer and then headed back to the bungalow tired and smiling.

When I got back inside, I opened the back sliding doors to let in a cool breeze and saw a pelican sitting on the cement table in the backyard. "Could it be Terry?" I thought to myself.

"Impossible," I thought. "That was a long time ago. How long do pelicans live?"

I smiled and moved slowly out onto the sunporch and sat down on a chaise lounge watching the bird and remembering all the fun I had as a kid in this little yellow house. The pelican seemed content to just sit there, and I did the same until I drifted off to a sleep full of childhood dreams of laughter and waves and crazy eights.

When I awoke, with groggy, nap brain, it was getting dark, and the pelican was gone. Although I'm sure he really was there before, it all seemed like a dream in my fuzzy state of mind.

I looked in the fridge to see what I had to eat and only saw a couple of cups of yogurt and some fruit. Not enough to satisfy the hunger I'd worked up in the waves, so I maneuvered around the maze of discarded shingles in the front yard and walked out to the car and headed to the supermarket where I asked the lady at the seafood counter if they had any fresh grouper.

"Hon, we're all outta grouper, but we got some nice mahimahi. It's delicious grilled and blackened. Why not try some?" the lady behind the counter asked with a thick southern accent.

"I'm afraid my grilling skills often blackens what I'm cooking," I laughed.

She laughed too and then enthusiastically told me how she sprayed the cooking surface of the grill with a nonstick cooking spray before she lit the grill. Then she told me what seasonings to buy and advised that I turn the fish every two minutes.

"You've sold me," I told her. "You must be quite the cook."

"I do love food," she admitted. "Not just the eating, but the cooking too. I used to be afraid to try new ways to cook. But then I got a poor cholesterol reading from the doctor and my husband bought me a cookbook about eating healthy and wrote inside it, 'You are an incredible force of nature and can do whatever you set your mind to. So if you love cooking, stop worrying about it and get back to what you enjoy!' Now how could I argue with that? In fact, I'm working on my own cookbook of healthy grilling recipes!"

"Good luck with the book and thanks for the grilling tips! I hope I do your recipe proud," I said as she handed me wrapped fish.

"You will!" she laughed in a wonderful Southern drawl, "'cause you can do anything you set your mind on."

When I got back to the bungalow it was dark. I lit the grill and went inside to start preparing dinner. As I chopped up the vegetables I'd bought, I caught myself smiling again. How was it that something that seemed so foreign just a few weeks ago could seem so natural now?

Well, for one thing, I was relaxed, which I hadn't been for a long time. I was also following Fin's advice of testing out new ideas and seeing what worked for me and which ideas from my past no longer worked for me. In fact, I was learning to go with the flow of life just like Fin had us say in his bodysurfers' oath. "Hmmmmmmmm," I thought to myself, "maybe that bodysurfers' oath wasn't just for the kids after all. But I don't think I'd ever remember that elaborate funky chicken handshake."

I laughed and shook my head as I carried my dinner out to the grill.

After I laid the meat on the cooking surface, I smelled the first whiff of the seasonings heating up and releasing their fragrance into the night air.

"I'm exactly where I'm supposed to be," I thought to myself smiling.

Then I sat down and something soft tickled my leg. Reaching down I found a long brownish feather from the pelican that had visited earlier that day.

"Yes," I thought to myself, "I'm exactly where I'm supposed to be."

DAY 18

The next morning I was up early, had already said my affirmation, and was enjoying breakfast outside when Vinnie pulled up. I waved and walked over to greet him.

He was a bit pinker than he was the other day and figured that he had enjoyed a beach day with Ricky. "I hope everything worked out the way you were hoping with your child," I said.

"It all turned out just fine," he said. "Thanks for asking. Now today we should get most of that roof on. It'll be loud."

"I've got my beach stuff already packed and ready to evacuate," I laughed.

"Smart man," Vinnie said as he started to unload the new shingles.

I was inside doing the dishes when I heard the truck radio of Vinnie's crew blaring up the street. I hurriedly finished up and headed out the door, beach gear in hand.

"There's cold water in the fridge," I called to Vinnie as I maneuvered the obstacle course of old shingles in the yard and headed toward the ocean.

It was still early, and as I passed Velma's house I saw her in the front yard. I walked over to say hello.

"Hey, Jack!" She smiled.

"Hi, Velma," I replied. "You all set for the luau?"

"Just about. I just have to bake my cookies and brownies for the traveling horde," she answered smiling.

"Man, I've been so busy worrying about whether the place will be ready that I haven't even thought about what to serve. What did my aunt usually serve?"

"Well, she always served this delicious fruit punch, but the rest was different each time, as I recall. I remember one year I was swamped for days on end before the luau. She'd come into the hair salon where I was working to get her hair done, and while I was cutting her hair, I was telling her how I didn't have time to make anything to serve the neighbors. That evening I had just been home a few minutes when down the street walked your aunt and uncle with trays of homemade goodies for me to serve the guests the next day. She was a good woman."

"That she was," I said, thinking that this was exactly like something she would do. "I always loved her fish dip on crackers."

"That was good. In fact, she gave me the recipe if you want to make it," Velma said.

"Hmmm. I might just do that. Let me think about it. Can I come by later to get the recipe?"

"No problem." Velma smiled.

"Is there anything I can help you with before I head off to the beach?" I asked.

"You've already done more than enough," she said. "But you let me know if I can help you. Okay?"

I assured her I would let her know if I needed any help and headed off to what I thought would be my last full day at the beach for a while. In two days I was to drive to Jacksonville to pick up my uncle, so I wanted everything ready before then. I had hoped for some more beach time, but wasn't sure what to expect.

When I got to the beach the water was smooth as glass.

"I must be meant to practice patience and just enjoy this beautiful morning," I thought to myself.

I claimed my beach real estate for the day and headed off for a walk toward the pier.

Hardly anyone was out yet, and it felt like I had the whole beach to myself. "This is the life," I thought.

Then it dawned on me that my time here was almost over, and I'd have to go back to the real world of unemployment and look for a job and work on my own home. No bodysurfing. No beach guru. Just me, reentering my old life again. Although I hadn't set a definite time to go back, I figured that my uncle would stay a few days and then put the house on the market, and I would head back home to return to my old life.

As I walked along the shore, my thoughts continued in this vein, and I was not exactly enjoying the morning the way I had planned.

"Whoa, Jack! Kleishas again?" I heard Fin say from behind me. (How did he do that?)

"I don't know if it's kleishas," I replied.

"Well, whatever it is, it isn't very positive I can tell that," Fin said. "What's up?

So I explained my sadness about leaving and my worries about returning to my old life.

"I hate to break this to you," Fin said. "But your old life is gone."

"What?" I exclaimed.

"So's the old you," Fin continued. "Remember the bodysurfers' oath we took the other day?"

(So it wasn't just for the kids!)

"Yes," I said trying to remember the whole thing.

Fin saw the perplexed look on my face and repeated the oath for me.

"Do you solemnly swear to use the secrets of bodysurfing to enjoy life more? And do you solemnly swear to keep from hurting yourself or anyone else while riding the energy in the awesome ocean on the most awesome of waves?"

"I do," I said smiling.

"Do you solemnly swear to realize that there are an abundance of awesome waves out there, and to understand that not every wave's awesomeness is meant just for you? And that there is enough awesomeness to go around, but when the right wave offers its awesomeness to you, do you promise to jump in and enjoy the ride of you life?" Fin continued.

"I do. Now please don't make me do the funky chicken handshake," I said smiling.

"Nah, that was just for the kids." Fin smiled back. "But you shouldn't take yourself so seriously that doing something silly would embarrass you. You know I've seen you sand dance."

I laughed, "That you have."

"But while the handshake was for the kids. The oath was for you," Fin said.

"I had a feeling that was the case," I said, remembering how thoughts of it came back to me the night before.

"so? . . . ," Fin said.

"So what?" I asked a little confused.

"So do you realize that there are an abundance of awesome waves out there, and do you understand that not every wave's awesomeness is meant just for you? And do you realize that there is enough awesomeness to go around? And *when* the right wave offers its awesomeness to you, do you realize you need to jump in and enjoy the ride of you life?" Fin asked smiling.

"Oh, so you're saying not to stress out about the future and enjoy the moment," I asked.

"Bingo, Jack. I know that the future seems very uncertain, but you really are exactly where you're supposed to be to get to where you're supposed to go," Fin said, patting my shoulder.

"It's just that this has been such a great time, and I don't want it to end," I said.

"But is this your dream?" Fin asked.

I had to admit that it wasn't.

"Then as Thoreau said, 'Go confidently in the direction of your dreams. Live the life you've imagined.'"

"But that can be scary. What if I fail?" I said.

"What if you don't?" Fin countered. "What if everything in your life has led up to this moment so that you can take this next step in making your dreams a reality?"

"But what if it doesn't?" I asked. "It's fine to dream when I'm on vacation away from reality. But it's different when I'm going right back into the middle of all the confusion of my life."

"I don't know what you call confusion," Fin said, "but I think most people would agree that house renovation is confusing when it's your own house, and you've been working on someone else's. You've handled that okay."

I hadn't thought of that, but he did have a point.

"Look," he continued. "Imagine you have two oceans. One is full of kindness, love, and compassion and the other is full of hate, insecurity, fear, and revenge. Which one will have the biggest wave?"

I just looked at him.

"Think, Jack. What causes a wave?"

"Energy," I said.

"Good. So which ocean will have the biggest wave?"

"Whichever one I put the most energy into?" I said hesitantly.

"Exactly! So the choice is yours. Where do you want to put your energy?" Fin asked.

"Into the positive," I replied.

"Glad to hear it," Fin laughed. "You know, you still have a few days left in Daytona. Why are you wasting them worrying about the future that might or might not be?"

"Remain in the moment," I laughed.

"Great idea!" Fin exclaimed. "I wish I'd said it."

"Uh, I think you did," I laughed.

"Maybe so," Fin agreed. "Just remember to embrace the unknown and know that the universe wants you to succeed. Now where are we headed?"

As we had talked, I hadn't paid attention to where we were walking and found that we had walked way past the pier.

"I think we need to walk back in the other direction," I said.

We turned around and walked a zigzagged trail back as we picked up trash in the surf and then walked up to deposit it in the garbage cans located close to the sea wall.

We were silent for a while and then Fin suddenly said, "Jack, expand your vision. Stop looking downward caught up in your own world and look toward the horizon. How can you enjoy the journey if you're not looking forward to the destination?"

"Are we talking about life or just our walk on the beach?" I asked.

"Both," Fin said definitively.

"I should have known. But didn't you just tell me to not worry about the future?" I smiled.

"You see, here you are on this beautiful beach on this beautiful day, but you're not enjoying it. You're a million miles away. You're all caught up in the possible pitfalls of the future. You weren't looking to your dreams happening," he said.

He was right (as usual).

"Don't get caught up in your own world of kleishas or what ifs, engage with what you are doing or the person that you're talking to. Make contact. Get involved. It makes life a lot more interesting."

"Sorry," I said.

"No worries," Fin said. "I just hate to see you wasting perfectly good beach time worrying about things you can't do anything about from the beach."

"You've got a point." I smiled. "Thanks for pulling me back into the *awesomeness* of life at the beach."

"Well, that's what fellow bodysurfers do. Remind each other to use the secrets of bodysurfing to enjoy life. I took the oath too you know." Fin smiled.

"You're right, Fin. I was already stressing about going back home, and I still have a few days left here."

"I call that end-of-vacation syndrome," Fin laughed. "It's a common malady here at the beach. People escape their lives for a while and really enjoy unwinding and getting back into the natural rhythm of life and then, poof! With days left of their vacation they're already worrying about the very things they took the vacation to escape."

"I can totally relate to that," I agreed. "But what can I do about it?"

"Enjoy the ride,' Fin replied.

"What?" I asked.

"Enjoy the ride. Just like when you're bodysurfing you don't pull out of a wave until it is over, the same should be true with anything in life that you enjoy. If you have the time, and you've taken the effort to go to a place to destress and enjoy life, why cut it short?"

"But how can I keep my worries from blindsiding me?" I asked.

"Be in the moment. You know how when you are riding a wave and the only thing you're doing is enjoying the ride and feeling the rush of energy around you?" Fin asked.

I nodded.

"Same thing with anything in life. Be engaged in what you're doing and where you are. Just like a few minutes ago, we were walking in the surf of a beautiful ocean. I bet you didn't even the see the dolphin swim past."

I admitted that I didn't and was disappointed about it.

"That's just part of life at the beach," Fin said. "And part of what you're missing not being engaged in where you are. Remember, you are exactly where you are supposed to be to get to where you're supposed to go. So enjoy being here while you're here. Figure out what you want to do next, and enjoy being where you go next, once you get there. Otherwise, you might be looking forward but missing the journey. And the journey is life my friend. So enjoy the ride of your life."

I laughed, "You're right. But it isn't always easy to stay in the moment."

"Of course it's not," Fin agreed. "But it is worth the effort."

"Oh no, another thing that needs practice!" I groaned, smiling.

"You've already been practicing it," Fin laughed.

"What?"

"Sure. What do you think meditation is, but being in the moment? Remember when you were meditating and when you were engaged in watching the pelicans fly and the sunrise?"

"Yeah."

"Well, you were in engaged in the moment and the rhythm of life at the beach," Fin said. "And just now you had the energy of life at the beach swirling around you and you missed it all by worrying about what just might, possibly, could, perhaps, happen in the future."

"But worrying seems to be one of the things I do best," I protested with a smile.

"That's because you are putting all your energy into the ocean of worry and so have created wave after wave of worry for you to ride. Is that what you want out of life?"

"No," I replied.

"Then channel your energy to positive things, not worries. By worrying you can't change anything except missing the opportunity of living life in the moment. So do your best to release control of the outcome. Worry restricts our growth, creativity, happiness, and energy and can negatively affect our health. If it turns to fear, it can even draw what we're worrying about to us."

"You mean like an affirmation?" I asked.

"Yes. Worry is no more than an affirmation that you don't have control of life and don't trust the universe to get you where you need to be, so you try to second guess the outcome. Sometimes you're right, and sometimes you're wrong, but rarely do you have control over the situation. You may think you do, but it's usually only an illusion."

"That's a scary thought," I said.

"It can be. But remember that the universe that is guiding the turtle to where she needs to build her nest is also guiding you. If the turtle spent all of her time worrying about how far up she needs to build her nest when she finally gets on land, she might miss the dangers around her in the water and never make it to land to build her nest. She needs to be in the moment to do what she is meant to do, and you need to be in the moment to do what you are supposed to do."

"Are you saying that planning is bad?" I asked.

"No." Fin smiled. "Planning is good. But how often do things go exactly as you have planned?"

"Not very often," I admitted thinking of my job, past relationships, and how long it was taking to get the work on the bungalow finished.

"So what I'm saying is, do your best to plan for the future and stop worrying. Your goals can point you in the right direction to get you to where you are supposed to be. Your plans will either work out, or they won't, and all the worrying in the world won't change that. And when your plans don't work out, think of it as synchronicity moving you in the direction you are supposed to go. It may not be the easiest direction to move in, but it will lead you to who you are supposed to become. Most of us don't get our strength from the good times in our life. We get our strength from the challenges that we've faced."

"Just like all the time I spent worrying about losing my job and working hard to keep it only to have lost it anyway?" I asked.

"Exactly," Fin agreed. "Think of all the time you spent worrying about losing your job. Did that help you keep it?"

"No."

"Did that help you enjoy life more?"

"No."

"Did that do you any good at all?" Fin asked.

"Okay, okay. I get it. But it's not so easy to just give up worrying."

"I was worried you'd say that," Fin joked.

I rolled my eyes.

"Seriously, though, recognizing that you are worrying is a big first step," he said, ignoring my eye roll.

"So when I find myself worrying, I should acknowledge what I'm doing?" I asked.

"Yes, and then ask yourself, 'Is worrying about this going to solve the problem?' If the answer is no, then ask yourself, 'What am I missing out on because I am worrying about this?' You'll be surprised about all that you are missing in the present because you are worried about things that may or may not happen in the future."

"So you're saying adopt a 'no worries' policy?" I asked.

"Well said," Fin agreed. "But also keep in mind your forgiveness policy to forgive yourself and others when things don't go as you wanted them to. Or when you catch yourself worrying even after you have chosen to stop worrying."

"In other words, one more thing I need to practice!" I moaned.

"Yes. But it gets easier in time. And as it becomes a part of you, you'll be surprised at how easy it can be," Fin said reassuringly.

"Well, I need to get out of this end of vacation syndrome right now," I said.

"Then I say immerse yourself in the moment, dive in, and enjoy the ride," Fin laughed as he pointed to some small waves just off the beach.

In seconds I was riding a wave toward shore with a smile on my face and a big "wahoo!" in my heart. It was hard to believe that I could've missed this by worrying.

After wearing ourselves out in the waves, we continued our walk back to where my beach gear was, and we both plopped down exhausted and smiling.

As we sat contentedly on the beach, I watched as the sun streamed through the clouds radiating out in shafts of light.

"You see how the sun shines through the clouds over there?" Fin asked pointing to where I was looking.

I nodded.

"Those are Buddha's fingers," he continued. "A childhood friend told me that every time you see Buddha's fingers it is the universe reminding you that you are loved."

"I like that thought," I said smiling.

"Me too," Fin added. "But I was curious about what they really were and did some research. I found out that they are technically crepuscular rays and are formed when something, like that cloud, blocks some of the rays of light from the sun, causing a shadow. This makes the rays of light that are not blocked seem brighter and enhances the beam's definition as it shines toward the earth. In other words, the shadows can make the universe's loving light more visible to us."

"I thought I heard a lesson coming on," I teased.

"You are very astute," Fin laughed. "So just like your losing your job is a shadow in your life, coming to the beach to rediscover who you are helped you find the light guiding you toward all that you can become. Compared to who you were three weeks ago, how do you feel?"

"There's no comparison!" I said happily.

"You are a good student," Fin said. "You beat me to the lesson."

"Huh?"

"It's all about comparison. Sometimes we need the contrast of shadows and light in our lives to show us the difference between what our lives are, filled with egocentric beliefs and actions, and what our lives could be—filled with loving, compassionate beliefs and actions)."

"So you're saying that if it wasn't for the darkness in our lives, we wouldn't find the lightness in them?" I asked.

"I'm not sure about that. But I know for myself whenever I've hit a dark part of my life I work harder at searching for and finding a way to a brighter existence," Fin replied.

"Just like I've been doing here at the beach?" I asked.

"Exactly," Fin said. "A month ago what were you thinking of?"

"My exorbitant workload," I replied.

"Were you even thinking of going to the beach or any kind of happiness?" Fin continued.

"No. Just trying to keep my head above the proverbial water," I replied, frowning a little.

"And now, even if they offered you your old job back, would you take it?" Fin asked.

I thought for a minute. "A sure job would be a good thing," I said, "but no, I don't think I would. I want more out of life than what I had before."

"And you wouldn't have known that unless you experienced both the light and shadows of this particular stage of your life." Fin smiled. "So the Buddha's fingers remind us that there is an abundance of loving light around us always. But it sometimes takes a shadow to show us that the light has been there all along."

I nodded grasping what he was saying as I watched the light stream from the clouds.

"The problem I'm having right now is that I don't know what I'm supposed to do. You've really inspired me into delving deeper into who I am spiritually, but aren't I also a human being for a reason?" I asked a little perplexed.

"Good question!" Fin exclaimed clapping. "The trick is to find the balance between spirituality and the physicality of being in the human world. It's like riding a wave. You feel all the possibilities of how the ride could turn out, and yet you feel the energy of the wave as it pulls you ahead or drops you off. That's life. Don't be afraid to jump in and enjoy the energy of life. Make plans, but realize that plans often must change and morph as the energy of life shifts and carries you along."

"But how do I know if I'm on the right path?" I asked and then realized the answer as I joined Fin in saying, "Synchronicity."

"But that's easier to talk about when I'm at the beach, instead of searching for a job."

"Well, it all goes back to that promise you made," Fin said.

"What promise?" I asked.

"Do you solemnly swear to use the secrets of bodysurfing to enjoy life more? And do you solemnly swear to keep from hurting yourself or anyone else while riding the energy in the awesome ocean on the most awesome of waves?"

"I do," I said smiling.

"Do you solemnly swear to realize that there are an abundance of awesome waves out there, and to understand that not every wave's awesomeness is meant just for you? And that there is enough awesomeness to go around, but when the right wave offers its awesomeness to you, do you promise to jump in and enjoy the ride of you life?" Fin continued.

"Oh, that promise," I said. (How could something that sounded so childlike be so complicated?)

"It goes for more than just bodysurfing, Jack. It goes for life too," Fin said seriously. "I know it can be scary. But life is like bodysurfing. There's the possibility of being tossed about or looking foolish if you jump in with all you've got, but there's also the chance of enjoying . . ."

"The ride of your life," I chimed in laughing. "I know, I know. But real life is looming on the horizon again. I guess I'm just feeling apprehensive."

"Life at the beach is real life. In fact, wherever you are, real life is happening, whether you're on vacation or not. No one is guaranteed one hundred years or even tomorrow, so you better start living the life you want today."

"I guess I'd better start getting my super job affirmation going," I joked.

"Sending positive thoughts about your career into the universe is always a good idea," Fin replied. "So what do you think it should say?"

"Something about making millions of dollars would be nice," I said.

"Maybe, maybe not," Fin said. "I know a number of well-to-do people who aren't happy and don't enjoy life. You see, money can't make you happy. No thing and no one can make you truly happy. That comes from deep inside yourself. If you are truly happy, you can enjoy life whether you dine on lobster or potato chips, vacation in Europe or in a local park. Besides, you shouldn't use affirmation for selfish gain. Instead, use them to better the world. Remember, we're all connected. What you do for others, you're really doing for yourself."

"So I need to be more altruistic about my career?" I asked.

"Not necessarily, Jack," Fin replied. "You are a unique person with unique experiences and talents. Find where your uniqueness can help make the world a better place. It doesn't have to be working for a nonprofit group. It could be helping any organization to grow in a way that you believe is helping others. The important thing is that you understand that you have the ability to make the world a better place. Synchronicity will guide you to where you need to be. Just follow the signs and enjoy the ride."

"Whoa!" I said. "Getting a charge to make the world a better place is a big expectation."

"It would be if it were just up to you," Fin laughed. "But it's up to everyone. Just do your part."

"Yeah, but how do I know what my part is?" I asked.

"You'll know," Fin laughed reassuringly. "Think about it and live up to your standards, not someone else's. If you are living your life to please others, you're not doing what you were put on earth to do. You are here in your form and with your talents to make the world a better place. Living by someone else's standards not only diminishes your light, but also makes the whole world a bit darker. Reach for your higher good and remember that the universe wants you to succeed.

"That's a lot to think about," Fin continued. "But remember you're still at the beach. Enjoy your time here while you have it. Don't lose the rest of this beautiful day lost in career choices. There'll be time enough for that.

"Now I have to get going," Fin added, and he was off in a flash humming a happy-sounding tune.

I sat there mulling around the idea of my career making a difference in the world. It seemed to be a tall order, but I also knew that I was exactly where I needed to be to get to where I needed to go.

I sat and watched the waves shimmering below the Buddha fingers and reminded myself that the universe was sending love in the direction I was headed. Even though I wasn't sure which way that was.

I was enjoying the afternoon at the beach when my cell phone rang. It was Vinnie telling me that the roof was finished and asking if I wanted to come and inspect it.

I packed up my gear and hurried toward the bungalow.

As I was walking down the street, I saw the blue-gray color of the roofing shingles contrasting nicely with the bright yellow bungalow. It looked good from afar, and I hoped from up close.

The closer I got, the better it looked. I really didn't know how to inspect a roofing job but looked it over as best I could. "It looks good," I said. "You guys are fast."

"It's a small house," Vinnie laughed. "The real test will be after the next rainstorm. So let us know if you have any trouble."

I assured him that I would tell my uncle to call if there were any leaks.

"The guys did a magnet sweep to catch any of the roofing nails that may have fallen. It's not a guarantee that one or two haven't escaped their notice, but they're usually pretty careful. Just make sure to wear shoes in the yard and be careful if you're digging in the dirt with your hands."

"Got it," I said. "Thanks for getting this done before the luau."

"No worries," Vinnie laughed. "Besides, Mrs. Vargas told me it had to be done and swept clear of nails so it wouldn't ruin the party. I try to always do what she tells me to. She scares me a little,"

"I know what you mean," I laughed.

Vinnie hopped in his truck and took off. I was just about to go inside the bungalow when Mrs. V came out of her place and called out to me, "It sure was loud around here. I thought they'd never finish."

"That's funny," I said. "I was just thinking about how quickly they finished the job."

"That's because you ran off to the beach while the rest of us had to put up with the incessant hammering. It looks good though."

"Sorry about the noise. I know my uncle appreciates your patience as much as I do," I said replying with kindness (or at least giving it my best shot). "I should've invited you to the beach with me."

"Are trying to hit on me?" she asked, tousling my hair.

"Uhhhh, mmmmmm, no," I said.

"Well good, I'm particular about who I strut my stuff in front of," she cackled and, with an exaggerated shake of her hips, turned and walked back leaving me speechless and chuckling on the inside.

I put away my beach stuff and went back out to see what needed to be done in the flower beds and to determine how many plants I should buy. There wasn't much worth saving except for the two big yellow blooming hibiscus on the side of the house.

I grabbed a pencil and paper and measured the space by walking heel to toe through the flower beds to determine how many plants to buy. Then I headed off to the home-improvement store, once again, in search of the perfect plants.

As I wandered the aisles, I tried to remember all the different plants that seemed to be doing well on the Hibiscus Lane. Then I searched for those plants. It took quite awhile, but I finally decided on a row of plumbago bushes that bloomed the color of Mrs. V's bungalow, for the front of the house. For the back of the house I found several brightly colored crotons, yellow blooming beach daisies, and some beautiful hibiscus with the colors of a sunset sky in its bloom.

On the way home I stopped at the supermarket and picked up some fresh fish and a few shrimp for myself and an extra piece of fish just in case the pelican returned. (He hadn't.) I fired up the grill and began unloading the plants from my car, putting each container where I would plant them the next day. They looked bright and cheerful.

I went back in, seasoned the fish, and carried them to the grill, when to my surprise I saw the pelican sitting on the cement table. I laughed and carefully approached the grill not wanting to scare him away.

"Here ya go, fella," I said as I tossed him a shrimp. "I hope you don't mind, but I think I'll call you, Terry."

He opened his mouth and caught it in midair, pointed his beak toward the heavens, and swallowed. It seemed like a lot of work for such a little shrimp, but I enjoyed watching him, so I tossed him another, and then another, and another.

Soon, all that was left was the two pieces of fish, so I cut up one while I tossed the other on the grill.

While my fish cooked, I tossed the pieces of fish to Terry. Soon there was only my fish left, and I watched it cook, while Terry watched me watching it cook. When it was done, I took it back inside to prepare the rest of my meal; I then went back out to join Terry for dinner. He watched as I ate and chatted to him about my reservations about being jobless and worries about the job interview process.

Then I remembered about setting my intention for a new job. Fin had said that it shouldn't be self-serving, so the only thing I could think of was, "The universe is guiding me to the career where abundance of joy, money, and opportunities to help others flow freely to me."

I asked Terry what he thought about my affirmation. He sat there and blinked occasionally. When I'd finished eating, I thanked Terry for listening and headed inside. He remained there a few more minutes and then flew off toward the Halifax River, where I guessed his nest was located.

I turned my attention back to the mural, but still couldn't figure out what it was missing. Then I picked up a book and started reading, but dozed several times before I decided it was time for bed. The next day would be busy, getting the bungalow ready for both my uncle and the luau.

DAY 19

The next morning I was up early, set my intention for the day, and remembered to add the new part about the job. I plugged in the coffeemaker and went out to watch the sunrise. I watched the pelicans fly toward the beach against an orange and purple sky, thinking how fortunate I was to have this time at the beach. The smell of coffee pulled me from the moment, and I went inside, fixed breakfast, and brought it out to the cement table.

As I ate, I watched the colors of the sky change to a beautiful electric light blue. There were very few clouds, and so I thought I should get the plants in the ground before the heat of the day took over.

After all the planning I had done yesterday, the plumbago I'd placed in a row in the front of the bungalow now seemed rather boring. I was disappointed, but then remembered that Fin had told me that plans were to get us moving in the right direction so that synchronicity could lead us to where we were supposed to go.

"Let's see if this works," I said to myself and went inside to grab a pencil and paper. In just a few moments, I had figured out a new landscape layout with the plants I had brought home. It resembled a cottage garden and, if it worked it, would add a lot of color to the front of the house.

I moved the plants around and was very pleased with the results. It wasn't what I had intended; in fact, it was much better.

"All this or something better," I said as I smiled remembering my morning affirmation.

The soil was easy to dig, and I was finished planting in a very short time. I pulled out the hose, watered the plants, mulched the flower beds, and then watered the plants again.

I was standing back enjoying the result of my efforts when Mrs. V walked up.

"Gees, Jack!" she exclaimed. "You do know that a hedge around a house is supposed to be all one kind of plant, don't you?"

"But this isn't a hedge, it's a garden," I said.

"Hmmmmm," she said. "I like all the different colors."

Why didn't that surprise me?

"Thanks," I said, and really meant it.

"Good job," she said, giving my arm a punch and walking away.

Now that was something that I wasn't expecting. But it felt good. Was Mrs. V changing? Or was it the fact that I was changing in how I interacted with her? Either way, I was happy with the result.

I was hosing the dirt and grime off me when I heard my cell phone ringing. It was my uncle calling.

"Hey, Uncle Doug!" I said truly excited. "I just finished the landscaping."

"I'm sure it looks great, sport," he said.

"It does!" I said celebrating in the moment.

"I'm planning on picking you up tomorrow around ten. Is that okay?" I asked.

"Well, that's why I'm calling," my uncle said. "There's a slight change of plans."

My heart sank as I thought that my uncle was canceling out. "You're still coming, aren't you?"

"With all the work you've done, of course, I coming. But you won't have to pick me up."

"Huh?'

"Well, sport, I need to ask you one more favor," my uncle continued. "A good friend of mine, named Irving, is having a real rough time right now, and I was thinking that he could drive me down and stay with me at the beach for a while. He can drive, so you won't have to come up here to pick me up."

"If you're having a tough time, the beach is certainly a great place to go," I said. "I can certainly attest to that."

"The problem is the sleeping arrangements," my uncle continued, sounding a little worried.

"He can have the guest room, and I can sleep out on the sunporch. I just slept out there a couple of nights ago," I said.

"I hate to ask it after all you've done," Uncle Doug said. "But he really needs to get away from his current situation for a little bit."

I assured him I understood completely, "Besides that'll give me a little more time on the beach."

My uncle laughed, "You sound just like you did when you were twelve."

I laughed too, "I'm beginning to feel like that again."

"That's the great thing about the beach. It always brings out the kid in me too," my uncle agreed. "I've been away for far too long."

He then told me they planned to arrive midafternoon the next day, and after a bit more conversation he said, "I really appreciate all that you've done for me, Jack. I can't wait to see the old place again."

I was excited for him to see the place too, but I just smiled and said, "I hope I did you proud."

"You always do, sport. You always do," he replied.

We chatted a few more minutes, and when I hung up, I had a wonderful feeling from being able to do something to help this kind, loving man.

I had just been given the gift of more beach time. So with the plants planted and the bungalow in order, I headed off to the beach, smiling and enjoying the moment.

As I reached the beach, I saw Fin sitting meditation style on his towel. I quietly walked toward him from behind, but when I got within fifteen feet of him, he said, "Hey, Jack! How did your house project go today?"

(How did he do that?)

I told him of my landscaping plan and how it had changed to become a garden, and of Mrs. V's approval.

He laughed, "Sounds like all is right with the world. Let's take a walk."

"Yes. I believe it is," I said, dropping my beach gear.

While we walked, I told him about my uncle driving down with a friend who was having some troubles.

"Your uncle is a good man," he said.

"He is. He's always seemed to know that the beach can rejuvenate a person. I'm just figuring that out," I said, feeling a bit sad that it had taken me so long to understand this lesson, and thinking about all the beach time I'd missed even though it was just over-an-hour's drive from my home.

"We all get the lesson when we need it most," Fin said. "The important thing is that we understand the lesson, not our age when we understand it. Because from that moment on, we have that specific knowledge that can help us change the direction of our lives."

"But don't they say you can't teach an old dog new tricks?" I asked.

Fin stopped and said, "Look behind us. Do you see your footprints?'

I nodded.

"Where do they lead to?" he asked.

"To where I'm standing," I replied.

"Good. Now from where you are standing in which direction can you go?"

"In any direction I want," I said.

"And it's the same with life." Fin smiled. "Life happens, and how we've reacted has led us to where we are right now. But by learning from life, our next step can be in any direction and take us toward where we want to go."

"But isn't reacting just letting something else control your destiny?" I asked.

"Not really," Fin said thoughtfully. "We really don't have control over anything but our response to things."

"I guess," I said.

can't control what I'm going to do next can you?" Fin

t's for sure," I laughed.

"And for all your planning, you couldn't control how your uncle was to come down to Daytona. Right?" he asked.

"Right. So all I can control is what I do in response to my circumstances," I said, starting to understand where this was going.

"That's right, and that's life," Fin said, looking out to the waves coming into shore. "The waves we bodysurf on are like people. They have more alike than not alike, but it's how we handle the surprises that can make or break the ride."

I laughed, "Well, my life has certainly had a lot of surprises."

"And you're handling them well," Fin agreed.

"Well, I could do with a few less surprises and a little more security," I said.

"There's an old proverb that says, 'A ship in the harbor is safe, but that's not what a ship is for," Fin said. "Yes, it's nice to have a feeling of security. But that's not what life is about. It's not about feeling secure, it's about living the life you were meant to live. That means living with integrity and having the courage to love, laugh, serve, and forgive."

"You think it takes courage to do those things?" I asked.

"To do them, well, I think it does," Fin answered. "To love unconditionally takes a lot of courage. It means loving even when there is a chance you won't receive love or even be liked by the person you love."

"But isn't that just being used?" I asked.

"No. If you are expecting something in return, you can be used. But if you truly love someone unconditionally, you don't expect anything in return. Loving someone unconditionally doesn't mean giving him everything he wants. It means loving someone and understanding that he or she is on their own life journey. That the energy that makes the molecules in my body dance to make me who I am is also dancing in the bodies of everyone and everything else. We are all one big dancing celebration of life. And in the end, no matter where our journeys travel, we all wash up on the same shore. So why not have the courage to catch a wave and enjoy the ride and wash up on that distant shore with an open heart?"

"That's easier said than done," I said.

"That's where the courage comes in," Fin smiled.

I laughed, "Okay, but what about laughing? That doesn't take courage."

"Sure it does. How many people do you know that take life and themselves so seriously that they don't enjoy either?" Fin asked.

"I can think of a few. Me included," I said, chagrined.

"Why do you think that is?" Fin asked.

"Because life is serious stuff," I said.

"Does that mean it can't be enjoyed?" Fin asked.

"Well . . ."

"Remember how serious you were when you first got here?" Fin asked.

"Yeah. I've noticed I've been smiling a lot more lately."

"What's changed? Your circumstances?"

"No, I have," I said.

"Right. And that took courage to look at life in a different way and not have to prove you are right all of the time," Fin said.

"So by understanding that I don't have to be right, as long as I am learning helps me take myself less seriously?" I asked.

"Exactly. But so many of us feel that being right is more important, no matter the cost, and so the lesson is lost. Not forever though, it will keep coming around until it is learned." Fin smiled.

"Is that really true?" I questioned doubtfully.

"Sure it is," Fin laughed. "The universe is very patient and will continue to bring to you the lessons you need to learn."

"Oh right, like karma keeps giving you a different vantage point of the lesson until you learn it," I said, remembering our talk from the other day.

"Exactly."

"What happens after it's learned?" I asked.

"It's no longer an issue. You've learned to handle that situation and know what to do if it arises again."

"Okay, but what about courage to serve?" I queried.

"It's similar to love. You have to do it with no expectation of reciprocity."

"You mean do it because it feels right, and not because you expect to get anything out of it?" I asked.

"Exactly. It takes a lot of courage to do someone a favor and not expect a thank-you."

"But shouldn't someone say thank you if you do them a favor?" I asked.

"What people should do and what they do are two different things. For example, I used to get so angry when I'd be in traffic, and I'd let someone in front of me, and they didn't wave thanks back. I thought it was disrespectful, and it would send me into thoughts about the state of the world and how disrespectful people were. Then I realized that if my actions depended only on what I received, then they were nothing more than a form of ego-centered living. That was hard to admit. But once I did admit it, I understood that I could recognize those thoughts and work on changing them. If I hadn't, we'd have never met."

"What do you mean?" I asked.

"The first day I saw you, I could tell you were struggling with some major life problem. So I had the choice to let you struggle or to offer my help and risk being rejected. I chose to offer my help, and it took you awhile to accept. You probably thought I was a crazy old beach bum."

"Well, I didn't know you," I said half-heartedly, defending my actions.

"It's okay. It wouldn't be the first time," Fin laughed. "But you see, if I was afraid of you rejecting or judging me, I probably wouldn't have even made the initial effort."

"And yet you went out of your way to help me," I said, taking in the risk he had taken.

"Because I've been where you were and knew I could help," Fin said.

"Thanks!" I said. "Really thanks."

"It's been my pleasure," Fin replied. "Thank you for being willing to laugh."

"That has been my pleasure," I said, "literally."

We both laughed.

"Now, tell me about why we need courage to forgive," I said.

"Forgiveness isn't about a scorecard where you are counting errors and saying, 'I'm so good because I forgive you.' Real forgiveness comes from within."

"So forgiving someone doesn't make me a better person?" I asked.

"You don't do a good deed and magically become a good person. You are a good person, so your actions follow."

"So if this is true, then some people are good and some are bad?" I asked totally confused.

"No, all people have goodness within them, but in a world so full of ego-based thinking, it takes courage to let that goodness show."

"So saying, 'I forgive you,' isn't enough. You have to feel it," I pondered out loud.

"Well said." Fin smiled. "But at least saying, 'I forgive you,' is a start. Then you can start examining the feelings you have around the issue. Sometimes you might have to forgive yourself before you can forgive someone else. That takes away the ego-need to be right and helps you see the situation from a different point of view. Try to see things as neutral and realize that you can't control other people's actions only your reaction. Just like you can't control the waves, you can only control your choice of which waves to ride."

"This is going to take some work," I said thoughtfully. "I see where courage comes in."

Fin agreed, "It takes work, but the ability to love, laugh, serve, and forgive make it worth the while."

We were back to at our beach gear.

"The waves look great," I said. "Shall we?"

And we jumped into the ocean and caught wave, after wave, after wave.

We were floating in the water enjoying the combination of the feel of the cool water on our bodies and the sun's warmth on our faces when a small wave washed a dollar bill under my chin.

"Whoa! Look what just came my way," I said to Fin, holding the found dollar.

"Abundance seems to be flowing to you." Fin smiled. "Don't forget to be grateful."

Instantly I thanked the universe for the abundance in my life. Not just for the dollar, but for the ability to enjoy life and feel the sun on my skin and the opportunity to help my uncle and enjoy the sound of children laughing at the beach and a thousand other things. It was a wonderful moment of realization of just how incredible it was to be connected to the energy that is flowing through everything, always.

Finally we got out of the water, and Fin said, "I've got to get going. But before I go, I have a little present for you."

He reached into his knapsack and pulled out a conch shell. "It's to remind you of your time here," he said, holding out the shell.

I took it from him and smiled. "When I need a break from life, I'll hold it up to my ear and listen to the surf sound it makes." I was amazed at how truly touched I was by this gift.

"Well, that's nice," Fin said. "But the reason I'm giving it to you is to remind you that the energy of life is all around you. That sound of the surf is also like the sound of the flow of traffic and lots of other things. It's the energy of life. This is to remind you that the energy of life flows all around you. How you use it is up to you."

And with that he was packing up his gear.

"Will you be here tomorrow?" I asked.

"You bet," he said. And he was off whistling.

I smiled and shook my head. What an interesting time at the beach this had been. Looking back, it was by this strange set of coincidences that I was where I was at that moment. "Coincidences, right. Synchronicity is more like it," I said while I laughed and marveled at how the universe really did seem to want me to succeed.

"Thanks!" I said to the universe, and really meant it!

After the sun had baked the saltwater off my skin, I packed up my bags and headed back to the bungalow to figure out what I was going to serve for the luau. On my way, I thought I'd drop by Velma's house to see if I could get my aunt's fish-dip recipe. I saw her car wasn't in the carport, so I pulled a pad and paper out of my knapsack and wrote a note asking her to call me when she returned. Then I headed across the street to the cheerful little home and watered the colorful garden once again. Just looking at it made me happy.

Once inside, I unpacked my beach gear and carefully put the shell that Fin had given me on the dining room table. I took a shower, and when I was coming out of the bathroom, I looked across the hall toward the dining room mural and saw the shell in front of it, and I knew instantly what the mural needed.

"Finally!" I said as I grabbed my paints and brushes and began to paint a conch shell on the beach in the lower left-hand side of the mural.

I liked the fact that synchronicity brought me exactly what I needed when I needed it. I liked the fact that the shell had come from Fin. And I especially liked the fact that to me the shell represented a reminder of going with the flow of life.

It took several hours, but when I was finished, I stepped back, took a look, and smiled. Were there better murals? Sure. But when I looked at this mural, I didn't just see a picture of a sunrise, but I also saw a symbol of the dawn rising on my new life.

"Life is good!" I said. It's funny, I couldn't remember saying it that often before I had come to the beach, and now it was a common phrase. I know it wasn't that my situation had changed so drastically; I had. "Thanks!" I said again to the universe.

It was getting dark, and Velma still hadn't come back, so I thought I would get busy stringing the tiki lights along the back of the house. The shades were yellow, green, and orange and reminded me vaguely of some lights that my aunt and uncle had strung along the back of the house thirty years ago.

I remembered painting the hooks hanging down from the eaves of the house, so I found an extension cord and hung the lights in the same place others had been strung many years before. The familiarity made me smile.

They put out a very small amount of light, so I flipped on the sunporch lights. It was still dark toward the back of the small yard, so I lit the tiki torches. The flames cast dancing shadows across the back of the yard and made it look very festive.

I had grabbed the hose and was watering the plants in the backyard again when a voice said, "It looks good."

I turned around, and there was Velma smiling.

"Thanks," I said.

"Here's the fish-dip recipe," Velma said, holding out a yellowed recipe card in her hand. "I copied it down for myself but thought you might want the recipe written in your aunt's handwriting."

I looked down at the yellowed card and saw the familiar loops and curls. It brought back all the letters she had written to me over the years and all the support that familiar writing had provided throughout my life.

"Thanks for thinking of that," I said. "This really means a lot."

"It's my pleasure," Velma said, and I could tell that she had thought about it long and hard before she gave me this little token of my aunt's life. She had done it out of love and had hoped it would mean to me what it meant to her, and it did.

"I finally finished the mural," I said proudly as I put the recipe card in my pocket. "Come take a look."

"I'd love to," Velma replied.

"Love to what?" came a raspy voice from the shadows.

"Love to see Jack's mural, Gladys," said Velma as Mrs. V came out of the darkness and stood so close to one of the tiki torches that the shadows danced across her face in a foreboding way.

"Let's take a look," Mrs. V said as she started toward us. "Oh damn, I dropped my cigarette!"

As she bent her head down toward where she had dropped her cigarette, the wind blew slightly, and a flame caught onto her giant head scarf.

At first it looked like a trick of the dancing shadows, but as she stood up, the rush of air must've fanned the flames, and the fire ignited.

It's amazing how things seem to move in slow motion at a time like this. Velma started to run toward her. Mrs. V had a strange look on her face seeing Velma coming toward her, and I realized she didn't know that she was on fire. I just stood there for a second thinking, "What the . . ." when I realized that I had a hose in my hand. I pointed it toward her and pulled the trigger dousing the flame and a very shocked and unhappy Mrs. V.

"What the hell did you do that for?" she yelled and gave me a look that should be next to the phrase "if looks could kill" in the encyclopedia.

"You, you were on fire," I stuttered out.

She reached up and touched the dripping, burned scarf and partially melted rollers, and a look came over her face that made me want to reach out and hug her. But Velma was already doing just that.

For once, Mrs. V was speechless as Velma led her away toward her periwinkle bungalow saying, "I don't think it's as bad as it looks."

I started to follow, but Velma stopped me and said, "She'll be fine. Her skin wasn't burned. This is a private moment. Let her have her space."

"Man, life can change in an instant," I thought to myself as I watched Velma and Mrs. V go into the house and close the door. I, too, was shaken up by this and just sat at the cement table and pondered what had just happened. "What are the odds?" I asked myself. Then the thought of synchronicity popped into my head.

No, surely synchronicity wouldn't cause something like this to happen. I got up and turned off the hose, put out the tiki torches, and decided to ask Fin about this.

Once inside, I put away all my paints and brushes and made a list of the supplies I would need for the luau. My mind kept going back to Mrs. V on fire and how fast it had happened. I was sitting at the table lost in thought when Velma knocked on my door.

"Is she okay?" I asked.

"A little shook up. But she'll be okay. I need you to run to my house, and in the top drawer of my vanity you'll find my hair-cutting supplies rolled up in a black leather case. Bring them back over to Gladys's house."

"You got it," I said and headed off. I was almost to the door when I thought, "I don't have the keys." But as I tried the door, it was really no surprise to find that it was unlocked.

I found the leather kit and ran over to Mrs. V's.

"Thanks," Velma said, meeting me at the door. "Now don't you worry. She wasn't hurt except for her pride. It'll all be okay. It was a good thing you had that hose in your hand, or it could've been a lot worse. Someone was sure looking out for her."

Then she closed the door.

While I walked back to the yellow bungalow, I wondered why I was watering plants again. I had just watered them an hour before, and they wouldn't have needed it, even if they were newly planted.

Was it synchronicity? Could something good come out of this? "I must ask Fin about this," I said to myself.

By this time the adrenaline rush was over, and I was feeling exhausted. I climbed into bed and said one more thanks to the universe for how everything turned out. It had been an exciting day, and no one had gotten seriously hurt, so life was good.

DAY 20

The next morning, I was up before the sun and sat out at the cement table watching the morning light break through the darkness, the beginning of a new day. It occurred to me that this was my last day of self-reflective beach time before my uncle and his friend came to stay at this happy little bungalow. Since his friend would be staying with him, my uncle wouldn't need me, and I could go back to my old life and begin the process of picking up the pieces and begin living the life the universe was guiding me toward. "Whatever that is," I thought to myself.

As the sky lightened, I saw the pelicans fly toward the beach and wondered to myself if I would be able to keep this contented feeling after I left Daytona and headed back to the world of unemployment and all that lay ahead of me. "You're where you're supposed to be to get to where the universe wants you to go," I heard Fin saying in my head. I smiled, said thanks, and was shocked to hear back.

"For what?"

I turned, and there stood Mrs. V, her platinum blond hair cut stylishly short with just a flip in the back. I was doubly surprised, first by having my morning meditation interrupted and then by seeing how nice she looked without a big glaring scarf tied around her head.

I stared at her for a moment and then said, "You look great!"

"Yeah, yeah," she said discounting what I was saying, but I could tell she was happy I thought so.

"No, really. You look great! You should have done this years ago," I said.

"Well, I guess I had to wait until just the right time to let you catch me on fire," she replied.

"Ummm. It wasn't me that caught you on fire, I'm the one that hosed you down," I said smiling.

She chuckled, "Yeah, I guess you're right. Thanks for that."

"You're welcome. I'm glad you're okay. And honestly you look years younger. Velma gave you a great look."

"Yes, she did. You know I'd always kept my hair the way my husband liked to see me wearing it, but it was a lot of bother," she said as her hand gently tugged at the short hair at the side of her head. "Last night I got the first good night's sleep I've had in years."

"Really?" I asked surprised.

"Yeah, those damned curlers are uncomfortable." She smiled.

I laughed, "Can I help you do anything to get ready for the luau?"

"Nope. I just got an extra hour because my hair is already done."

"What are you going to tell people about your hair?" I asked.

"Well, at first I was going to tell people I just felt it was time for a change. But then I figured, 'Hell, this makes a great story.' So I just decided to tell them the truth. Really, how many people can say they got a great haircut from setting their head on fire? Plus you'll be the envy of the neighborhood. Do you know how many people have wanted to turn a hose on me over the years?"

I laughed, "You have a point. And a good sense of humor about the whole thing."

She smiled. "Now, we both better get a move on if we're going to be ready for tonight's activities."

With that, she was heading off toward her blue bungalow, and I thought I noticed a little spring in her step that wasn't there before.

After breakfast I double-checked my grocery list and added the kind of breakfast cereal I remembered my uncle liked, as well as milk and a few other necessities so that when he and Irving arrived they wouldn't have to run to the grocery. Then I headed off to do my shopping. As I was driving back home, I saw Velma in her front yard.

Once I'd parked I walked across to her yard. "Great job on Mrs. V," I said.

"Well, if it's one thing I learned from my cancer, it was how to make do with whatever hair you got," she said smiling.

"I think you did more than 'make do,'" I replied.

"We did. In fact, we made up," she said smiling. "My working on her hair gave me the time to tell her how bad I felt about yelling at her for cutting my hibiscus. I think she was in the right frame of mind for listening 'cause she said she understood and not to give it a second thought. I was also able to thank her for working in my garden these past few weeks. She even hugged me before I left."

"Wow! This haircut might be the beginning of a whole new Mrs. V," I said.

"It could be at that," Velma said thoughtfully. "It takes more than a haircut to change a person, but sometimes one small change can lead to something bigger."

"Can I help you with anything to get ready for tonight?" I asked.

"I'm in pretty good shape, thanks to all your help," she said.

"Then I'm gonna get going," I said.

"Enjoy the beach," she laughed.

That's exactly what I intended to do as soon as I made the fish dip. Happily, it was easier than I thought.

Once the dip was in the refrigerator and I had cleaned up the kitchen, I grabbed my gear and headed off to enjoy my last day at the beach for a little while.

Fin was already there, sitting meditation style, facing the ocean. And of course, no sooner had I set foot on the sand then I saw him wave to me, even though he was facing away from me. (How did he do that?)

"Hey, Fin!" I called out.

"Hello, my friend." Fin smiled. "The universe has brought you some wonderful waves today. Care to join me?'

"You bet!" I said, setting up my beach chair, taking off my flip-flops, and dashing toward the ocean.

The waves were perfect, and I was riding one onto the beach and letting out a loud "wahoo!" before I knew it. Fin smiled a big ear-to-ear grin as I swam toward him.

"What's that grin for?" I asked.

"I was just wondering to myself which I enjoyed more, watching you ride that wave or watching you celebrate the ride."

I laughed, "It's a big difference from three weeks ago, isn't it?"

"It's amazing what a little time will do," Fin said.

"And a little help from the universe, and you," I countered.

"I didn't tell you anything you didn't already know deep inside yourself. I just helped bring it back up to the surface. Remember, it's the same energy dancing through you that is dancing through me and through these waves. That energy carried you here and carried those messages to you."

"You know, I'm really starting to feel that's the case," I said thoughtfully. "But I'm wondering, 'Now what?'"

"Well, my friend, at any time in their lives, people are capable of doing what they dream of."

"Now I've just got to figure that out," I said.

"Oh, it'll come to you," Fin laughed as he jumped into a wave and rode it to shore. And I had no doubt he was right.

Later I told him about the excitement of the night before and how Mrs. V had actually seemed happier this morning.

"She's just shedding her old layers, just like you did. We all need to drop the things that are no longer working in our lives, whether it's old hairstyles that tie us to the past or old habits that keep us from our future," Fin said and smiled. "Life is full of possibilities if we only open ourselves to them."

We spent the rest of the morning playing in the surf like little children until we were both exhausted.

As we got out of the water, I said, "My uncle is coming in this afternoon, and I'll be heading home in a day or so. I just want to thank you for all that you've taught me."

"No worries, my friend." Fin smiled. "Chatting with you has reminded me of how incredible life really is. I realize it every day, but once I start vocalizing about it, everything becomes clearer, so you've helped me too."

"The way you live life, I'm surprised to hear that you need any reminders," I laughed.

"Everyone needs a reminder now and then." He smiled. "Now I have to take off. Jack, I hope to see you again soon, and when I do, I expect to see you enjoying the ride of your life."

And with that he was packed up and headed down the beach humming the same happy tune.

"Thanks again and enjoy the ride!" I called to him.

He turned and waved with a big ear-to-ear grin as he continued walking.

I smiled to myself, and yet I was a little sad that this might be the last time I saw Fin for a while. But at the same time, it also seemed a new part of my lessons as a student of life was about to begin.

I enjoyed the sun for a while longer before I packed up my beach gear and headed back to what I'd come to know as my home on the beach.

My uncle and his friend hadn't arrived yet. So I jumped in the shower and then cleaned out the dresser drawers by repacking my suitcase. As I was emptying out the last drawer, I found the list I had made of the things I was doing in my life that I felt were bringing me down. I looked at the list and laughed. Most of those things were no longer an issue for me. And the list of things that I did that lifted my spirits looked so incomplete compared to what I had been doing daily for the last few weeks. Could three weeks really make that much difference?

I was out on the sunporch reading when I heard my uncle's voice say, "Jack, you outdid yourself, sport!" and then heard the car door slam.

I jumped up excitedly and ran out to greet him.

He opened his big arms and gave me a bear hug. "You done me proud, sport! It looks great!"

I smiled, and even though Fin said I shouldn't do anything for the payoff of a thank-you, this was the exact response I had been hoping for.

Doug introduced me to Irving, who looked like he had seen much better days. "Let me get the luggage," I said, pulling out their two bags and following them into the bungalow.

As I went to the front door, I saw my uncle standing with his mouth open staring at the mural.

"I found the old drawing," I said.

Tears welled up in his eyes, and he said, "You done Anita proud too."

Hearing these words made my eyes tear up too as I remembered how much I loved my aunt and uncle.

I could've stayed in that moment for quite a while, but my uncle seemed embarrassed, and so I changed the subject by saying, "Check out the rest of the house while I put your bags in your rooms."

Doug showed Irving around, and I caught up with them on the sunporch.

"It looks just the way I remember it," Doug said appreciatively.

"It was too happy a place for me to want to change much." I smiled.

He understood the meaning of my words and began to tear up again.

"But not everything is the same around here." I smiled as I saw Mrs. V coming across the back lawn.

Doug did a double take as he saw the new Mrs. V sans rollers and scarf.

They chatted and laughed for quite a while. I'd never seen Mrs. V so animated, in a pleasant way. I guess that's part of the magic of reuniting with old friends and shedding things that seem to be holding one back.

The next thing I knew Doug was bringing her inside to see the mural. I wasn't sure if I was ready for her critique, but I told myself I was exactly where I needed to be to get to where I needed to go.

"So that's what he's been doing with all his spare time," Mrs. V said. "It looks good. I like all the color. Really brightens up the old place."

My jaw dropped for a second before I said, "Thanks."

"Your nephew's been a damn good neighbor," she said to my uncle as she was leaving. "He plays the stereo too loud and imagines bears in the night, but kids do that."

A big smile crossed my face at the notion of being called a kid. But then I thought to myself, "This is the happiest I've been since I was a kid. So maybe I am acting like one."

My uncle and Irving went in their rooms to unpack. A few minutes later my uncle came out holding a conch shell. I thought it must've been mine until I saw the one Fin gave me on the coffee table.

"When I saw the shell in the mural, I wanted to show you this one, sport. You see, this shell was given to me by a very dear friend. Now hold it up to your ear," he said, handing me the shell.

I did as I was told and smiled as I listened.

"That there is the energy of life reminding you that life is all around you, and is yours for the taking. At least that's what my friend Fin told me forty years ago when we first came to Daytona for a visit. I've always kept it with me to remind me to have the courage to live life to the fullest."

"Love, laugh, serve and forgive," I said, smiling as Doug stared, looking like he'd seen a ghost.

"Fin's been helping me too," I said and showed him my conch shell. "In fact, that's why the conch shell is in the mural."

"Well, I don't know how it's possible. He was old when I knew him forty years ago. One day he just disappeared, and I assumed he'd passed away."

I assured my uncle that Fin was very much alive. In fact, more alive than anyone I ever knew. Then we chatted about life and our hopes and dreams and memories.

That night, the party was a big success. Everyone was happy to see my uncle and made both Irving and myself feel like we were part of the neighborhood. Mrs. V was the sensation of the evening and smiled more than I had ever seen her smile.

After the party, as I lay on the lounge chair in the sunporch, I reflected back on my time at the beach. It had seemed like everything I had done in those three weeks was preparing for the party, which seemed to go by in a blink of an eye. But what I had learned in those three weeks would stay with me for a lifetime. Then, I remembered Fin telling me, "Life happens between waves too."

"Yes, it certainly does," I thought to myself as I smiled and drifted off to sleep, grateful for the time between waves where I could just enjoy life and know I was exactly where I needed to be to get to the greater good the universe knew I could achieve.

DAY 21 & BEYOND

The next day, I awoke happy and refreshed.

At breakfast my uncle announced that he couldn't bear to sell the beach place with all the happiness it still held in store for our family.

Later, Irving, my uncle, and I went to the beach, and my uncle promised to teach Irving how to bodysurf. At first, Irving protested that he was too old, but soon the three of us were having a grand time in the waves. When we got back to shore, my uncle told Irving, "You know, bodysurfing is a lot like life . . ." At that moment I knew both my uncle and Irving would be okay.

That evening, as we were having dinner at the cement table in the backyard, Terry showed up to mooch food, and it delighted my uncle and his guest. After dinner, Mrs. V and Velma dropped by, and we stayed out laughing in the backyard for quite a while.

I stayed with them another day and then decided to head back to my home and the new life that lay ahead for me.

As I drove across the causeway to the mainland, the wind blew through the windows as I headed toward my future, and I swear I heard Fin say, "Trust your gut, jump in, and enjoy the ride of your life!"

I smiled all the way home.

CPSIA information can be obtained at www.ICGtesting.com
Printed in the USA
BVOW05s1129150315

391741BV00001BC/98/P